MATT CHRISTOPHER'S
ALL-STAR LINEUP

MATT CHRISTOPHER'S ALL-STAR LINEUP

Five Volumes in One

THE KID WHO ONLY HIT HOMERS

RETURN OF THE HOME RUN KID

BASEBALL PALS

CATCHER WITH A GLASS ARM

CHALLENGE AT SECOND BASE

BLACK DOG
& LEVENTHAL
PUBLISHERS
NEW YORK

This edition published by arrangement with
Little, Brown and Company, (Inc.)

Published by

Black Dog & Leventhal Publishers, Inc.
151 West 19th Street
New York, NY 10011

Distributed by

Workman Publishing Company
708 Broadway
New York, NY 10003

Manufactured in the United States of America

j i h g f e d c b

ISBN: 1-884822-68-1

Library of Congress Cataloging -in-Publication Data

Christopher, Matt.
    Matt Christopher's All-Star lineup.
        p.   cm.
    Contents: The kid who only hit homers — Return of the Home Run
Kid —   Baseball pals — Catcher with a glass arm — Challenge at
second base.
    ISBN: 1-884822-68-1
    (1. Baseball — Fiction.)   I. Title.
PZ7.C458Mat   1997
(Fic) — dc21   — dc21   96-52601
                                                        CIP
                                                        AC

Contents

The Kid
Who Only Hit Homers

for my son,
Dale

The Kid Who Only Hit Homers

by Matt Christopher

Illustrated by Harvey Kidder

Author's Note

This story was told to the author by a person whose expressed wish is that he remain anonymous. Every word in it is true (so he said), except that names have been changed to protect the innocent (and those not so innocent).

The author was left to form his own opinion on whether the incidents have actually happened, and he prefers to keep that opinion to himself.

It is left to the judgment of the reader whether he wishes to do likewise.

Matt Christopher

1

THE HOOPER REDBIRDS were having their third practice session of the spring season and Sylvester Coddmyer III, a right-hander, was batting.

Rick Wilson hurled in the first pitch. It looked good and Sylvester swung.

Swish! He missed it by six inches.

"Just meet it, Sylvester," advised Coach Stan Corbin. "You're trying to kill it."

Sylvester tried to "just meet" Rick's next pitch, and fouled it to the backstop screen. He hit the next one to Rick. It was a drib-

11

bler that took almost five seconds to reach the mound.

"Hold it up for him, Rick!" shouted Jim Cowley, the Redbirds' second baseman.

"Think that would help, Jim?" yelled Jerry Ash.

A rumble of laughter broke from the other players on the field. Sylvester didn't let it bother him, though. He was pretty used to it by now.

"Okay, Sylvester," said the coach. "Lay it down and run it out."

Sylvester bunted Rick's next pitch down to third and beelined to first base. His stocky build and short legs didn't exactly help him be a very fast runner.

He had hoped that by now he would show some improvement in his playing. If there was any, it was so slight no one seemed to notice.

His performance in the outfield wasn't any better than it was at the plate. Mr. Beach, the assistant coach, was knocking flies out to the outfielders, and Sylvester missed three out of four that were hit to him.

"Remind me to bring you my mom's clothes basket at the next practice," said Ted Sobel, one of the outfielders who was sure to make the team. "Maybe *then* you can catch it."

"Funny," said Sylvester. "Ha ha."

Twenty minutes later practice was over. The boys walked tiredly to the locker room, showered, and went home.

"Well, are you going to sign up to play?" asked Jim Cowley.

"Tomorrow the last day to sign?"

"That's right."

"I'll think about it," said Sylvester.

13

He thought about it at the supper table, on the swing in the yard, and in bed before he fell asleep, and decided he wouldn't sign. He was sure he'd just sit on the bench, anyway. And who'd like to sit on the bench all the time?

The next afternoon he sat in the bleachers and watched the Hooper Redbirds practice. No one seemed to miss him on the field. No one, that is, except Jim Cowley, who ran over from first base after batting practice.

"Syl! Why aren't you on the field?"

"I didn't sign up," answered Sylvester.

"Why not?"

Sylvester shrugged. "Why? To warm the bench? Anyway, I don't care that much about playing."

"Then why are you here?"

"Nothing else to do," replied Sylvester.

"I bet," said Jim, and ran back to the infield.

Sylvester folded his hands over his knees, glad that Cowley had left. The guy was starting to get on his nerves.

"Why did you lie to the boy, Syl?" said a voice.

Startled, he looked and saw a man climb up the bleachers and sit beside him. He had never seen the man before, but figured he must be the father of one of the players.

He blushed.

The man smiled and put out his hand. Sylvester put his into it and felt the man's warm grip. "I'm George Baruth," said the man. "You're Sylvester Coddmyer the third, aren't you?"

"Yes, I am," said Sylvester, and frowned. George Baruth? There was no

Baruth going to Hooper Junior High that he knew of. "Are . . . are you looking for me?"

George Baruth's blue eyes crinkled at the corners. He was a big man with a round face and a nose like a large strawberry. He was wearing a coat over a thin white jersey, brown pants and a baseball cap with the letters NY on the front of it.

"Well, hardly," said George Baruth. "I just figured you'd be here."

Sylvester heard a sharp *crack!* and looked just in time to see catcher Eddie Exton blast a pitch over short.

"Why did you lie to the boy, Syl?" George Baruth asked again. "You do want to play baseball with the team, don't you?"

Sylvester nodded, thinking: *How could he know that? He never saw me before.* "Yes, I do," he admitted.

"Well, don't lie about it. You didn't fool Jim, and" — he grinned broadly — "you don't fool me."

Sylvester's smile didn't quite match Mr. Baruth's. He tried to think of something to say, but couldn't. He never was much of a talker.

"Syl," said Mr. Baruth, "I don't like to see a boy watch a game from the bleachers while his heart bleeds to play."

"But I would never make a ballplayer, Mr. Baruth," said Sylvester, hopelessly. "Ballplayers are good catchers and good hitters, and I don't fit into that picture at all."

"Well, you've played *some* baseball, haven't you?"

"Yes. Some."

"Okay. Stick around after the Redbirds finish their practice."

Sylvester stared at him. "Why?"

"I'm going to teach you to become a better baseball player, that's why. As a matter of fact . . ." and now Mr. Baruth's eyes twinkled, "I think I'll teach you to become one of the best players ever to play in Hooper!"

Sylvester's eyes popped. "How are you going to do that, Mr. Baruth?"

George Baruth chuckled. "You'll see, my boy. See you after practice."

He got up and left the bleachers, and once again Sylvester Coddmyer III was by himself. He kept watching the Hooper Redbirds practice hitting, and then watched the coach knock grounders to the infielders. But all the time he kept thinking about George Baruth and his promise.

He's just pulling my leg, thought Sylvester. *Nobody in the world could ever help me become a good ballplayer.*

19

Sylvester looked over his shoulder, expecting to see Mr. Baruth getting into a car or walking on the sidewalk. The man was nowhere in sight.

He sure could vanish fast, thought Sylvester, and turned his attention back to the practice session.

Finally the Redbirds were finished and left the field. All except Jim Cowley. He came over and looked at Sylvester. "Practice is over, Syl. Aren't you going home?"

"In a little while," replied Sylvester.

Jim frowned, then smiled. "Well, just make sure you don't stay all night. So long."

No sooner had he left than George Baruth came around the bleachers. He was carrying a baseball bat and a glove, and his coat pockets were filled with baseballs.

"Here, take the bat," said Mr. Baruth, tossing it to Sylvester. "And walk over to the backstop screen. I'll pitch to you."

Syl caught the bat, trotted to the backstop screen and Mr. Baruth approached the small, worn area between home plate and the pitcher's mound. It was the same spot the Redbird pitchers had used during batting practice.

Syl stood at the left side of the plate facing Mr. Baruth who, he saw, was left-handed.

"Keep the toes of your feet parallel with the plate," advised Mr. Baruth. "Hold your bat a few inches off your shoulder. That's right. Okay. Here we go."

He wound up and delivered. The ball came in moderately fast, heading for the plate. Sylvester swung. *Crack!* The ball blazed in a straight line to short.

21

"Hey! How about that?" cried George Baruth. "Nice hit!"

Sylvester smiled. He had even surprised himself!

George Baruth threw in another pitch. This one was too far inside. "Let it go!" he yelled.

Sylvester jumped back and let it go.

The third pitch blazed across the plate again and Sylvester belted it to left center field. He hit the next to right center and the next to deep left. Now and then a pitch was too high or too wide and he would let it go. But every pitch that came over the plate he swung at and hit every time.

He couldn't understand it. Why couldn't he hit Rick's pitches as well as he did Mr. Baruth's?

After Mr. Baruth had thrown the last ball — there were eight altogether — he and Sylvester ran out to the outfield, collected them, and came back to continue the pitching and hitting.

After the fourth time of doing this Mr. Baruth called it quits. He pushed back his cap and wiped his sweaty forehead, and Sylvester noticed his short crop of black hair with wisps of gray around the edge.

"Tomorrow tell the coach that you've changed your mind," said Mr. Baruth. "You really want to play. You have a good pair of eyes and strong, fine wrists. You're going to make a great hitter, Syl. Take my word for it."

Sylvester looked at him unbelievingly. "What about my legs, Mr. Baruth?"

"What about them? You're going to play baseball, Syl, not run in a horse race."

2

I T WASN'T TILL the end of the fifth
period in school on Monday when Sylvester had collected enough courage to
ask Coach Corbin if it was too late to sign
up with the Redbirds. The coach, dressed
in a brown suit, was walking toward him
in the corridor.

"Oh, Co — Coach," Sylvester stammered. "Can I see you a minute, please?"

"Of course, Sylvester," said Coach Corbin, and looked at Sylvester with dark,
friendly eyes. "What is it?"

"Is it too late to sign up for baseball?"

Dark brows twitched briefly then squeezed together so that they almost touched.

"Friday was the last day to sign, Sylvester. And I've got too many players now. Why didn't you sign up earlier? Didn't you see the notice on the bulletin board?"

"Yes. But I —" Sylvester shrugged. "Okay. Thanks, Mr. Corbin."

He walked down the corridor to his homeroom, his head bowed and his hands in his pockets. He wasn't surprised at Coach Corbin's reply. He had hoped, though, that the coach would've let him sign up. At least then he'd have had a chance to show what he could do.

After school he walked home alone. Hooper was a small town in the Finger Lakes region of New York State. Tourists

26

drove through it all the time, but no one as much as stopped there to fill up for gas.

The school, Hooper Junior High, stood on a hill overlooking the village. Most kids lived close enough to walk to it. A few had to ride on one of the buses.

Sylvester still had two blocks to go when he heard footsteps pounding behind him, and then a familiar voice. "Syl! Wait a minute!"

He turned and there was George Baruth, running toward him.

"Oh, hi, Mr. Baruth!" he said, and stopped to wait.

George Baruth came up beside him, breathing tiredly. "Did you ask the coach?"

"Yes," said Sylvester. "He said he's got too many players now."

27

"I was afraid of that," said George Baruth. "Dang it, I've got to get you on the team somehow, Syl."

Sylvester looked at him. "Can't we just forget about it, Mr. Baruth? He doesn't want me to play. He probably thinks I'd just be in the way."

Mr. Baruth's eyes flashed. "That's just what we don't want him to think, Syl. We have to get him to change his mind about you and put you on the team. Now, let me think a minute."

He shoved his baseball cap back, scratched his head and looked at the sidewalk as if among the spidery cracks he might be able to find the solution.

He started talking, but his words were low and mumbly, and Sylvester knew that he was just talking to himself.

Suddenly he jerked his cap down hard

and tapped a sharp finger against Sylvester's shoulder. "I've got it, Syl!" he cried. "The team's practicing now, isn't it?"

"Yes, it is."

"Okay. Is your glove at home?"

"Yes."

"Get it, and let's go to the field. I have an idea and it's burning a hole in my head!"

Sylvester ran the two blocks to his house, got his glove, and ran out again, yelling "Hi, Mom!" to his mother, who was stirring up something in a large bowl.

"Sylvester!" she called. "Where's the fire?"

Mom was short and blond and a little on the stocky side. Ever since Sylvester was born she had wished for a daughter, too, but so far there was only Sylvester. Dad, a traveling salesman, had said just a few nights ago that Sylvester was more than he had bargained for and that they should be thankful to have him.

"I'll be back, Mom!" Sylvester shouted over his shoulder.

Suddenly, just outside the door, he paused. He couldn't keep Mr. Baruth waiting — not with that idea burning a hole in his head — but he had to tell Mom whom he was with.

"I'm going to be with Mr. Baruth, Mom!" he shouted to her. "He's going to help me play baseball!"

"Mr. Baruth? Who's he?"

"I don't know! But he lives in Hooper . . . somewhere! And he wants to teach me to play better baseball so that I can play with the Redbirds! He's just great, Mom! See ya later!"

He met George Baruth and together

they headed back for the school. The baseball field was south of it. The guys were already on it, taking batting practice. George Baruth climbed up the bleachers behind first base and sat down near the end of the third row. Sylvester sat beside him, wondering exactly what could be burning a hole in Mr. Baruth's head.

They sat through batting practice. Then Coach Corbin hit grounders to the infielders and a man whom Sylvester recognized as Mr. Beach, the math teacher and Mr. Corbin's assistant coach, began hitting fly balls to the outfielders clustered in center field.

"Watch the kid in the yellow pants," said Mr. Baruth.

Sylvester watched and saw the kid misjudge one fly after another and then drop one that had fallen smack into his glove.

"That's Lou Masters," he said. "He's not doing very well, is he?"

Mr. Baruth chuckled. "He's not doing well at all, Syl. And if your coach has any sense he'd know it. Look. Run down there and ask that fella hitting the ball to let you try catching a few flies, too."

Sylvester stared at him. "But Coach Corbin told me it was too late, Mr. Baruth!"

"How can it be too late? The league doesn't start till next week. Get going. He shouldn't mind letting you try to catch a few, at least."

Reluctantly Sylvester climbed down the bleachers and walked over to Mr. Beach. He waited till Mr. Beach blasted out a fly then gathered up all the courage he could and said, "Mr. Beach."

32

The tall man, pantlegs flapping in the wind, looked at him. "Hi, Sylvester," he said. "What's up?"

"Can I . . . can I go out there, too?"

Mr. Beach smiled. "Have you signed up to play?"

"No."

"Then why do you want to go out there?"

Sylvester shrugged. "Well, I'd like to play if I can. I thought that if I did pretty good, you — or Mr. Corbin — would let me sign up."

Mr. Beach laughed. "Okay, Syl. Get out there and I'll hit you a few."

"Thank you!"

Sylvester ran out to the field, flashing a smile at George Baruth and receiving one in return. Mr. Baruth made a circle with his right thumb and forefinger.

"This one's for Syl!" yelled Mr. Beach, and hit one about as high as a ten-story building. Sylvester got under it and caught it easily.

Mr. Beach knocked out much higher flies to the other boys who seemed to have trouble judging the ball. It was Sylvester's turn again and this time Mr. Beach hit the ball just as high as he did for the other boys. The ball soared into the blue sky until it looked no larger than a pea, came down and dropped into Sylvester's glove.

"Hey! Nice catch, Syl!" yelled Mr. Beach. "Let's try another high one!"

He blasted another ball high into the sky. Sylvester ran some twenty feet to the spot where it was coming down, put out his mitt and plop! He had it.

The other outfielders stared at him unbelievingly.

"Hey! What's happened?" observed Ted Sobel. "You couldn't catch worth beans last week!"

Sylvester shrugged. "I'm not very good at it, yet," he said modestly.

After they finished outfield practice Sylvester returned to the bleachers and sat down beside George Baruth.

"Good work, Syl," George smiled broadly. "Did you see their eyes pop when you made those fine catches?"

Sylvester grinned. "Well . . . I kind of surprised myself," he said honestly. Then he thought of something and looked at Mr. Baruth curiously. "You're really not from Hooper, are you, Mr. Baruth?"

The big man chuckled. "No. I'm a stranger here, Syl. Every year I spend my vacation in a different town. This year I picked Hooper. This region is one of the most beautiful in the world, Syl. Did you know that?"

Sylvester smiled. "Yes, sir. I think so, too, Mr. Baruth." He paused a moment. "Mr. Baruth, how come you picked me out to help? Aren't there other kids who are better?"

Mr. Baruth chuckled again. "Why should I try to help someone who is better? I saw that you really loved baseball, and tried your best to play. But you had problems. You couldn't play well, so you got discouraged and wanted to quit. Right away I knew you were a boy who needed help."

Sylvester grinned. "Do you really think you could help me, Mr. Baruth? Man, I don't think there's anybody lousier than I am."

"I not only *think* I can help you, young

37

buddy," replied Mr. Baruth, a glimmer in his eyes. "I *know* I can!"

Suddenly there was a shout from near home plate and Sylvester saw Coach Corbin waving to him. With the coach was Mr. Beach, who looked as if he had just uncovered a box of some very valuable treasure.

"Sylvester Coddmyer!" yelled the coach. "Come here, will you?"

"I'd better see what he wants," he said. "Excuse me, Mr. Baruth."

"You bet, Syl," said George Baruth.

Sylvester clattered down the bleachers and ran across the green, mowed grass toward the tiny group clustered near home plate. When he reached it Coach Corbin smiled at him and placed an arm around his shoulders. "Mr. Beach told me you looked very good catching fly balls to-day, Sylvester," he said.

Sylvester shrugged. "I'm better at hit-ting, too," he said proudly.

"Oh? Mind trying to prove it to me?"

"No."

"Okay. Pick up a bat. Rick, throw a few to Sylvester."

Sylvester found a bat he liked and stepped in front of the backstop screen. Rick Wilson walked out to the temporary pitching box, waited for Sylvester to get ready, then blazed one in.

Smack! Sylvester laid into it and blasted it over the left field fence.

"Jumping codfish!" cried Coach Corbin. "Look at that blast! Pitch another, Rick!"

Rick did. *Pow!* The second ball rock-eted out almost as far as the first. Rick threw in another. Again Sylvester swung and again the ball shot like a rocket over the left field fence.

"That's enough!" said Coach Corbin. "We can't afford to lose baseballs! Sylvester!"

"Yes, Coach?"

"I don't know what you've been doing since last Friday, but you're sure a different ballplayer now. Be in my office in the morning to sign up. I think I might be able to fit you in."

"Thanks, sir!" said Sylvester happily.

3

THE HOOPER REDBIRDS played a practice game with the Macon Falcons on Tuesday. Coach Corbin assigned Sylvester Coddmyer III to right field and put him fourth in the batting order. Fourth, as everybody knew, was the cleanup position.

The Redbirds' batting order was:

> Cowley 2b
> Sobel lf
> Stevens ss
> Coddmyer rf
> Ash 1b

Kent   cf

Francis   3b

Exton   c

Barnes   p

The Falcons had first raps. Terry Barnes, the Redbirds' alternate pitcher, was a little wild on the leadoff hitter and walked him. The next Falcon laid a neat bunt down the third-base line which Duane Francis fielded and pegged to first on time. The bunt advanced the base runner to second, putting him in position to score.

The next Falcon blasted a fly back to Terry. Terry caught it, spun, and shot the ball to second to nab the man before he could tag up.

Three outs.

Sylvester came trotting out of right field and saw several people sitting in different places in the bleachers. And, there in the third row from the bottom just behind first base, sat Mr. Baruth.

"Hi, Mr. Baruth!" cried Sylvester.

"Hi, Syl!" answered Mr. Baruth, smiling. "Go get 'em, kid!"

Jim Cowley led off with a grounder to short, an easy out. Ted Sobel singled and Milt Stevens walked, bringing up Sylvester Coddmyer III.

"Knock 'em in, Syl!" yelled the coach.

Duke Farrel, the Falcons' tall right-hander, blazed his first pitch down the heart of the plate. Sylvester leaned into it, swung — and missed.

The next pitch was slightly high. That was Sylvester's opinion. The umpire's opinion was different. "Strike two!" he yelled.

The next pitch looked high, too. But

43

Sylvester didn't want to take a chance on striking out. He swung. Missed!

"Strike three!"

He couldn't believe it. The first time at bat and he struck out. What would the coach think? What would Mr. Baruth think?

He turned glumly, tossed his bat onto the pile and went to the dugout.

"Chin up, Sylvester," said the coach. "You'll be up again."

Jerry Ash popped up to short and the side retired.

The Falcons scored a run at their turn at bat and then the Redbirds came to bat. Bobby Kent singled. Duane Francis' bunt put him on second, and Eddie Exton's triple scored him. Pitcher Terry Barnes's single scored Eddie.

The Falcons' leadoff man lambasted a

long clout to deep right field, sending Sylvester running back toward the fence. His short legs were a blur as he ran, while all the time he kept his eyes on the ball. Then he reached up. The ball came down, brushed the tip of his glove, and bounced against the fence.

The Falcon ran all around to third on the hit.

The next hitter blasted a line drive over first baseman Jerry Ash's head. The ball struck the ground in front of Sylvester. But, instead of bouncing up into Sylvester's waiting glove, it skidded through his legs.

Once again he spun and sprinted after the ball. A run scored by the time he pegged it in.

Man, oh, man! he thought. What's wrong with me? I'm not doing anything right! Mr. Baruth will give up on me for sure.

Terry fanned the next hitter. Then Bobby caught a long fly in deep center field, and another run scored after the runner tagged up. Eddie Exton caught a pop fly to end the half inning.

"Hey, Syl," said Jim Cowley, "what're you doing out there? Playing baseball or running a track meet?"

"Ha ha," said Sylvester.

Milt Stevens led off the bottom of the third with a double over the shortstop's head. Up came Sylvester for the second time.

"Okay, Syl," said Jerry Ash, kneeling with his bat in front of the dugout. "Make up for those errors."

The pitch. It looked good. Sylvester swung. *Crack!* A long blast to center field!

46

Sylvester dropped his bat and bolted for first, but slowed up before he got to it. The center fielder had caught the ball.

"Tough luck, kid," said a voice from the bleachers. "But don't give up. Hang in there."

Sylvester looked at Mr. Baruth. His smile was weak. *I've got to, Mr. Baruth,* he thought, *or Coach Corbin will bench me.*

Jerry Ash singled, scoring Milt. Bobby and Duane both got out, ending the half inning. Falcons 3, Redbirds 3.

The Falcons got a man on and threatened to score when Steve Button, their cleanup hitter and a left-hander, clouted a skyscraping fly to right field. Bobby Kent started to run over from center, but Sylvester yelled, "I'll take it! I'll take it!"

"Take it!" shouted Bobby.

The ball dropped into Sylvester's glove and stuck there. A shout sprang from the scattered Redbird fans as Sylvester heaved the ball in, holding the runner on second base.

He felt much better now. He *needed* that catch.

The next two Falcons failed to hit and the half inning ended with a zero on the scoreboard.

"Nice catch, Syl," said Mr. Baruth as Sylvester trotted in from right field.

"Thanks, sir," Sylvester smiled.

Neither team scored again until the bottom of the fifth. With one out Sylvester socked a single, a scratch hit to shortstop. Jerry Ash's triple scored him.

Falcons 3, Redbirds 4.

"Hold 'em, Redbirds!" yelled a fan.

Terry walked the first Falcon and the

next was safe on Milt's error at short. Then Steve Button blasted another fly to right field. Sylvester got under it, shouting, "I'll take it! I'll take it!"

Then, just for an instant, he lost sight of the ball against the white clouds. When he spotted it again it was too late. The ball skimmed past his glove and struck the ground. He caught the high bounce and pegged it in, but not before two Falcons crossed home plate.

When the Redbirds came to bat they failed to score and the game went to the Falcons, 5 to 4.

"I can't figure it out, Sylvester," said Coach Corbin, wonderingly. "You hardly looked like the same kid out there who practiced with us yesterday."

"Are — are you going to drop me, Coach?" asked Sylvester worriedly.

"No. But if you don't do better than you did today . . ." The coach shrugged. "I'll just have to keep you on the bench most of the time."

4

SYLVESTER CODDMYER III wrote a composition that night on snakes and how they benefit man. It was for English. He had wanted to write on baseball because he loved it so. But Miss Carroll, his English teacher, suggested that he write about something else for a change.

He researched his material from a couple of magazine articles and the encyclopedia. He wasn't especially crazy about snakes, but after reading up on them he realized that they were really interesting creatures.

Nevertheless, he enjoyed baseball more than anything else. He liked to read about its history, and about old-time ballplayers.

He thought of himself becoming a great outfielder or a great hitter. Man! Wouldn't that be something?

He knew he was just dreaming, though. He would never be *half* as great as any of those hitters whose names he'd read in the baseball encyclopedia.

He picked up the big book from the shelf near the desk and leafed through it to the section where the names of the home-run hitters were listed. Right on top was Babe Ruth, with 714 home runs. Man! 714!

George Herman "Babe" Ruth had been a pitcher for the Boston Red Sox. Then he went to the New York Yankees, where he played outfield and became a batting champion. He hit sixty home runs in 1927 and held the record until it was broken by Roger Maris in 1961. When he died in 1948 he held seventeen World Series records.

There were other great hitters — Willie Mays, Mickey Mantle, Jimmy Foxx. But no one had hit as many home runs as the "Babe."

Sylvester closed the book, shut his eyes and dreamed again. Wouldn't it be something to be good enough to have *his* name in the encyclopedia some day?

He opened his eyes and laughed. He'd never!

The Hooper Redbirds' first league game was on April 28 against the Tigers from Broton. Coach Corbin assigned Sylvester to right field and put him at the bottom of the batting order.

Sylvester wasn't surprised. He felt he was lucky to be in the lineup at all.

The Redbirds batted first. They got two men on but failed to score. Sylvester trotted out to right field, hardly glancing at the fans that sat scattered in the bleachers.

The Redbird cheerleaders, wearing white sweaters and short red skirts, whooped up a cheer from the first-base bleachers side, followed by a cheer from the Tiger cheerleaders, who wore yellow jerseys and blue skirts and were at the third-base bleachers side.

Thinking of George Baruth made Sylvester look briefly at the bleachers, near the end. He really didn't expect to see Mr. Baruth there.

But he was! He was sitting at the end of the third row from the bottom, where he always sat.

The perplexed look on Sylvester's face changed to a smile. He waved, and Mr. Baruth, smiling, waved back.

Rick Wilson, on the mound for the Redbirds, whiffed the first Tiger, then got into a hole with the second and walked him. An error by shortstop Milt Stevens, and then a clean single through the pitcher's box, scored a run before the Redbirds could smother the Tigers.

Duane Francis led off in the top of the second with a drive to center field that the fielder caught for the first out. Eddie Exton grounded out and Rick came to bat, looking as if he were going to be the third victim for sure.

He walked on four straight balls, and up came Sylvester Coddmyer III.

Sylvester pulled on his protective helmet and stepped into position in the box. All three outfielders were standing with their legs wide apart and their arms crossed over their chests. The Tigers' infielders were making the usual noises, while, in the stands, several of the fans yawned boringly.

"Strike one!" yelled the ump as Jim Smith blazed the first pitch over the plate.

Then, "Ball!" And "Ball two!"

He swung at the next pitch. "Strike two!"

The fans of both teams began yelling loudly. Sylvester felt sweat on his brow. Was he going to strike out and let both the coach and Mr. Baruth down? Was he going to disappoint them again?

The pitch. It headed for the inside corner. He swung.

Crack! A hard, solid blow! The ball shot like a white streak toward left field. And then — over the fence!

Sylvester dropped his bat and trotted around the bases for his first home run of the season.

The entire team was waiting for him behind home plate. Each member shook his hand as he crossed it.

"Nice sock, Syl!"

"Great blast, man!"

Even Coach Corbin and Mr. Beach shook his hand. "You came through that time, Syl!" exclaimed the coach, beaming.

Sylvester smiled.

Jim Cowley got up and flied out.

The Tigers went down without scoring in the bottom of the second. The Redbirds came to bat and Jim Smith seemed to have some kind of jinx on the ball as he mowed down Sobel, Stevens, and Ash with ten pitches. The Tigers came to bat again.

Rick fired in two strikes on the leadoff

57

batter, then got a little wild and walked him. The next Tiger bunted, advancing the runner to second and getting safely to first himself as third baseman Duane Francis muffed the wiggling grounder.

A left-handed hitter stepped to the plate. A big kid with pants halfway down his legs and wisps of black hair sticking out from under his helmet.

Duane turned and motioned to Sylvester. "Back up, Syl! About twenty steps!"

Sylvester backed up exactly twenty steps and crouched, hoping that the guy would either strike out, hit a grounder, or knock the ball to some other field. Even though he had caught some high flies in practice, he had missed them in a practice game.

Smack! A high soaring fly heading for

right field! Sylvester figured that it was going over his head and started to run back.

His feet slipped and down he went.

5

PANIC GRIPPED Sylvester as he looked skyward, searching frantically for the ball which he had momentarily lost sight of.

There it was, coming right at him! Without rising to his feet — he didn't have time, anyway — he lifted his glove and made a one-handed catch.

Then he scrambled to his feet and pegged the ball in to the infield. Jim Cowley caught it and quickly turned, ready to throw it. But the runners had returned to their bases — one to first, the other to second. Calmly, Jim threw the ball to Rick.

The Redbird fans cheered Sylvester for his great catch, and he blushed. It was just lucky, he thought, that he had fallen in the right spot and turned in time.

Two singles in a row scored two runs for the Tigers. Then Rick whiffed a left-handed hitter. The next blasted a triple, scoring two more runs. Eddie Exton caught a pop-up to end the inning. Redbirds 2, Tigers 5.

Bobby Kent led off in the top of the fourth.

"Come on, Bobby," said Coach Corbin. "We need runs, and the only way to get them is by getting hits."

The Tigers were a determined, fighting bunch as they kept up a steady chatter on the field. The will to win was in every move they made.

Bobby took two balls and a strike before moving the bat off his shoulder. He fouled a pitch for strike two, and the noise in the infield grew louder than ever. Then he blasted a high throw to center field which the Tiger outfielder caught without trouble.

Coach Corbin's groan could be heard throughout the Redbirds' dugout.

Duane Francis had a problem with his pants. He kept pulling them up after each swing. His third swing resulted in a sharp single over short.

"Nice hit," yelled the coach.

Eddie Exton must have looked pretty dangerous to Jim because the Tiger pitcher threw four straight balls to him, none of which was within five inches of the plate. Eddie walked.

Two men on. Only a homer could tie the score.

Rick Wilson looked dangerous, too. He seemed to be glowering at the pitcher, daring him. Sylvester knew, though, that it was just Rick's natural look whenever he came to bat.

Rick pounded out Jim's third pitch for an easy out to left field. And up came Sylvester Coddmyer III.

"Don't be too anxious, Sylvester," advised Coach Corbin. "Just a nice easy poke will be fine."

Jim Smith stepped to the mound, stretched his arms up high, brought them down, looked at the runners, then threw. The pitch blazed in. Sylvester stepped into it, saw that it was too high and let it go.

"Ball one!" cried the ump.

Jim repeated his movements with hardly a change. This time the pitch was too far outside.

"Ball two!"

"Don't be afraid of 'im, Jim!" shouted the Tiger catcher. "He was just lucky before!"

Jim drilled the third pitch over the heart of the plate. Sylvester stepped into it and swung. He didn't know how to hit "just a nice easy poke." He swung hard, just like he had always done.

There was the solid sound of wood meeting horsehide, and then the horsehide shooting out to deep left center field, rising steadily and then falling . . . fall-

ing far beyond the fence for a home run.

The Redbird fans stood up and applauded and the cheerleaders went crazy clapping and cheering and doing cartwheels. Sylvester trotted around the bases, shook hands with the guys waiting for him at the plate, and sat down. He hadn't even run hard enough to work up a sweat.

Jim Cowley walked, then Ted Sobel grounded out to end the half inning. Redbirds 5, Tigers 5.

Sylvester saw the coach looking at him. Mr. Corbin's mouth hung open, but he seemed too numbed to speak.

The Tigers' leadoff man socked a scratch single past Jerry Ash, then ran to second on a sacrifice bunt. The next Tiger blasted a high fly to right field. Sylvester sprinted after it. At the last moment he dove with his glove hand stretched out. He landed on his stomach at the same time that the ball landed in his glove.

He rose quickly and winged the ball to Jerry, who sped to first base and touched it before the runner could tag up. Obviously the Tiger didn't think that the Redbird right fielder was going to get within miles of the ball.

Two outs, and a runner on second base.

Rick fired in two pitches, a strike and a ball. Then the Tiger hit one back to him which Rick caught and tossed to Jerry for the third out.

"For a slow runner you sure can cover a lot of ground fast!" exclaimed Jim Cowley as Sylvester tossed his glove to the side of the dugout and sat down.

"I guess it just takes that extra effort," said Sylvester.

Glenn Higgins, pinch-hitting for Stevens in the top of the fifth, cracked the first pitch for a single over second base. Jerry flied out to left and Lou Masters, pinch-hitting for Bobby Kent, walked. Duane struck out and Eddie Exton walked, filling the bases.

The fans applauded Rick as he stepped to the plate. So far he had walked and flied out. "You're due, Rick!" shouted Jim Cowley.

Rick flied out to left field.

6

THE TIGERS came to bat, gnashing their teeth. The leadoff man waited out Rick's pitches, got two balls and two strikes on him, then drilled Rick's next pitch through the hole between left and center fields for two bases.

Milt Stevens fumbled a hot grounder, chalking up an error.

Men on first and second.

Crack! A sharp blow over first baseman Jerry Ash's head. Sylvester ran in a couple of steps, caught the ball on a hop and fired it in. It was a long, hard throw, heading directly for Eddie Exton, who was crouched over home plate, waiting for it. Rick caught it instead, turned and whipped it to Eddie just as the runner slid in between Eddie's legs.

"Out!" yelled the ump.

A grounder to third ended the threat.

"Okay, Syl," said Coach Corbin. "This is the last inning and you're first man up. What're you going to do?"

Sylvester shrugged. "I don't know. I never led off before. Shall I wait him out?"

The coach grinned. "Use your judgment, Syl. It's been working pretty good for you so far."

Sylvester smiled. "Okay, sir. Thanks."

He pulled on his helmet, picked up his favorite bat and stepped to the plate. The stands and bleachers turned into a beehive.

71

Jim blazed in a pitch. Sylvester let it go, thinking it a little bit too close.

"Strike!" yelled the ump.

Sylvester let another pitch blaze by, believing it was outside.

"Strike two!" yelled the ump.

Sylvester stepped back and looked at him. The umpire smiled pleasantly. "Don't grumble, Sylvester," he said. "That cut the outside corner."

Sylvester stepped back into the box. Jim Smith's next pitch came in and looked almost exactly like the one before it. Man, he couldn't let this one go by and be called out on strikes. He swung.

Smack! The ball shot toward right field, climbing higher and higher the farther it went, and dropped inches on the other side of the fence. A home run.

The fans and cheerleaders went wild.

They yelled and jumped and someone screamed, "Hold it! Ya wanna break down the bleachers?"

"You're terrific, Sylvester," commended Coach Corbin as he shook hands with Sylvester Coddmyer III. "Three homers in your first game! That's a record, son!"

Sylvester blushed. "You mean no one has hit three homers in a first game before?"

"I don't think so," said the coach. "Not for Hooper Junior High, anyway."

Jim Cowley walked, but the next three guys failed to get on and the Redbirds retired. The Tigers leadoff man flied out to center. Glen missed another hot grounder, his second, and the Tigers had a man on.

The next Tiger smashed out a single, and the runner on first dashed around to

73

third, sliding in to the bag in a close play.

"Safe!" yelled the man in blue.

Rick fanned the next man. Two outs. Then Rick caught a pop-up, ending the game. Redbirds 6, Tigers 5.

Sylvester picked up his glove and barely turned around to head for home when the mob swooped on him like a flock of pigeons onto a pile of corn. They shook his hands. They patted him on the back. They ruffled his hair. They praised him. He had never expected anything like this in his life.

When they finally broke away there was one kid still standing there, smiling at him. He was much shorter than Sylvester, and younger. His hair was blond and sort of long, and he wore tinted, black-rimmed glasses.

Snooky Malone was the only kid Sylvester knew who read everything he could get his hands on about astrology. It was his belief that every person was born under a certain star and that that star ruled his destiny.

"Hi, Sylvester," said Snooky, his eyes like large black periods behind the tinted lenses.

"Hi, Snooky," said Sylvester, straightening up his clothes and his cap and starting for home.

Snooky Malone ran after him. "I was just wondering, Syl. When's your birthday? The day and month . . . I don't need the year."

Sylvester looked at him curiously. Snooky couldn't weigh over eighty-six pounds.

"What do you mean you don't need the year?"

Snooky's smile faded and came back. "I want to read your horoscope, that's why. Bet you were born under the sign of Scorpio."

"When's that?"

"Between October twenty-fourth and November twenty-second."

"Wrong," said Sylvester. "I was born between May first and May thirtieth. May twenty-seventh, to be exact."

"Gemini!" Snooky's smile brightened like a star itself.

"What's so exciting about that?" asked Sylvester, not especially sharing Snooky's enthusiasm.

"It's your star! You're a Geminian!" said Snooky.

Sylvester frowned. "Is that good or bad?"

Snooky laughed. "How could it be bad?

You're knocking out home runs, aren't you?"

A voice called from near the dugout. "Sylvester!" It was Coach Corbin. "I'm inviting the team to an ice cream treat at Chris an' Greens! Can you come?"

"Right now?"

"Right now."

"I'll be there," said Sylvester.

He looked around and saw Snooky running toward the gate. Then he looked toward the first-base bleachers and saw George Baruth standing in front of them, waving to him.

"Nice hitting, Sylvester!" cried Mr. Baruth.

"Thanks!"

"Oh, that's okay, Syl. As a matter of fact, you deserve it."

Sylvester stopped dead in his tracks,

turned and saw Coach Corbin smiling at him.

It was the coach who had answered him. When he looked back toward the bleachers George Baruth was gone.

7

SYLVESTER put down a banana split that was bigger, "bananier" and nuttier than he had ever had before. And just because he was the hero of today's game.

The team then went home. After Sylvester showered and got into clean, everyday clothes he ate supper with Mom. Dad was out on "the road," as he called it. He wasn't coming home till Friday night.

"You probably won't want dessert after having a banana split," said Mom, whose color of eyes and hair matched his.

"What have you got?" he asked. He felt

full, but if Mom had baked something he liked he'd make room for it.

"Apple pie," she said.

Apple pie? No pie made was tastier and more delicious than the apple pie Mom made.

"I'll have a piece," he said.

His mother stared at him. "Are you sure?"

"Yes, I'm sure," he answered and settled back to wait for it.

She took the pie — a large, puffy, crusty thing — out of the oven, set it on the counter and cut him a piece. She placed it on a small dish and put it before him. His mouth watered just looking at the soft, juicy apples oozing from under the crust.

He made a noise like a hungry tiger, cut a chunk of it with his fork, and stuck it into his mouth. While he chewed he looked up at his mother, his eyes big as stoplights. "Mom," he said, "it tastes just as delicious as it looks!"

"Thank you, son," she said. "But don't make a hog of yourself."

Five minutes after he was finished he felt sick. Mom cleared off the table and he still sat there.

"Something wrong, Sylvester?" she asked.

"I think I made a hog of myself," he replied frankly.

"Ate too much, didn't you?"

He nodded. "Can I lie down?"

"Not on a full stomach. Sit in the living room till your food digests a bit. Later on you may lie down."

He got up, went into the living room and sat down. He didn't even feel like turning on the television set. He sat with his legs sprawled out and his head resting against the side of the easy chair. Man, did he feel sick.

After a while Mom let him go to bed.

"You'll feel much better in an hour or so," she said.

He closed his eyes. He didn't know whether he had slept or not, but when he opened them again there sat George Baruth, looking at him sourly.

"Hi, kid," said George.

"Well, hi, Mr. Baruth," replied Sylvester. "I didn't hear you come in. I guess I must have fallen asleep."

"I understand you overloaded yourself," said George Baruth.

Sylvester grinned weakly. "A little," he admitted.

"Little, my eye," grunted George Baruth. "If it were a little you wouldn't be lying there. First a big banana split, then a chunk of apple pie on top of a big dinner. If that isn't being a glutton I don't know what is."

"Yeah. You're right, Mr. Baruth. But how did you know I was sick? How did you know I had a banana split and then an apple pie on top of my dinner?"

George Baruth's eyes twinkled and he reached over and patted Sylvester's hand. "Don't worry about it, kid," he said softly. "Just don't make a hog of yourself again or you'll find yourself sitting on the sidelines instead of playing."

He rose. "Take care, kid. See you at the next game."

"Okay, Mr. Baruth. Thanks for coming."

After George Baruth left, Sylvester lay

there, thinking. How did he know I was sick? he wondered. Only Mom knew that.

Presently Mom came in, smiling. "Feel better?" she asked.

"Yeah." He looked at her seriously. "Mom, did Mr. Baruth call or something?"

She frowned. "Mr. Baruth?"

"Yes. He's the guy who's helping me play baseball. Did he call? Did you tell him I was sick?"

"What do you mean, Sylvester? I didn't see any Mr. Baruth."

He stared at her. "He was here a few minutes ago, Mom. You . . . you must have let him in."

She looked at him worriedly, came nearer and put a hand on his forehead. "You're cool now," she observed. "You must have had a fever, or were dreaming."

"No, I wasn't, Mom," he insisted. "He was here, visiting me!"

The worried look disappeared and she smiled. "Okay, okay. Don't get excited. But please try to understand, son. No one came in here. I would have seen him if he did. You must have dreamed it all."

8

THE HOOPER REDBIRDS had first raps against the Lansing Wildcats in their second league game on the Lansing athletic field. Apparently Coach Corbin's faith in Sylvester Coddmyer III had improved for he was lifting Sylvester's position in the batting order from ninth to eighth.

Sylvester glanced at the first-base bleachers. Sure enough, George Baruth was sitting at the end of the third row, wearing the same pants, same jersey, same coat, same cap. Mr. Baruth must have caught his eye for he lifted a hand in a wave, and Sylvester waved back.

He thought of that evening last week when he was sick and had that dream — or whatever it was — of George Baruth's coming to visit him. If it was a dream it sure was as real as could be.

Jim Cowley, leading off, lambasted a high pitch to center field for the first out. Ted Sobel struck out, Milt Stevens walked, and Jerry Ash flied out to end the top half of the inning.

Right-hander Terry Barnes, slender as a reed and slow as molasses, had trouble finding the plate and walked the first two Wildcats. Up came Bongo Daley, the short, stout Wildcat pitcher.

"A pitcher batting third?" muttered Jim Cowley. "Must be a hitter, too."

Apparently Bongo was. He drilled

Terry's first pitch to left center for a double, scoring one run. The cleanup hitter stepped to the plate.

Terry bore down and struck him out with five pitches. Bobby Kent caught a long fly in center field. The runner on third tagged up and raced in for the second run. A pop-up to short ended the inning.

"Come on, you guys," snapped Coach Corbin. "This isn't tiddlywinks. It's baseball. Let's get going!"

Bobby, leading off, smashed a liner down the left-field foul line that just missed going fair by inches. He lambasted another almost in the same spot.

"Straighten it out, Bobby!" yelled the coach.

Bobby did. The third baseman caught the next line drive without moving a step.

The ball hadn't risen more than five feet off the ground. One out.

Duane walked. Eddie popped to short for the second out, and up to the plate stepped Sylvester Coddmyer III.

The crowd cheered. The cheerleaders led with:

> *Fee! Fie! Fo! Fum!*
> *We want a home run!*
> *Sylvester Coddmyer!*
> *Hooraaaay!*

Suddenly Sylvester remembered that he had forgotten to look for the coach's signal. He stepped out of the box, glanced at the coach sitting in the dugout, received a smile in return and the sign to "hit away," and stepped back into the box.

"Ball!" cried the ump as Bongo blazed in the first pitch.

"Ball two!"

Then, "Strike!"

Wasn't that a little too low? thought Sylvester.

"Ball three!"

"He's going to walk you, Syl!" yelled Jim Cowley.

"Steeeeerike!"

Three and two. Bongo caught the ball from his catcher, stepped off the mound, loosened his belt, tightened it, yanked his cap and finally stepped on the rubber. He stretched, delivered, and bang!

Sylvester's bat connected with the ball and for a moment he watched the white sphere drill a hole through the sky as it shot to deep center field. Then he dropped the bat and started his easy run around the bases while the cheers of the fans and cheerleaders rang in his ears.

"It's fantastic, Syl!" cried the coach as he shook Sylvester's hand at the plate. "Just fantastic!"

"How do you do it?" asked Jerry Ash, who was supposed to be the team's clean-up hitter.

"I just pick the good one and swing," replied Sylvester honestly.

"And blast it out of the park," added the coach.

Terry went down on three straight pitches. Three outs.

Redbirds 2, Wildcats 2.

Terry Barnes's first pitch to the Wildcat leadoff man was drilled sharply through the hole between first and second bases. Sylvester stooped to field the low, sizzling roller, but the ball squirted through his legs. He spun, raced after it, picked it up near the fence and heaved it in. Sick over the error, he saw the Wildcat pulling up safely at third.

"Forget to drop your tailgate, Syl?" asked Ted Sobel, grinning.

"Guess so," replied Sylvester.

A pop fly to third, and then a one-hopper slammed back to Terry, accounted for two outs, and Sylvester felt better. The Wildcat whose ball he had let skid through his legs was still on third.

Ted Sobel caught a long, high fly for the third out.

Bobby Kent belted a single that half inning, scoring two runs.

Bongo's home run over the left-field fence with nobody on was the Wildcats' only hit in the bottom of the third.

Eddie Exton, leading off for the Red-birds in the top of the fourth, popped out to second. And even before Sylvester started for the plate the Redbird cheer-leaders were yelling:

Hey! Hey! Who do we admire?
Sylvester Coddmyer!
The third!

The girls jumped and clapped, joined in an applause by the Redbird fans.

Sylvester, blushing, stepped to the plate.

9

BONGO DALEY FIRED the first pitch high and outside for ball one. He didn't look worried that the batter might blast a pitch out of the lot.

But the next two pitches weren't over the plate either.

His catcher called time and ran out to the mound to talk with him. So did the first and third basemen. The huddle lasted half a minute.

The guys returned to their positions and Bongo toed the rubber again. He wound up, delivered, and the ball nipped the inside corner for a strike.

He fired another in the same spot for strike two. "You have 'im now, Bongo!" yelled the catcher.

The next pitch was almost over the heart of the plate, chest-high. Sylvester liked the looks of it and swung. The solid blow alone told the story. It was another blast over the right field fence.

The Redbird cheerleaders and fans went wild.

It was their only run that inning. The Wildcats scored once, and held the Redbirds scoreless in the top of the fifth inning with Sylvester waiting for his third trip to the plate.

Redbirds 5, Wildcats 4.

He tossed his bat aside and ran out to

his position in right field, smiling and waving to George Baruth sitting in the bleachers behind first base. George smiled and waved back, but so did several other people, as if they thought that Sylvester was smiling and waving at them.

The Wildcats scored a run on an error by Milt and then a line drive over second base. Redbirds 5, Wildcats 5.

Coach Corbin was clasping and unclasping his hands, and now and then wiping his forehead with his handkerchief. He never said very much, and he seldom got angry. But he sure did get extremely nervous whenever the game was close.

And it was close now. Too close. This was the top of the sixth inning. It was their last chance to break the tie. It was either that, or lose.

"Don't ever be ashamed to lose," the coach had once said. "Everybody loses sometime. But play to win."

"Hit away, Syl," he said to Sylvester, who was looking at him for instructions.

The fans yelled wildly as he stepped to the plate. He glanced at the scoreboard. 5 to 5. He'd try to sock another out of the ball park — if he could.

The pitch. It was low, but not too low. He swung. Missed!

"Oh, no!" groaned Terry.

The next pitch was wide.

"Ball one!"

Then, "Stri – " the umpire started to say, but didn't finish. Sylvester had swung at the pitch and the ball was soaring like a loose balloon out toward deep center field. The Wildcat fielder raced out to the fence, then stood there and watched the ball sail over his head.

For the third time that day Sylvester Coddmyer III trotted around the bases, not slowing down his pace till he crossed home plate. He was given the usual reception from the coach and players, and applause from the fans and cheerleaders.

Bongo, apparently shaken by Sylvester's third homer, walked the next two batters. The next two got out. Then Terry singled, scoring Jerry, and Bobby Kent grounded out to short.

The Wildcats pushed across a run at their turn at bat, but that was all. The Redbirds came out on the big end, 7 to 6.

There was more than just yelling, handshaking and back-patting this time. A photographer from the *Hooper Star* took pictures of Sylvester, and a *Star* reporter, carrying a small tape recorder in one hand and a microphone in the other, popped questions at him. He was never so embarrassed in his life.

"Is your name really Sylvester Coddmyer the third?"

"Yes."

"How many years have you played baseball, Sylvester?"

"I never played before."

"Are you sure?"

"I'm sure."

"Then how do you account for getting a home run every time you bat?"

"I just hit the ball squarely on the nose."

"Yes, but — no one else in the world hits a home run every time up. Do you think there is something . . . well, uh . . . unusual about you, Sylvester?"

"No. Why should there be?"

The reporter shrugged. "Well, there shouldn't." He grinned faintly. "What other sports are you interested in, Sylvester?"

"No other sport."

"Okay, Sylvester. Thanks very much."

The reporter and photographer left, and he breathed a sigh of relief. He had barely relaxed when someone nudged his elbow. "Hi, Sylvester."

It was Snooky Malone, grinning that funny grin of his. He was carrying a small booklet, something about "Your Horoscope." Sylvester wasn't able to see the whole title.

"What's it now, Snooky?" he asked, becoming a little annoyed with Snooky's pestering him.

"Being a Gemini makes you have more

ability than the average person, Sylvester," said Snooky proudly.

"Thanks, Snooky," replied Sylvester. "But I haven't got time to listen to that stuff now. I'm tired."

He started for home and Snooky hopped alongside of him. "This book says that you are ruled by the planet Mercury," went on Snooky. "It also says that when the planet Venus, or the Moon, draws close to Mercury as they are seen from Earth, a Gemini's powers are sharpened. That's why you knock home runs every time you bat, Sylvester."

"I'm glad to hear that," said Sylvester, not very impressed.

"But that's not the only reason why."

Sylvester stared at the big periods behind the dark-green glasses. "What do you mean by that?"

"I read quite a lot about occultism, too."

"Occultism?" Sylvester frowned, perplexed. "What's that?"

The dark eyes held onto his unflinchingly. "It's a science dealing with the mysterious," said Snooky. He paused, as if to give time for that information to sink in. "Who do you keep looking at and waving to in the bleachers behind first base, Sylvester?"

"George Baruth. Why?"

"George Baruth? Who's he?"

"A friend."

"From around here?"

Sylvester shrugged. "No. He's vacationing here."

"Oh?"

Sylvester looked at him again, then plunged on ahead, determined this time not to stop. "Sorry, Snooky, but I can't hang around any longer."

"See you again, Sylvester," said Snooky.

Don't be in a hurry about it, thought Sylvester.

10

THE REDBIRDS and the Macon Falcons clashed on the eighth. It seemed that the poor Falcons didn't have enough nourishment even to flutter their wings, let alone play baseball. They crumbled under the Redbirds' attack, 11 to 1.

Sylvester Coddmyer III was up to bat four times and knocked four home runs to keep his streak unbroken. He had nine runs batted in and three put-outs.

"I marked down a home run for you the last time up even before you batted, Syl," said the scorekeeper, proudly.

"Don't you think that's going a little bit too far?" said Sylvester.

There was no school on Monday, the eighteenth. It was Teachers Conference Day. Two hours before game time against the Teaburg Giants, Sylvester Coddmyer III was on his way home with a load of groceries when a combined sound of running footsteps and a high-pitched voice thundered in his ears.

"Hi, Sylvester!" greeted Snooky Malone, coming up beside him and grinning that elfish grin of his.

"Hi, Snooky," said Sylvester, and made a face. "You're not going to start on that horoscope and occult stuff again, are you?"

"As a matter of fact" — Snooky paused — "I was. But not here."

"Good," said Sylvester, and picked up speed.

Snooky grabbed his arm. "At Chris an' Greens, Sylvester. I want to treat you to a delicious pie à la mode."

Sylvester slowed down to almost a stop. "Pie à la mode?" His mouth watered. "Pie à la mode's my favorite dessert."

Snooky's smile was almost fiendish. "I know." He coaxed Sylvester to the corner and across the street to Chris an' Greens, Sylvester fighting against the impulse every step of the way. It was a losing battle, and the way he tackled the pie à la mode he didn't mind having lost at all.

"We're friends, aren't we, Sylvester?" said Snooky, taking an occasional sip of his lemon soda.

Sylvester looked at him. "If I didn't

109

know you, Snooky, I'd think you were trying to sell me something."

Snooky laughed. "All I want you to do is trust me," he said.

"Who said I didn't?"

"Okay. Tell me your secret. George Baruth is no real person, is he? He's someone you've made up."

"Snooky, you've got bats in your head. He's as real as you are."

"No, he isn't. He's a figment of your imagination."

Sylvester stared at him. "Snooky," he said, "I'm beginning to think that *you're* a figment of my imagination!"

"That's because I'm different from most kids," smiled Snooky.

"You can say that again," said Sylvester. He turned to what was left of the pie à la mode and finished it.

"Want more?" asked Snooky. "I've been saving up my allowance for a new book on astrology, but I can wait another week."

The thought of eating another pie à la mode hit Sylvester like a sledgehammer. "You sure it's okay?" he asked.

"I wouldn't ask you if it weren't," answered Snooky, and ordered another pie à la mode for Sylvester.

For a while both boys held their silence. Sylvester took his time devouring his second pie à la mode, Snooky took his time sipping his first lemon soda.

Snooky must have bats in his head, thought Sylvester sourly. Saying that George Baruth wasn't real was plain ridiculous.

"I've got an idea," said Snooky, the smile on his face broadening. "How about

111

introducing me to him this afternoon at the game?"

"Sure. Why not?"

Suddenly he didn't feel good. He was full of pie à la mode — so full his stomach was beginning to rebel.

"I've got to get home, Snooky," he said, sliding off the stool and grabbing the bag of groceries. "I don't feel good."

"Gee, Sylvester!" cried Snooky. "I hope you're not getting sick!"

"It's too late," muttered Sylvester. "I'm sick already."

He hurried home, plopped the bag of groceries into his mother's arms and headed directly to his room, where he toppled on the bed, so hot he felt he was burning. His mother came in.

"Sylvester!" she cried. "What's hap-

112

pened to you? Where have you been for the last hour?"

"Snoo — Snooky Malone . . . treated me to . . . two pie à la modes," he said, and moaned.

"Two pie à la modes? No wonder you're sick!" She lifted his feet onto the bed and covered him with a blanket. "You made a pig of yourself. When are you going to learn?"

He moaned again, too sick to agree with her. He closed his eyes and heard his mother leave and the door latch click shut.

Sometime later he was awakened from his sleep and his mother said there were several boys here to see him. "Do you feel better?" she asked. "Or shall I tell them you'll see them tomorrow?"

"I feel better," he said. "Send them in."

She left and a moment later in came Jim Cowley, Terry Barnes and Eddie Exton. "What happened to you?" asked Jim.

"Stuffed myself with pie à la modes," replied Sylvester. "How did the game come out?"

"We lost," said Eddie. "Ten to four."

"It was your fault," said Terry. "You and your pie à la modes." Then he grinned. "Know what? I'm nuts about 'em, too."

11

THERE WAS A CHANGE in the line-up when the Seneca Indians played the Redbirds. Coach Corbin moved Sylvester up to fourth in the batting order. Sylvester had been up there before, in a scrimmage game. Would he perform well enough today to earn the position for good?

The Indians were leading by one run when Sylvester came to bat in the bottom of the first inning. Jim Cowley was on first after uncorking a single.

Bert Riley, a tall, loose-jointed kid with

a funny way of throwing the ball, was on the mound. He toed the rubber, stretched, and threw. Every part of his body seemed to go into motion before the ball actually left his hand.

The pitch was wide. "Ball!"

Bert went through his peculiar motions again, and pitched. *Pow!* The hit was as solid as it sounded. The ball took off like a shot and cleared the left-field fence by at least twenty feet. The crowd roared and Sylvester started his slow, easy trot around the bases.

He glanced at the bleachers as he reached first base and saw George Baruth sitting there at the end of the third row, smiling that boyish smile of his. He waved and Sylvester waved back.

Then Sylvester saw the kid sitting next to Mr. Baruth waving to him, too, and he recognized Snooky Malone.

"Nice blast, Sylvester!" Snooky shouted.

H'm, thought Sylvester. Apparently Snooky had taken it upon himself to meet George Baruth.

The Indians picked up two runs in the top of the third. Then Sylvester hit his second home run in the bottom of the fourth. Indians 3, Redbirds 3.

As Sylvester ran out to the field he looked over at George Baruth and Snooky Malone. He expected to see Snooky talking Mr. Baruth's head off. Snooky was busy talking, all right, but it was with the kid on his left side. Maybe Snooky wasn't interested in getting into a conversation with an old guy like Mr. Baruth.

Terry's first pitch was blasted out to deep right, directly at Sylvester. Sylvester sprinted forward a few steps, then suddenly panicked. The ball was hit farther than he expected!

He turned and ran in the opposite direction. His short legs were a blur as he ran. He looked over his left shoulder, then his right. There was the ball, dropping ahead of him!

Somehow he picked up more speed, stretched out his glove hand, and caught the ball.

The applause from the Redbird fans was tremendous. A double between left and center fields braced up the Indians' hopes of scoring, but a pop fly and then a one-hopper to Terry ended the top half of the fifth inning.

Jim, leading off, flied out to center. Ted walked and advanced to second on Milt's single over short. Up came Sylvester Coddmyer III and the Redbird fans went wild again.

The Indians called time. The infielders

ran in toward the mound, surrounding their pitcher, Bert Riley. They held a quiet, lengthy discussion, then returned to their positions.

What now? thought Sylvester, as Bert Riley faced him for the third time.

"Ball!" shouted the ump, as Bert blazed one in — a mile outside.

"Ball two!" shouted the ump. Another one outside.

"Ball three!" And another.

"He's afraid of you, Syl!" yelled Snooky Malone. "He's gonna walk you!"

And that's just what Bert did. Sylvester was walked his first time ever.

12

ALL KINDS of noises exploded from the Redbird fans. Some of them yelled. Some of them hissed.

Sylvester didn't care. He didn't get out, that was the important thing.

The bases were loaded and Jerry Ash was up. The fans and the team gave Jerry all kinds of verbal support, but it did no good. Bert struck him out.

Bobby Kent did a little better. His swinging bat connected with the ball. But the ball hopped up into the Indian shortstop's glove just like a trained rabbit.

The shortstop whipped the ball to second, throwing Sylvester out and ending the Redbirds' threat.

Top of the sixth. A hard blow to short! Milt muffed the ball, picked it up and pegged it to first. A short throw. Jerry Ash stretched for it. The ball struck the tip of his mitt and rolled aside.

Oh, come on! thought Sylvester. We can't flub the ball now!

Terry motioned Duane to come in a bit. The third baseman advanced till he was ahead of the bag by a few steps, then bent forward, hands on his knees.

A bunt! Duane rushed in, fielded it and pegged it to second. Too late! The base umpire's hands fanned out with the "safe" sign. Jim fired to first, but there, too, the hitter beat the throw.

Two on, no outs, and a tied score, 3 and 3.

Terry wiped his forehead, tugged on his cap, toed the rubber. He stretched, delivered. A blow over second! A run scored! Bobby Kent fielded the ball and threw it in, holding the Indians on third and first.

"Bear down, Terry!" yelled Sylvester.

A smashing grounder down to Jim! He caught the hop, snapped it to Milt. Milt stepped on second, rifled the ball to first. A double play!

Jerry pivoted to throw home, but held up. The Indian on third wasn't taking any chances.

Terry caught the soft throw from Jerry, then climbed to the mound, got Eddie's sign and pitched. Ball one. He zipped two over the heart of the plate. The Indian batter swung at the first and missed. He blasted the second one over short for a clean single, scoring another run.

Terry struck out the next batter. Indians 5, Redbirds 3.

"Last chance to pull this game out of the fire," said Coach Corbin. "Start it off, Duane. Make 'em be in there."

Duane waited for 'em to be in there and got a two-two count. Bert's next pitch was letter-high and Duane corked it out to short left field. The Indian outfielder raced in and made a shoestring catch.

Eddie waited for a pitch he liked and blasted it for a single. The hit livened the Redbirds' bench. The players had been sitting there as if their tail feathers had already been clipped.

Terry socked a hard grounder to third which the baseman caught and pegged to second. The throw was wild!

A cheer exploded from the Redbirds' bench and the cheerleaders as Terry made his turn and came back to stand safely on first base.

Then Jim popped up to the catcher for the second out, and it looked as if the Seneca Indians were about to scalp the Redbirds for sure.

Ted Sobel let two strikes go by, then knocked the third pitch between right and center fields for a double! Eddie and Terry scored to tie it up.

What a ball game this was!

Milt walked and once again Sylvester Coddmyer III came to the plate.

"Out of the lot, Syl!" shouted Snooky Malone.

A hit out of the lot would mean eight runs and victory. But was Sylvester going to be given the chance to do that? Not if Bert Riley, who had called a time out, and the infielders, who were running toward the mound, were planning the same strategy they had planned before.

"Booooooo!" yelled Snooky Malone.

The discussion around the pitcher's box took only half as long as it did the first time. The players returned to their positions. Bert Riley toed the rubber, pitched, and the ball zipped wide of the plate.

Bert pitched three more almost in the same spot and for the second time that day, and in his life, Sylvester Coddmyer III walked.

The bases were loaded.

"Your baby, Jerry!" yelled Snooky Malone.

Crack! A sock over second base! Ted and Milt scored and that was it. The game was over. Indians 5, Redbirds 7.

The next morning's *Hooper Star* had an item on the sports page that read:

REDBIRDS PLAYER CONTINUES SENSATIONAL HITTING STREAK

Sylvester Coddmyer III smashed out two homers and was walked twice to keep his batting record unmarred as the Hooper Redbirds beat the Seneca Indians 7 to 5 in the Valley Junior High School League.

His 1.000 batting average, and a home run each time at bat (except for the two walks), is unprecedented in Hooper Redbirds baseball history.

As a matter of fact, it may possibly be unprecedented in national baseball history.

The least impressed person about this sensational hitting, however, is Sylvester himself.

This week two national magazines printed his picture and writeups about him. Sylvester's comment:

"I just can't see why they're making all the fuss."

The Hooper Redbirds played the Broton Tigers that evening and took the game, 8 to 4. Sylvester was walked the first time up, hit homers his next two times up. One was a grand-slammer.

Newspaper reporters, photographers and a television crew from Syracuse made him their center of attraction after he had won the game against the Lansing Wildcats practically singlehanded. The score was 4 to 0 and he had made all the runs himself — by homers.

"Do you think you'd like to play in the

big leagues after you get out of school, Sylvester?" asked a reporter.

"I don't know. I might."

"Do you practice batting a lot? Do you think that's why you keep on hitting home runs?"

"I don't practice any more than the other guys do," replied Sylvester sincerely.

"Do you suppose it's the way you stand at the plate that gives you so much power?"

"Maybe. I never gave it much thought."

He felt a gnawing ache growing achier and achier in his stomach and forced a smile. "Do — do you mind if we stop now? I'm getting awfully hungry."

"Of course, Sylvester. Thanks very much for your time," said the reporter.

Sylvester started to ease through the

crowd, smiling at the many faces smiling at him. He looked for the one he was most anxious to see, and finally saw it near the edge of the crowd.

"Hi, Mr. Baruth," he greeted.

"Hi, Sylvester," said George Baruth. "Boy! Are you a celebrity!"

"Yeah, I guess I am."

"Just make sure you don't get swell-headed from all the fuss," warned George Baruth.

"Swellheaded?" Sylvester looked up at Mr. Baruth with large question marks in his eyes.

"Yes. You know — strutting around like a cocky rooster. Ignoring your friends. Not listening to your mother and father. Thinking you have suddenly become a lot better than other people. That's being swellheaded. It's the worst kind of thing

130

that could happen to a person who becomes famous."

The possibility of his becoming like that frightened Sylvester. "That would be awful, Mr. Baruth. I think I'd rather not play baseball again than get swellheaded."

George Baruth smiled and patted him on the shoulder. "That's the way to talk, son. You're a level-headed boy."

"Hey, Sylvester!" someone shouted from behind him. "Wait!"

Sylvester recognized the screechy voice even before he turned.

It was Snooky Malone's.

13

"AH . . . SYLVESTER," said George Baruth. "This is where I'll leave you. See you later."

"Okay, Mr. Baruth."

Snooky came pounding up the sidewalk and stopped beside him, smiling broadly.

"Man! What publicity you're getting!" he cried, breathing hard. "Even television! Wow!"

Sylvester shrugged, unimpressed. "I just hope they don't do it too often," he said. "What time is it, Snooky?"

Snooky looked at his wristwatch. "Five-thirty."

"Oh, man! Mom's probably wondering what happened to me!" He started to run. "Sorry, Snooky, but I've got to get home!"

He realized then that George Baruth wasn't ahead of him. Nor was George behind him. He looked back toward the houses he had passed but couldn't see his friend anywhere.

"What are you looking for?" asked Snooky, running along beside him.

"Mr. Baruth," said Sylvester. "He was with me just before you came."

"Mr. Baruth? The man you told me about?"

"Yes."

"He was with you just before I came?"

"Yes. You must have seen him."

133

Snooky chuckled. "No, I didn't. I didn't see anybody with you, Sylvester."

Sylvester looked at him perplexedly. "You're lying."

"I am not lying."

"But he was with me!"

Snooky smiled mischievously. "I believe you."

Sylvester's jaw dropped. "Why should you if you didn't see him?"

"Because I know you're a Gemini and are ruled by a special Sun-Sign that makes it possible for you to see into the beyond."

"You're talking crazy, Snooky," said Sylvester, still staring at the periodlike eyes behind the dark lenses of Snooky's glasses.

"A common response," said Snooky. "But I'm surprised to hear it from you."

"But you've met him!" cried Sylvester. "You were talking to him at the baseball field!"

"Syl, how could I have talked to him when I have never even seen the guy?" said Snooky.

Sylvester's eyes grew wider. "But you were sitting beside him in the bleachers the other day."

"I was? I didn't see anybody I didn't know." Snooky smiled and put a hand on Sylvester's shoulder. "I envy you, Syl. I really do."

They reached the intersection and Snooky paused. "Well, here's where I turn off, Syl. See you later."

" 'Bye, Snook."

Snooky wasn't a bad name for him, thought Sylvester as he continued up the street alone. But Snoopy would be more fitting.

Mom had supper ready, just as Sylvester had figured. She wondered what had delayed him and he told her. She listened to him, eyes fixed on him.

"It's the truth, Mom," he said. "Every word of it."

"I believe you," she said. "But why you, Sylvester?"

" 'Cause I'm the only one who hits a home run every time. And I've been walked only three times."

"And that's unusual?" asked his mother.

He grinned. "Yes, Mom. I guess it is."

Sylvester knocked three home runs against the Macon Falcons on June 3, but the Redbirds lost in spite of it, 7 to 6.

The next morning's *Hooper Star* read:

REDBIRDS LOSE
IN SPITE OF
CODDMYER'S
THREE HOMERS

Sylvester Coddmyer III's three home runs were not enough to help the Redbirds in their game against the Macon Falcons yesterday. It was the Redbirds' second loss of their first highly successful season, thanks to the powerful bat of Sylvester Coddmyer III.

So far he has compiled a record of twenty-one home runs, an unprecedented record.

He has never struck out nor scored any hits other than home runs, leaving him with a batting average of 1.000.

Asked by this reporter what he makes of the youth's exceptional hitting, Redbirds Coach Stan Corbin says he doesn't know. The fact is, neither does anyone else.

As for Sylvester Coddmyer III, his bat is doing all the talking.

That evening a Mr. Johnson from one of the nation's most popular magazines came to the house and said that his magazine was offering Sylvester fifteen thousand dollars if he would let them publish his biography.

"Since you are under age one of your parents would have to sign, too," said Mr. Johnson.

Sylvester and his mother seemed paralyzed for awhile. They stood staring at the man like wax figures.

Mr. Johnson smiled. "Of course there will be more money coming to you from other sources," he said. "We are thinking of sponsoring an hour special on a television network and taking you to New York for an appearance on two or three national television shows. You and your husband may go along with him, of course, Mrs. Coddmyer, with all expenses paid."

"We . . . we may?"

That was all Mrs. Coddmyer could say. As for Sylvester, he was unable to say anything. Just listen. He wasn't sure whether this was all real or just a dream.

"What do you think, Ma?" he asked after he realized that Mr. Johnson was waiting for an answer.

"What? Oh — I think it's absolutely fine." Her eyes bounced worriedly back and forth between Sylvester and Mr. Johnson. "It'd help to pay up our bills, wouldn't it?"

"Part of the money will be put in a trust fund for Sylvester's education," explained Mr. Johnson.

"Oh, yes, of course," said Mrs. Coddmyer. She was sitting down now and twisting a handkerchief round and round on her lap.

Mr. Johnson placed a couple of sheets of paper, with carbon between them, on the table. "This is the contract binding you and our company," he explained. "I'll leave it with you to read over thoroughly at your convenience. You may want to have your lawyer read it."

"We don't have a lawyer," said Mrs. Coddmyer.

"You really don't need one. But read over the contract before you sign it. I assure you it contains all I have discussed with you and that it is perfectly legitimate."

"Oh, we're sure of that, Mr. Johnson," said Mrs. Coddmyer.

Mr. Johnson smiled, rose and shook hands with them. "I'll telephone in a day or two," he said, and left.

Sylvester sat thinking hard. All these great things happening to him were not just by accident. He had been helped, and the person who had helped him was his friend, George Baruth.

If anyone was able to offer advice it was Mr. Baruth. Dad wasn't home, anyway. He wouldn't be for almost a week.

"I know who we can ask for advice, Ma," said Sylvester. "He's not a lawyer, but I know he'd be glad to give us advice about this."

"We should ask your father, Sylvester."

"Oh, Mom! He won't be home for almost a week! And he usually agrees with you on important things, anyway!"

"Who's this man you're talking about, Sylvester?"

"George Baruth. That friend of mine I told you about."

Mom frowned. "George Baruth? Sylvester, are you sure you know what you're saying? I've heard you talk about him, yes. But I have never seen the man, nor have I ever heard of him except from you."

"I don't care, Mom," said Sylvester seriously. "He's a great guy and he's my friend. And he helped me become what I am. I know he'll be glad to help us on this."

Mom sighed. "Okay, if you say so. Do you know his phone number?"

"He's on vacation here. But I'll see him."

14

H E WAS RETURNING from school the next day when who should he meet coming toward him from Winslow Street but George Baruth himself.

"Good afternoon, kid," said George. "Fancy meeting you."

"Yeah," said Sylvester. "Me, too." Excitement suddenly overwhelmed him. "Got something very important to ask you, Mr. Baruth," he said.

"Oh? What?"

"Mr. Johnson, from a famous magazine, was at our house last evening and left a contract for me to sign," said Sylvester. "He says that his company wants to publish my biography and will pay me a lot of money for it. They'll also put money into a trust fund for my education. And I'll be on TV shows and Mom and Dad can come along with all expenses paid. Mr. Johnson says we can have our lawyer read the contract before we sign it, because either Mom or Dad has to sign it, too. But we don't have a lawyer."

He paused to catch his breath.

"And you'd like me to read the contract and advise you on what to do. Is that it?" asked George Baruth.

Sylvester's head bobbed like a cork on a wavy sea.

"Well," said George Baruth, starting down the street, Sylvester pacing beside

144

him like a pup, "I don't know for sure what to say myself."

"Don't you want to read the contract?"

"I don't have to. I know what it says. You told me. It's honest, that's for sure. As for signing it . . ." He halted and looked at Sylvester with a deep, haunting look in his eyes Sylvester had not ever seen before.

"It's a lot of publicity and money, Sylvester. But fame could be a dangerous thing. It could ruin one's life. The first taste of it is sweet. So you'd want more. It's human nature. But something bad could happen. Suppose your hitting dropped to rock bottom? People would laugh at you. Your own friends would mock you. You'd wish you'd never seen a baseball."

Mr. Baruth paused, took out a handkerchief and wiped his face.

"Something else about it bothers me, too," he said.

"What, Mr. Baruth?"

"Well . . . me. What I did to make you into a great baseball hitter. You see, Syl," suddenly his eyes looked dim and sad, "I won't be around much longer. And, with me gone, you may not be hitting like you used to . . ." He paused.

"I'll sure miss you, Mr. Baruth."

"And I'll miss you."

"Then you . . . you don't think I should sign the contract?"

George Baruth eyed him silently for a long while, then said, "Suppose you decide that yourself, Syl?"

Sylvester shrugged. "Okay. Thanks, Mr. Baruth. You've been awfully kind to me."

"You've been a joy to me, too, Syl."

They shook hands.

"Will you be at the next game?"

"You bet," said George Baruth.

Sylvester turned, started to run, and bumped into Snooky Malone, hitting the little guy so hard that Snooky fell to the sidewalk, his glasses falling off and his books spilling out of his hands.

"Hey, watch it!" yelled Snooky.

"Oh, sorry, Snooky!" cried Sylvester. "I didn't see you!"

"I guess you didn't!" exclaimed Snooky, rising to his feet.

Sylvester gathered up the dark glasses, handed them to the little guy, then gathered up the books.

"I heard you talking," said Snooky.

Sylvester looked at the huge periods behind the glasses. "What did I say?"

147

" 'Thanks, Mr. Baruth. You've been awfully kind to me. Will you be at the next game?' "

"That's all?"

Snooky nodded, and smiled. "You were talking with George Baruth, weren't you?"

Sylvester nodded. Darn Snooky, snooping around all the time.

"What were you talking about?"

"Something very important, but I can't tell you about it, Snooky. Sorry."

He and Mom talked a lot about the contract that night. Mr. Johnson called the next morning and arrived that afternoon. He looked at the contract and frowned.

"It's not signed," he observed.

"No, it isn't," said Sylvester. "We decided it was best that I didn't."

"Why, Sylvester? Isn't the money enough?"

"Oh, it's not the money, Mr. Johnson. It's just that I don't deserve it and all that publicity. I'd be thinking about it all my life, and I wouldn't want to do that. I'm sorry, Mr. Johnson, but that's how Mom and I decided."

15

THE HOOPER REDBIRDS beat the Teaburg Giants 8 to 3 on June 8, leaving one more game to play for the Redbirds. Sylvester's home-run streak went unbroken. He had three in three times up, twice with no runners on, once with two on. Mr. Baruth was at the game, sitting in his usual place.

Immediately after the game, and all the way home, Snooky Malone clung to Sylvester like a leech. Now and then Sylvester looked around for George Baruth but didn't see him. Was he staying away because of snoopy Snooky? Probably.

It wasn't till the next day after supper, while Sylvester was brooding about George Baruth on the front porch steps, that Mr. Baruth stopped by.

"Oh, hi, Mr. Baruth!" Sylvester greeted him happily.

"Hi, kid," said George. "Did you sign the contract?"

"No, sir. Mom and I talked about it and decided against it."

"Did you tell your Mom about me?"

"Of course. That was all right, wasn't it, Mr. Baruth?"

George Baruth's face lighted up as if someone had turned on a switch inside him. "Sure it was all right. It's all right all the way down the line, kid." He paused. "Well, good-bye, kid. And keep happy, hear?"

Sylvester nodded, and stood up. "Are you — are you leaving now, Mr. Baruth?" he asked.

The big man nodded and walked down the street, head bowed, till he was out of sight.

The crowd on Thursday was the biggest ever. People filled the grandstand and the bleachers, and were lying down or standing behind both foul lines. The game was against the Seneca Indians, and the Redbirds had first raps.

Left-handed Bert Riley was on the mound again for the Indians and walked the first three men up. For a while no one was advancing toward the plate, and Coach Corbin said, "Sylvester, wake up."

Sylvester rose from the on-deck circle and walked to the plate. He had been looking at the end of the third-row bleacher seats — looking for George Baruth. But, for the first time since the season had started, George Baruth wasn't there.

"Steerike!" yelled the ump as Bert blazed in a pitch.

"Ball!"

"Ball two!"

Then, "Strike two!"

Sylvester stepped out of the box, wiped his face with a handkerchief and stepped in again. Tensely, he waited for the next pitch. The crowd was hushed. Bert stretched, delivered. The throw looked good. Sylvester leaned into it and swung.

Plop! sounded the ball as it struck the catcher's mitt. The next second the crowd roared and it was as if a gigantic bomb had exploded. Sylvester Coddmyer III had struck out.

He walked to the bench, his head bowed.

"Don't worry about it, Syl!" yelled a familiar voice. "You'll bat again!" It sounded like Snooky Malone.

Jerry Ash flied out. Then Bobby Kent singled, scoring two runs, and Duane Francis grounded out.

The Indians scored once, and that was it till the fourth inning when Eddie Exton doubled and came in on Terry Barnes's neat single over first base.

The Indians made up for the run and more besides. With two men on, a left-handed hitter socked a clothesline drive out to right field. The ball grazed the top of Sylvester's glove and bounced out to the fence. Sylvester ran as hard as he could after it, picked it up and heaved it in.

Three runs scored. The Indians tallied

four runs that half inning, going ahead, 5 to 3.

Sylvester led off in the top of the fifth. He had looked once more for George Baruth in the seat at the end of the third row, hoping to see him. But the big man wasn't there.

Not until now was he sure that he would never see his friend again.

He struck out on three straight pitches.

Jerry doubled, though, and Bobby knocked him in for the Redbirds' only run that half inning.

Back bounced the Indians for three more runs to make their score 8. And back came the Redbirds for their last chance.

Jim walked. Ted singled. Milt flied out. And up came Sylvester.

"Knock it over the fence, Syl!" yelled Snooky Malone.

The pitch. Sylvester swung. *Crack!* A

hit! But not one of those long ones that he had been hitting all season. Not an over-the-fence blast that made the crowd draw in its collective breath.

It was a shallow drive but hard, with the ball rolling between the left and center fielders. Two runs scored and Sylvester reached second base for a double, the only hit he had made all season that wasn't a home run.

Both Jerry and Bobby got out and that was it. The Indians won, 8 to 6.

He thought it was all over then. He thought the people had suddenly forgotten him. But they hadn't. They crowded around him, patting him on the back and shaking his hand while photographers snapped pictures like crazy.

Then someone pushed through the crowd, and a silence fell like a curtain.

"Sylvester," said Coach Stan Corbin, standing there with a huge, bright trophy of a boy swinging a baseball bat, "in honor of our school, Hooper Junior High, and all the teachers and students and myself, I am happy to present this trophy to the greatest athlete Hooper Junior High School has ever had."

So choked up that he was unable to say a word, Sylvester accepted the trophy. Finally he was able to speak.

"Thanks," he said.

His mother and Snooky Malone walked on either side of him as he carried the trophy home.

But, somehow, it seemed that the trophy wasn't quite as heavy as it was when the coach had given it to him. It seemed lighter, as if someone else was helping him carry it.

FINAL STANDINGS

	WON	LOST
Redbirds	7	3
Giants	6	4
Wildcats	6	4
Tigers	5	5
Falcons	4	6
Indians	3	7

Return of the
Home Run Kid

Return of the
Home Run Kid

•

by Matt Christopher

Illustrated by Paul Casale

• Chapter 1 •

C rack!
*Sylvester Coddmyer III dropped the bat
and stared deep into the outfield. The ball soared
over the center fielder's outstretched glove. It was
heading toward the fence. It was going over. It
was* going . . . going . . .

"Wake up, Sylvester!" Coach Stan Corbin's raw
voice cut through the cool spring air. "Did you
come here to play baseball or nap?"

Pulling his cap over his thatch of blond hair,
Sylvester blinked and jumped up. He'd been doz-
ing there at the far end of the bench. The dugout
was so warm, and he really hadn't expected to
hear his name called. After all, he hardly ever got
to play these days.

165

It was such a nice dream, too. It reminded him of last season when he was the Hooper Redbirds' leading hitter. Back then it seemed as if he could hit nothing but home runs — except for the last game. He had struck out twice before getting a double, but that drove in what turned out to be the winning runs. That amazing season had earned Sylvester a trophy for being the best athlete in the history of Hooper Junior High.

To this day, he felt it was all due to Mr. Baruth. Sylvester wasn't even good enough to be considered a so-so player until that mysterious stranger showed up and started giving him pointers.

But Mr. Baruth had left town almost as suddenly as he had appeared. This season there was no outside help. At first Sylvester had figured he didn't need any. He thought he'd just show up and start belting the ball without a lot of effort or a lot of practice. It hadn't happened that way. Coasting along just didn't work, and his game had turned dismal. The coach really had no reason to let him play.

Now it was the top of the fourth inning, the

score 3–0 in the Seneca Indians' favor, and the coach had decided that Bobby Kent, the Redbirds' star outfielder, needed a rest.

"Grab your glove, Sylvester, and take Bobby's place out in center. Bobby, you've done well, kid. Take a break," said the coach.

The Redbirds' tall center fielder looked surprised. He glanced over at the short and stocky Sylvester and smirked as he flopped down on the bench.

Thanks for the vote of confidence, Bobby, Sylvester thought with a scowl. Just because you're hot out there now . . . Well, I can tell you it doesn't always last.

Glove in hand, Sylvester ran out of the dugout and nearly tripped on his straggling shoelaces. He'd loosened them when he felt his feet getting cramped from dangling off the bench. Quickly tying them, he ran off toward his playing position.

"Hi, Syl!" yelled Ted Sobel from his position in left field. Dressed in his Redbird red uniform with white trim, Ted looked neat and bright, like a Christmas ornament.

"Hi!" replied Sylvester. It felt good to be out on

167

the field with the sun shining down on him. It was a little bit like last year when, following Mr. Baruth's coaching tips, he'd made a series of fantastic catches on top of his great hitting. Maybe the coach and his teammates remembered how well he had played, after all.

"Hey, Syl," Les Kendall, the right fielder, greeted him offhandedly.

Les was the team's second leading hitter — right after that new kid, Trent Sturgis, who played shortstop. Trent did a good job fielding, but it was his hitting streak that made him the focus of everyone's attention.

As Syl mentally compared Trent's playing abilities to his own, his confidence sagged. He forgot all about Mr. Baruth and silently wished that any balls hit to the outfield would go to either left or right field.

The infield chatter rattled on as the Indians' catcher, Scott Corrigan, stepped into the batter's box. Wearing a black-trimmed yellow uniform, Scott was the Indians' cleanup hitter. So far he'd gotten a two-bagger.

Scott took two balls and a strike, then laced one deep to left.

"Back! Back!" Sylvester yelled to Ted as the ball rose in a high arc over the field.

Ted raced back as far as he could go, then watched as the ball soared over his head and disappeared behind the fence.

As he turned and watched Scott trot around the bases, Sylvester groaned. No need to hurry, he thought. I know just how he feels. A pang of envy pinched somewhere deep in his chest.

Rooster Adams was up next and slammed a low, clothesline drive straight out to center field. Sylvester's heart leapt into his throat as he saw the ball coming directly at him.

Mr. Baruth sprang into his mind. Remember what he told you. Keep your eye right on that ball and get under it. Sylvester ran forward, his arm stretched out in front of him.

Splat! The ball smacked into the pocket of his glove. And then it vanished.

He searched the green turf around his feet, thinking that he had dropped it.

169

"Your glove! Your glove, Syl!" Ted yelled at him from over in left field.

Sylvester looked at his glove and his heart uncoiled like an overwound spring. There, nesting in the center of the well-oiled glove, was the red-and-blue-threaded white ball.

He breathed a sigh of relief, picked out the ball, and tossed it to Jim Cowley, the Redbirds' second baseman.

"Good catch, Syl!" Jim called to him.

Syl's smile faded. Was Jim surprised he'd made a good catch or was he saying that to be nice?

He wondered whether Joyce Dancer was in the stands and what she thought of his catch. Joyce was twelve, a year younger than Sylvester, but they spent a lot of time with each other. They'd just started going to movies together.

There was no time to think about that. He had to pay attention to the game.

Stan Falls, up next, rapped out a single over shortstop. Then Jon Buckley struck out. Terry Barnes, the Redbirds' pitcher, was erratic today, first hot, then cold. Sylvester remembered the two batters he'd fanned in the first inning as well as the three runs he'd given up to the Indians in the second.

"C'mon, Terry! Strike 'm out!" Sylvester yelled as the Indians' shortstop, Dick Wasser, stepped into the box.

Dick hugged the plate as if he were defending it. He let two of Terry's pitches go by for strikes, then took a walk as Terry flubbed the next four.

Two out, two on as the Indians' pitcher, Burk Riley, came to bat.

"Easy out!" Sylvester yelled. "Easy out!" Burk's bat had hardly touched the ball so far today.

Burk took a called strike, then laced Terry's next pitch to right center field. Both Sylvester and Les Kendall raced toward the ball. Les got there first, scooped it up, and heaved it to third base. But his throw was short. Dick Wasser held up on third. Stan Falls raced in to score.

Bus Riley, the Indians' leadoff batter, then flied out to left to end the inning.

Seneca Indians 5, Hooper Redbirds 0.

Sylvester ran off the field, glad that the half

171

inning was over without any disasters on his part. He had made a good catch, but what if he had missed it? What would happen next time a ball came at him like that? Would he remember what he'd learned from Mr. Baruth again? All these thoughts seemed to bounce around in his head at the same time, making him nervous.

"Grab a bat, Sylvester!" the red-haired, freckle-faced scorekeeper Billy Haywood called to him as he came trotting off the field. "Start it off with a big one, pal!"

Start it off? Sylvester hadn't realized he'd be up at bat so soon. This made him even more nervous than he'd been in the field.

Sylvester took a couple of deep breaths, hoping that would help calm him down.

He yanked his maroon batting gloves out of his pocket, slipped them on, selected a bat — a brown one with white tape around the handle — put on a helmet, and strode to the plate.

Heart racing, he scraped the dirt with his shoes, pretending to get a better grip by digging them in. Time, just a little more time. That's all he needed. Time for his heartbeat to slow down.

Burk steamed in two pitches, a ball and a strike. Then came another pitch that looked as good as any Sylvester could hope for.

Clunk! Bat barely connected with ball, and the ball rolled away from the plate like a frightened worm.

Sylvester dropped his bat and raced for first base, knowing all the while that his short legs would never beat out the throw. It was a sure out. He could practically hear the call.

Suddenly, there was a yell from the crowd, and he saw the ball fly over the first baseman's head. It was a rotten throw! What a break!

He touched first and ran on to second, where he stayed, listening to applause from the Redbirds' supporters and boos from the Indians'.

"Hey, Codfish," yelled one of the Indians' fans. "You know what? You're just lucky!"

That stung, but Sylvester tried to brush it off. Sticks and stones, he thought. Mr. Baruth had pointed out that there were characters like that in every crowd — and that you just had to ignore them. Instead, he tried to concentrate on the next batter.

Duane Francis, the Redbirds' sandy-haired third baseman and Sylvester's closest friend on the team, took the first pitch — a strike — then rapped the next one between center and left field for a double, to score his pal.

"Nice going, Syl," second baseman Jim Cowley called as he came into the dugout.

Nobody else said anything. They hardly looked at him. It even seemed as though Trent Sturgis, bat in hand, deliberately turned away as Sylvester walked by him.

"Okay, bring him in, Eddie!" shouted Coach Corbin, standing and clapping in the third base coaching box.

Catcher Eddie Exton didn't. He fanned out. Terry, up next, bounced a one-hopper to the pitcher for the second out. Sylvester groaned with his teammates as they saw one of their best hitters go down.

174

It was now Jim Cowley's turn at bat.

"Out of the lot, Jim!" Sylvester yelled.

Jim's hit off the first pitch didn't go out of the lot, but it was good enough for a single, scoring Duane.

That was the last hit of the inning. Seneca Indians 5, Hooper Redbirds 2.

Terry and the Redbirds' defense held the Indians in check in the top of the fifth. In the bottom of the inning, with Les on first, thanks to a walk, and Trent on first by virtue of a clean single to short right field, the first baseman, Jerry Ash, flied out. That brought Sylvester up to the plate.

"Okay, Syl!" yelled the coach. "Let's see you clean the bases!"

Sylvester swung at Burk's first three pitches. He missed every one of them.

• Chapter 2 •

B ooooo!" yelled the same Indians' fan who'd called him names before. "You know what? You really stink! Like a dead codfish!"

Sylvester knew better, but the words still stung. As he headed for the dugout, he felt like a total failure. Of all the dumb times to strike out, he thought.

It wasn't like this last year, he reminded himself. He would have gotten a three-run homer if he was hitting like back then. That would have shut up that wise guy!

Yeah, but that was then. This is now. He couldn't avoid reminding himself of that, too.

"No sweat," said his pal Duane, as he passed

Sylvester on his way to the plate. "You'll get 'em next time."

Sure, thought Sylvester sourly. Next time.

Duane singled to keep things alive, but then Eddie Exton struck out.

Indians 5, Redbirds 3.

Stan Falls, leading off for the Indians in the top of the sixth and last inning, hit a three-two pitch to deep center field. As it came at him, Sylvester wished that it would be deep enough to sail over the fence.

It wasn't. Still, he only had to back up a few steps and it would be his.

But the ball hit the tip of his glove, not its pocket, and glanced off onto the ground.

"Oh, no!" he groaned, as he sprang forward, retrieved the ball, and pegged it in to second base to hold the runner at first.

He could almost hear that obnoxious Indians' fan yelling at him in the midst of all the shouting from the stands.

Jon Buckley grounded out, and Dick Wasser

flied out to right field. That brought up Burk Riley, the Indians' pitcher. It should have been an easy out, but Burk walked.

Two men on, two out, and Bus Riley, Burk's brother, came up next.

Crack! He lambasted Terry's first pitch directly at Trent, who caught it for the third out.

It was the Redbirds' final opportunity to win the game. As Sylvester joined his teammates in the dugout, Bobby Kent snorted.

"I don't know why the coach put you in, Coddmyer," Bobby said. "Maybe you were a hotshot last year, but you're nothin' but a cold turkey now."

Sylvester's face turned beet red.

"I didn't ask him to," he mumbled. "It was his own idea."

Trent, who was sitting nearby, cut in smugly. "Maybe he feels he has to, just because you're wearing a uniform." The tall shortstop had already acquired quite a reputation as an up-and-coming ballplayer with a batting average of over .400. Add

178

to this a really good throwing arm and the result was an inflated ego.

Sylvester's heart sank. After all, he thought, just because I love to play doesn't mean I'm any good for the team. I *was* great last year, but where does that put me now?

"Here we go, Terry!" The sound of Coach Corbin encouraging Terry Barnes called Syl back to the present. Terry gave it his best as he led off with a single between third base and shortstop. Syl joined in the cheers. He figured maybe if the Redbirds pulled it out in the end, the fans would forget about his stupid fielding error. Even his freak hit had been stupid. It was just by luck that he'd gotten on base.

"Way to go!" Coach Corbin called from the third base coaching box. "Okay, Jim! Let's keep it going!"

But Jim flied out, and so did Ted. Then Trent Sturgis stepped into the batter's box.

"C'mon, Trent!" Sylvester yelled, forgetting for a moment how Trent had snubbed him. Right now, all he wanted was for the Redbirds to win.

Trent walked.

The Redbirds were still alive!

"Atta boy, Trent!" Sylvester cheered along with the fans in the stands. "Let's keep it rolling, Les!"

Les didn't. He hit a pitch sky-high to the third baseman, and the Indians took the game, 5–3.

As the disappointed team left the dugout, Sylvester kept his cap pulled low over his forehead.

"Syl! Sylvester Coddmyer!"

Syl recognized the high-pitched voice calling to him. He got a little flustered when he turned and saw Joyce Dancer running toward him from the bleachers.

"Syl . . . oh, Syl!" he heard Bobby chant in a mocking, girlish voice, tickling Trent's funny bone as they drifted off in gales of laughter.

But the two wise guys made no impression on the young girl. Her deeply tanned arms, a result of long sessions on the tennis court, were wrapped around a healthy stack of books.

"Hi, Syl," she said, as she got closer to him. "Some game, huh?"

"Yeah," he mumbled, his voice barely audible.

He slowed his pace to make sure they wouldn't catch up with Bobby and Trent. It was no secret that he and Joyce were friends. But he didn't want to have to deal with those guys.

"Cheer up," Joyce said, breaking out in a big smile. "So you lost a ball game, not a war."

"To me it is a war," Sylvester grumbled.

"That's really nuts. But I know how you feel," Joyce said.

"You think so?"

"Sure I think so. I play tennis, remember? I've lost my share of matches. You don't think I like losing, do you?"

"'Course not. But you always look good, whether you win or lose," Sylvester said. Then he realized his words could be taken more than one way.

Joyce chuckled, hiking up the books in her arms. "Thanks, but I don't always feel good. I'm human, too!"

By now, they'd come to the end of a block.

"But you don't think that it's just like a war?" he asked.

181

"Nope." She laughed. "Not even a military conflict."

He finally laughed, too. "I guess you're right," he said. "It's just hard. I mean, I want to be good — at least some of the time — but it never happens lately."

"Yeah, being in a slump is the pits," she said. "Hey, you just have to do the best you can to get out of it. It's the only way it's going to happen."

"Thank you very much for your prescription, Dr. Dancer," he joked, a big grin on his face.

In fact, Joyce's cheerful nature was a little like medicine to him. He felt like taking her hand and squeezing it gently. Sometimes they held hands at the movies. But he wouldn't dare do that here, out in the open. He could imagine how the other guys would howl and jeer if they saw.

Still, it was nice and comfortable, just walking down the street with her. Without even asking, he leaned over and took some of her books as they chattered away in the late afternoon. There more and more shade these days as the leaves on the trees along the sidewalk grew greener and greener with the approach of summer.

Sylvester felt something else inside — hunger. His stomach was reminding him that he needed some nourishment. But that didn't stop him from enjoying his time with Joyce. He wished she lived five more blocks away instead of only two.

At last they were in front of her home, a white clapboard two-story house with shrubs and flowering bushes hugging its base.

Joyce took back her books and gave him what he liked to think was their secret wink.

"See you tomorrow," she said, then turned down the driveway toward the back door.

"Right," he said, winking back. "See you."

Still cozy and warm from the special feeling Joyce always seemed to impart, Sylvester walked slowly down the block and was about to cross over when a deep voice interrupted his thoughts.

"Sylvester! Sylvester Coddmyer the Third!"

For one split second, he flashed back to a year ago, to the moment when Mr. Baruth entered his life. But, no, even though this was a man's voice, it wasn't the same.

He turned around, his forehead creased with curiosity as he stared at the man walking toward him. The man was tall and lanky, had a stubble of a beard, and wore a white sweatshirt and a hat with an old-fashioned letter *C* on it. No, this was definitely not Mr. Baruth.

"Got a minute, Sylvester?" the man asked.

Sylvester was sure he'd never seen this man before. He wondered how he knew his name.

"Well, sort of," he answered. He was glad they were in a friendly neighborhood, not far from his home — just in case this guy turned out to be some kind of weirdo.

But the stranger had a really nice smile as he came forward and stretched out his right hand. Sylvester shook it cautiously, gazing into the man's dark eyes while he ran through his memory bank. Definitely, no one he'd ever seen before.

"Name's Cheeko," the man said. "Saw you play today. Whew! I hate to say it, but you sure have a lot of room for improvement, haven't you?"

184

He said it with a smile about a foot wide. Sylvester couldn't help but smile, too.

"You're right." He nodded.

"I bet you'd like to fill up that room and be a better ballplayer, right?"

"Right." The word had barely left Sylvester's lips when he suddenly recalled a conversation just like this with Mr. Baruth the first time they met.

"All right, then, listen to me," said the man named Cheeko. "I think I can help."

• Chapter 3 •

T he man's words raced on, fast and punchy, nothing like the mellow, steady sound of Mr. Baruth's voice.

"I know about that home run streak you were on last year. Great. But you missed one thing, one thing the guy who coached you left out. You have to be a lot tougher, more aggressive. You wanna be a winner in this world, you've got to make a few moves, take a few shortcuts, too. You've got to stand up for what's yours and let 'em know you're not some kind of bug that anyone can step on. Get what I mean?"

As Sylvester drank in every word, he wondered how this man, a perfect stranger, knew so much about him. Especially, he couldn't figure out how "Cheeko" knew about his hot streak last year. And Mr. Baruth's coaching.

"Wait a minute," he asked. "Do you know Mr. Baruth? Are you a friend of his?"

"Baruth?" Cheeko's eyes crinkled up at the corners as he flashed his big smile again. "Sure I do. It's like we're old buddies. Matter of fact, that's how I heard about you."

"He told you about me?" Sylvester relaxed a little as soon as he heard that Cheeko was a friend of Mr. Baruth's. That automatically made him a better than average guy in Sylvester's book.

"Exactly!" said Cheeko. "That's why I dropped by to see how you were doing. Not great, huh? Nothing to brag about, right?"

"Right," Sylvester admitted, looking down at the toe of his right shoe as he kicked at a pebble.

"Hey, I know you can do better," Cheeko went on. Despite his strong, almost pushy way of talking, Sylvester was interested in what he had to say.

187

Sylvester scowled. "Well, I sure would like to get out of this darn slump."

"You can," Cheeko insisted. "Hey, let me work out with you a little. Believe me, I can show you a few things the other guys on the field wouldn't ever even think of. Tell you what, I'll bring the baseballs. All you need to bring is a bat and your glove. Whaddya say? You up for it?"

A million questions raced through Sylvester's mind but he could only drag out a few.

"I . . . I want to be a better player," he said, "but how come you want to work out with me? Why not some other kid?"

"Hey, I told you, Mr. Baruth said you were an okay guy," Cheeko said, still smiling. "I hate to see anybody get a raw deal. There're still a lot of scores to settle."

Sylvester wasn't sure what he meant, but his heart was pounding at thoughts of his winning streak coming back to him.

"You sure you have the time to spend with me? Don't you have to work?" he asked.

Cheeko chuckled. "Time's the one thing I have.

Plenty of it. You might say I'm sort of retired. So, what's the word? Game?"

The vision of that blaze of glory that he felt every time the ball soared over the fence, every time he made an almost impossible catch, every time he crossed the plate at a steady trot, exploded in his mind. Sylvester would give almost anything to bring back those moments. There was no room in his mind for doubts now.

"Game!" he answered.

"Great!" said Cheeko. "See you after supper."

He put out a hand and Sylvester almost leapt to give him a high five.

As Cheeko headed off in the other direction, Sylvester started to run down the street toward his home. He hadn't gotten far when he realized he had a big step ahead: he'd have to ask permission from his parents to work out with Cheeko. After all, he was a stranger, just like Mr. Baruth. Maybe they'd want to meet him first.

Some of the other questions that he'd lost in his excitement started popping up in his brain now.

189

What did that *C* on Cheeko's hat stand for?

Where did he live?

Would he come to all the Redbirds' games the way Mr. Baruth had?

Sylvester was so lost in his thoughts, he almost missed his own driveway. But the minute he walked into the kitchen, he blurted out everything in a rush of words.

"Whoa! Hold it!" his father said, holding up his right hand like a traffic cop. "You met whom? Cheeko? Cheeko who?"

His mother walked into the kitchen and poured herself a glass of ice water from the dispenser on the refrigerator door.

She frowned. "Don't tell me you've met another mysterious stranger." She looked at Mr. Coddmyer and added, "Speaking of mysteries, you're home early. How come?"

"I worked through lunch and thought I'd put some time in the garden while there's light. They'll beep me if anything comes up," he replied. Mr. Coddmyer had a new job as a troubleshooter for a computer software company. He hardly ever

190

went into his office, but got his assignments from calls that came through on his beeper.

Sylvester wasn't really listening to their talk. He was too eager to get permission to practice with Cheeko.

"Cheeko didn't tell me his last name," he said. "He just introduced himself and told me he'd be willing to help me improve my game, you know, hitting and everything."

His father looked skeptical. "Didn't I hear that song before? Only a year ago . . . about a Mr. Baruth?"

"Yes, Dad," Sylvester said. "Cheeko's a friend of Mr. Baruth's. I mean, that's what he told me."

"We never got to meet your Mr. Baruth," said Mrs. Coddmyer. "But I will say that he did help you become a better player. That home run streak was incredible. And now there's another angel out of the blue who wants to help you again?"

"Angel?" Sylvester echoed. "I don't know if I'd go *that* far . . ."

"Well, whatever he is," replied his mother. "Listen, instead of just sitting around, let's get started on dinner. One of you get out the lettuce, wash it, and give it a whirl in the spinner. Someone else please set the table."

"First she manages the clerks in her store, now she puts us to work." Mr. Coddmyer laughed. "Don't push too hard. We're liable to go on strike."

As they set about their chores, Mr. and Mrs. Coddmyer continued to ask Sylvester about Cheeko.

"Maybe this Cheeko and Mr. Baruth are on some kind of coaching circuit," Mr. Coddmyer suggested. "I never heard of it before, but nothing would surprise me."

"Then I can go out after supper and practice with him?" Sylvester pleaded.

"I suppose I could give up clipping the hedge to meet this new supercoach," Mr. Coddmyer said. "Right after supper, I'll go over to the field with you."

"I'd like to meet him, too," said Mrs. Coddmyer, sitting down at the table in front of the salad bowl.

"But I have a huge inventory to go over tonight. It's going to take hours."

"That's okay, Mom," said Sylvester. "You can meet him if he comes to some Redbird games. Maybe you and Dad will be able to make a few more now." He'd never told them how much he missed seeing them in the stands this year. Maybe because he was a little embarrassed that he didn't get to play that much.

"By the way, why does Cheeko think you need help?" asked Mr. Coddmyer, dropping a pile of salad greens on his plate. "Has he seen you play?"

"I suppose so," said Sylvester. "I've never noticed him at a game, though."

"Gets more and more mysterious, our friend with the *C* on his cap," Mr. Coddmyer said with a frown. "I think . . ."

His thought was interrupted by the sound of his beeper. He shook his head as he went to dial the phone. Sylvester and his mother couldn't help overhearing him; the tone alone told them he wouldn't be finishing his meal, never mind going to watch his son practice.

193

"It's our biggest customer," he announced, hanging up the phone. "There's a major glitch in the system. I have to get over there right away."

"Can I still go practice with Cheeko, please?" Sylvester pleaded with both parents.

They glanced at each other in consultation.

"Well, all right," said his mother. "But only till it starts to get dark. Then you get right home, you hear?"

By the time she had finished saying that, Sylvester had picked up his glove and bat and was halfway out the door.

• Chapter 4 •

Sylvester was so eager to get to the field, he started to run the minute he reached the street. But after running nearly a block at a fast clip, he realized he might get tired and not perform as well as he should. So he slowed down to a brisk walk.

When he got to the field, Cheeko was already there, juggling three baseballs like someone in a carnival. There were three more balls on the ground next to him.

"Hi, Mr. Cheeko!" Sylvester greeted him.

Cheeko stopped juggling the balls and looked over at him. "Hi, yourself, kid," he said. "Hey, no mister stuff. It's just Cheeko."

"Okay," Sylvester smiled. "But . . ."

"No buts," said Cheeko. "You all set to hustle?"

"All set." Sylvester nodded.

"Good. First, we'll work on your fielding. Take a hike out to center."

Sylvester dropped his bat and ran deep into the outfield, his heart light as a feather. Boy, am I lucky, he thought, to be chosen by an expert — Cheeko sure sounded like an expert — to get help in fielding and batting. He wished his folks could be here to see how professional Cheeko acted, too.

There was another thing running through his mind, too, maybe just as important: if he got better at bat, he might be able to give the other wise guys on the team a little competition. Especially that smartmouth, Trent Sturgis, who looked down on everyone as if he were king of the Redbirds. Nothing would make Sylvester happier, he thought, than to start outhitting that swell-headed punk.

"Here we go!" Cheeko shouted, and knocked an easy fly ball out to him. Nevertheless, Syl got under it at the wrong time and the ball hit the heel of his glove and dropped to the green turf.

In a split second, his feeling of joy changed to disappointment and embarrassment. He knew it should have been an easy catch, yet he'd flubbed it like a rookie.

"Never mind that one, Syl!" Cheeko called out to him. "Spilled milk. Get the next one. Keep your eye on the ball."

Cheeko hit the next one slightly lower than the first, forcing Sylvester to run in about eight or nine steps. This time he got both his bare hand and his glove on the ball, even though it struck just below the pocket. He was determined to hang on to it — and he did.

Little by little, Cheeko started hitting them higher, and to the left or the right, making each catch more difficult. In the beginning of this shift, Sylvester missed a few. But Cheeko kept up his stream of encouraging comments — "Don't worry about the other guys. If it's anywhere near you, go for it. Let 'em eat your dust. Hustle! Show 'em

197

you're in charge out there. Step on 'em before they step on you."

He began to get the hang of it, and, after each catch, he gave himself a little mental pat on the back.

I'm getting better already, he told himself after about forty-five minutes of practice. I know I am.

"Okay, Syl," Cheeko called out to him a few minutes later. "That's enough of that for now."

His face glistening with sweat, Sylvester trotted in, smiling proudly. "How'd I do?" he asked.

Of course, he had his own opinion, but he wanted to know what Cheeko thought of his efforts.

"Good," said Cheeko. "Not perfect, but good. After all," he added, "you don't expect to be perfect right off, do you?"

"Sure can try." Sylvester laughed.

Cheeko laughed, too. "Right," he said seriously. "Grab your bat and get over there in front of the backstop screen." Then, turning to face the stands, he yelled, "Ladies and gentlemen, on the mound for the home team — the one and only —" he paused and he seemed to drift far away for an instant — "Cheeko! Batting leadoff for the opposition — Sylvester Coddmyer the third!"

Chuckling, he trotted out to the pitcher's mound. Cheeko didn't have a glove, but he wouldn't need one just to pitch.

As he trotted toward the batter's box, Syl felt Cheeko eying him. The would-be slugger tried to relax. Cheeko stretched, and delivered. Sylvester noticed that Cheeko was left-handed. The ball breezed in chest high. Sylvester swung at it as hard as he could. He missed it by a mile.

"Hey, hey, slow it down!" Cheeko called. He came off the mound toward Sylvester. "Don't be so anxious. Let's take one step back for a moment. First off, don't advertise to the pitcher that you're nervous. Give him the eye as you approach the batter's box; make him think you got him all figured out so nothing he throws at you will come as a surprise. Like this."

Cheeko took a few steps back, shouldered the bat, and stared at the pitcher's mound. His eyes never left that spot as he swaggered toward home

199

plate and tapped the dirt from his sneakers. Boy, thought Syl, shivering, I sure wouldn't want to be on the receiving end of that stare.

Cheeko turned and handed him the bat with his usual wide smile. "Now you try it, Syl. Wait for me to get on the mound." He ran back to position and yelled, "Look real mean, but don't lose control. Keep your eye on the ball, but don't attack it. Okay, let's see your stuff!"

Syl shouldered the bat as Cheeko had done and fixed his gaze on the left-handed pitcher. He pictured Trent and Bobby watching him and narrowed his eyes just a bit more. Cheeko tossed in another pitch, this one almost in the same spot as the first. Sylvester remembered his advice as he swung at it.

Crack! Bat met ball and sent it soaring to center field. It was one of the longest drives he'd hit since those over-the-fence homers he'd racked up last year. The throbbing in his chest returned.

Sturgis, get ready to eat dust! he wanted to shout.

"There you go," said Cheeko, nodding. "Caught on already. I knew you had it in you."

Sylvester smiled. Maybe that was my problem, he thought. I've been too anxious, wanting to kill the ball instead of just meeting it — and any pitcher could see that with no trouble at all.

He missed some of Cheeko's pitches but managed to connect with most of them. Some were grounders, some were fly balls to the outfield, and some even soared over the fence.

"Whew! All right, Sylvester," said Cheeko after two straight pitches ended up over the left field fence. "We'd better quit before we run out of baseballs. Not only that, but I'm getting winded."

"Can we get together again, Cheeko?" Sylvester asked hopefully.

"Of course. You don't expect to have it all after just one session, do you?"

"No, I don't."

"How about tomorrow, then? Same time, same place?"

"Sure, if . . . if you don't mind."

201

"Mind?" said Cheeko, wiping his face with a bright red handkerchief. "Why should I mind?"

"Well," Sylvester hesitated owning up to what was troubling him. "I mean, I don't want to take up a lot of your time. I mean, there's lots of kids who could use help, so . . ."

"Sew buttons." Cheeko laughed. "Ever hear that one? Hey, listen, I pick who I want to help and that's that. As long as you listen to what I say, we'll get somewhere. There's more than one way to win a ball game."

"What do you mean?" asked Sylvester.

"You'll find out," said Cheeko. "There's still plenty to learn. Little shortcuts you won't find in books, believe me. So just show up tomorrow and we'll go at it again. Okay, pal?" He gave Sylvester a gentle poke in the ribs.

Sylvester grinned and threw out his hand for a high five. "Okay!"

Cheeko tilted his cap and headed off down the road in the opposite direction.

Sylvester wondered where he lived. There were

no cars in the parking lot. Maybe he was staying at some motel within walking distance.

It was just starting to get dark as Sylvester picked up his bat and glove and started on his way. He couldn't help thinking about the future, when his practice sessions would, he hoped, pay off during some real games. Wouldn't it be dyna- mite if he could start getting home runs like last year? Super-dynamite! That would be better than getting a 100 on every test — history, spelling, and arithmetic included!

He was just about to cross an intersection a block from his house when a voice called out, "Sylvester! Wait a minute!"

Sylvester stopped, turned, and saw the familiar figure of Snooky Malone running toward him.

"Hey, where've you been?" Snooky asked.

Snooky had gone all the way through school with Sylvester since kindergarten. Sometimes they were real close friends. But lately Snooky had been more of a pain than a pal. With his great big wire-rimmed eyeglasses and his scruffy hair sticking out all over his head, Snooky looked like an owl. He tried to act wise, too, as if he knew it all, but he asked a million questions. Sylvester knew if he told him anything about what he'd just been doing, there'd be no letup. Snooky would pester him until Sylvester would be ready to strangle him.

"I was at the field. Hoped someone would show up to play a little, but nobody did," Sylvester admitted. He hoped this little white lie would hold Snooky off for a while.

Snooky glanced at his digital watch. "This time of day? I never saw anybody out at the field this time of day."

"Well, I just took a shot. You never know," said Sylvester, walking a little faster.

Snooky tagged along at his side.

"Hey, Sylvester, I was looking at your horoscope, you know, to see what the stars say, and . . ."

Sylvester stopped in his tracks. He didn't believe in star charts and stuff like that the way Snooky did, but he was a little curious at the moment. He played along with Snooky.

"Let me guess," he said. "They say my future looks good. That I'm heading for the top, just like last year. Right?"

Might as well take a shot, show him I know what he's all about, he thought, remembering Cheeko's advice. Couldn't do better than showing a little muscle to the wizard of the stars himself, one Snooky Malone.

"Well . . . yes . . . and no," Snooky replied, as though he weren't sure how to answer.

"Yes and no? What's that supposed to mean?"

"You're going to look good in some ways, but . . ." He paused, scratched his elbow, and stood there.

"But what?" asked Sylvester, suddenly impatient. Snooky usually wasn't at a loss for words.

"You won't like this, Syl, but I have to tell you. You're heading for some good things, but you're also asking for some trouble ahead."

"Trouble?" Sylvester frowned. "What kind of trouble?"

Snooky shrugged. "I don't know."

Sylvester snorted. "You're something else, you know that, Snooky? You're always into something, like reading bones, or fortune-telling cards, or tea leaves, or even stars. But you never have the full picture, that's your trouble. I'll tell you what's true — the first part. I am heading for some good things. And that's it. So sleep under the stars, Snooky. Maybe one of them will drop down and clue you in on what's happening now — never mind the future!"

Hiking his bat on his shoulder, he swaggered on down the street, leaving his old pal in a trail of dust.

• Chapter 5 •

At the Redbirds' practice the next afternoon, Sylvester could sense a big improvement in both his fielding and hitting — even though it didn't seem as if anyone else noticed. But he wasn't about to make a lot of noise about it. "Hey, guys, see me catch the ball? Anyone see that thump of the old beanbag?" That would grab attention, all right, but the worst kind.

All he had to do was keep it up and they'd see it. Eventually.

He could hardly wait to practice with Cheeko again.

That night, Mrs. Coddmyer was still struggling with her inventory figures. Mr. Coddmyer was working late. It seemed as though they'd never get to see Sylvester at bat again. Not even at practice.

He thought of asking Joyce to come watch but decided against it for now. It would be more fun to see the surprised look on her face after he started connecting with the ball in some actual games.

Cheeko was waiting for him on the field and they got right down to work. After a while, Sylvester could easily tell that he'd improved some more. Cheeko hit a lot of high fly balls and he caught most of them with ease. He hit a lot more of Cheeko's pitches, too. And there was no doubt about his accuracy. He was hitting long drives to the outfield, most of which cleared the fence by five to twenty feet.

"Hey, hey, pal, you're doin' pretty good," said Cheeko as they wound up for the evening. "I'd say you're about fifty percent better than yesterday. You're starting to get tougher, too. Meaner. Really digging in, you know. How're you feeling at the plate?"

"Great," said Sylvester, a little surprised at the question. He'd knocked so many over the fence, why shouldn't he feel great?

"I mean relaxing-wise," explained Cheeko, making fists of his hands and rolling his muscular shoulders back and forth. "Yesterday, you know, you were strung up tight as guitar strings. You a little looser today?"

"Oh, sure," replied Sylvester, understanding now what Cheeko meant. No big deal, he thought.

"Good, good," said Cheeko, tapping him on the shoulders. "You never want to let the suckers know you're nervous or anything, pal. Now look, I want to show you just a couple more things. Get out there and throw a few pitches."

"I'll never be a pitcher, Cheeko," Sylvester protested.

"No sweat, I just want you to look at what I do when the ball gets a little close," said Cheeko.

And as Sylvester threw one ball after another toward the plate, Cheeko taught him how to lean in just enough to let the ball graze him — and then fall down as though he were in agony. He

did it in such a way the ump would never be able to tell it was faked.

Sylvester wasn't sure he'd ever be able to do that — it looked a bit dangerous — but it was another lesson. Besides, a little physical pain might be worth it, if it got Trent and the others off his case.

When it was over, Cheeko wiped off his forehead.

"So, I'll see you again tomorrow night, right?"

Sylvester smiled. "Right."

Suddenly a light bulb popped on in his head. "Oh, I can't!" he said. "Tomorrow's Friday, and we're playing the Lansing Wildcats!"

"No problem." Cheeko shrugged. "We can get together Saturday morning, say around nine. Okay?"

"Sure. Will you be at the game tomorrow?"

"Wild horses couldn't keep me away," Cheeko replied with a big smile.

"Great. Well, see you then. Or, you'll see me!"

"You betcha," Cheeko said, and they parted company.

Sylvester didn't want to bump into Snooky Malone again, even accidentally, so he took a different route home. Snooky seemed to have a knack for showing up at the oddest places at just the wrong time. In fact, it was surprising that he hadn't been at the field this evening. Probably home gazing into a crystal ball . . . or watching *Star Trek: The Next Generation*. Yeah, he really freaked out on anything to do with the stars.

The next morning, Sylvester woke to discover a lazy drizzle falling. By noon he began to worry that it might be bad enough to postpone the game. With his gut feeling that he'd improved to the point where he could make a difference out there, the last thing he wanted to happen was a postponement.

But by mid-afternoon the sky had cleared, the sun had come out, and the stands filled up quickly with impatient Wildcat and Redbird fans. Sylvester could almost hear his heart singing "Take Me Out to the Ball Game," even though his stomach was so fidgety he couldn't even think about peanuts or Cracker Jack!

212

And just because the game was going to take place, chances were he'd probably sit out the first three or four innings on the bench. After all, he hadn't started since that one day back when Coach Corbin had to use him because only eight players had shown up.

With these thoughts running through his head, he got through infield and batting practice quietly and quickly. Then the field was cleared and the game was ready to begin.

Glove on his lap, arms crisscrossed over his chest, Sylvester sat in the middle of the dugout so that he had a good view of both the first base and third base sides of the bleachers. With the small crowd out there, it wouldn't be too difficult to spot Cheeko, he thought, unless his new pal had decided to sit somewhere directly behind him. No Cheeko came into view. That must be it.

The Lansing Wildcats, in their fresh, clean, white-trimmed green uniforms, were up at bat first.

As the Hooper Redbirds, in their bright red white-trimmed uniforms took the field to a roar of cheers from their fans, a shadow appeared in front of Sylvester.

"Syl! Look sharp! Sorry, I forgot to tell you, kid, but I want you to start in right field today."

Was he dreaming already? No, it was Coach Corbin, peering down at him.

Sylvester blinked as though he'd come out of a fog, then sprang out of the dugout as if he'd been shot from a gun. He ran about ten yards before he realized what a break this was. Turning around, he shouted back, "Thanks, Coach!"

Coach Corbin smiled. "Just do what you've been doing in practice," he said calmly.

Sylvester ignored the sudden rush of butterflies to his stomach and took his position at right field — where Les Kendall usually played. He pounded his fist into the pocket of his glove and shouted to the pitcher, Rick Wilson, "Get 'im outta there, Rick, ol' buddy! Make it one, two, three, guy!"

Mickey Evans, leading off for the Wildcats, watched two of right-hander Wilson's pitches blaze by him for a ball and a strike before he cocked the third pitch to short right field.

It was high and hard to see where it would come down. Sylvester sprinted after it, groaning in dismay that the very first hit had come his way.

He reached the ball in time to extend his glove — and caught it to make the first out.

There was a resounding cheer from the Redbirds' fans. It made him feel that he was back in the mainstream after wading in the shallows for so long. The cheers really raised his spirits.

Short, stalwart Georgie Talman stepped to the plate next. He took two balls and two strikes, then struck out. Two away.

Bongo Daley, the Wildcats' burly right-handed pitcher, was also their cleanup hitter. He lived up to his nickname as he slammed a two-bagger to right center field between Bobby Kent and Sylvester. Bobby got to the ball first and pegged it to second base to keep Bongo from stretching his hit to a triple. He never even glanced at Sylvester as they both got ready for the next batter.

Sylvester tried to ignore him, too. As tall, skinny Ken Tilton came to bat, he yelled, "C'mon, Rick! Get 'im outta there!"

215

Bobby, Ted Sobel in left field, and the entire infield joined in shouting encouragement.

Their yells didn't help. Ken singled, scoring Bongo. Then Leon Hollister, the Wildcats' third baseman, connected with a triple, scoring Ken. Finally, Rod Piper grounded out to end the two-run half inning.

"Okay, guys, are we gonna let those Wildcats get away with two runs? Or are we gonna do somethin' about it?" Coach Corbin shouted to his players.

"We're gonna do somethin' about it!" The answer came out loud and clear, as if from one powerful throat.

But the first two batters, Jim Cowley and Ted Sobel, hit pop flies for easy outs. Then Trent singled over first, and Sylvester, batting cleanup, approached the plate. His hands felt clammy, but he held the bat with confidence.

He stared down the pitcher and took the first pitch.

Crack! A high, long, cloud-piercing shot to deep left field! And over the fence for a home run!

216

The fans rose in their seats, cheered, whistled, and clapped wildly as Sylvester Coddmyer III trotted around the bases for the first time that season. He hadn't felt so good since last year, and that seemed so long, long ago.

Just about the whole team met him at home plate. They exchanged high fives and slapped him on the back, shouting "Way to go!" and stuff like that. He noticed a few who didn't come near him. Trent didn't make a move. And Bobby wasn't exactly jumping up and down, either.

Get used to it, guys, Sylvester thought. There's more where that one came from.

He turned and looked into the stands above the dugout. The space where his parents usually sat was empty, but at the end of the first row of the bleachers toward the first base side, he saw who he was looking for.

Proudly, he waved to Cheeko, who whistled and waved back.

The Wildcats got another run in the top of the second, and another in the third, putting them in the lead 4–2.

217

Then, in the bottom of the third, with two out and nobody on, Sylvester came up to bat again.

He tapped the plate and thought, No sweat, as he listened to the cheering fans. A question flashed through his mind — Was one of those voices Joyce's?

"Knock it out of the park, Sylvester!"

"Drive it into the next county, Syl!"

He didn't. He never even touched the ball with his bat. After two called strikes that whistled by him, he swung at a third right down the middle and struck out.

• Chapter 6 •

H ead bowed, eyes glued to the turf, Sylvester headed back to the dugout. He was so embarrassed he wished he could say a magic word and vanish.

He'd had three good, over-the-plate pitches. How could he have missed them all?

The Wildcats' fans laughed and mocked him with phony applause. The Redbirds' fans remained mute, as if they were stunned. How could their cleanup batter, who had hit a home run his first time up, swing at three pitches and miss every time?

None of the guys said a word to him as they picked up their gloves and headed out to the field. He avoided Trent's eyes. He could just imagine

219

the smile he'd see in them, and the smirk on Bobby's face.

He grabbed his glove and trotted out to right field, passing the Redbirds' first baseman, Jerry Ash, on the way. Jerry called, "Figure you were just lucky that first time, huh, Syl?"

Thanks a lot, thought Sylvester. What about my home run? I guess Jerry forgot that he struck out his first time up. Maybe that's what I ought to do now, just forget it.

But he couldn't. Sullen and ashamed, he sneaked a look into the stands at where he'd seen Cheeko. He wondered if his new pal had become disappointed, too, and left.

But Cheeko was still there, watching the Wildcats' first batter, who was approaching the plate.

The batter, A. C. Compton, fanned after six pitches. Mickey Evans went down swinging, too, drawing applause from the Redbirds' fans.

Then Georgie Talman, after fouling off four straight pitches, was given four straight balls, and walked.

Bongo Daley's fans gave him a rousing cheer as he stepped into the batter's box. It was plain that the tall, hefty blond pitcher was a favorite with the Wildcats' fans.

Bongo missed Rick's first pitch, but sliced the next one out between right and center fields. The slice took it on a curve directly toward Sylvester, who raced after it with lead weights pounding in his chest. It looked as though it might hit the ground before he got there, but he dove at it the very last second — and caught it as the back of his gloved hand touched the turf. Three out.

The Redbirds' fans cheered him as he ran off the field, tossing that ball into his glove again and again. He shot a brief glance toward Cheeko and saw him applauding along with the crowd.

Sylvester felt great. So what if that catch didn't make up for his strikeout? Hey, it kept another run from scoring, didn't it?

He'd barely settled down in the dugout, this time at the far end, when he heard a voice at his side say, "Hi, Sylvester!"

It was Snooky Malone.

"What are you doing here, Snooky?" he asked. "You're not on the team."

"Coach Corbin doesn't mind," said Snooky. "I did his horoscope for him. He's a Libra, nice and even tempered."

"Good for him," muttered Sylvester. I wonder what the sign is for a pest. That must be Snooky's sign, he thought.

"I just can't get over it, Syl," Snooky whispered.

"Over what?" Sylvester asked, softly, as though Snooky was in on a big secret.

"The way you're hitting. And the way you're not. And that catch. You haven't made a catch like that since last year, when you won that trophy, remember?"

"Look, Snooky." Syl's voice rose slightly. "I don't know what's with you these days, but lay off, huh? Don't bug me anymore."

Snooky frowned at him. "I know your sign, Sylvester. You're a Gemini. Geminis are great at whatever they do, and you prove it. Except for one thing."

222

"Oh, yeah? What?"

"What happened between last year and this year? You were hot and then you were cold and now you're getting hot again. I can't figure it," Snooky replied, his eyebrows raised high above his big wire-rimmed glasses.

"I don't know," Sylvester snapped. "And I don't care."

He nudged Snooky with his elbow and almost knocked him over.

"Scram, will you, Snook?" he said. "You're getting into my hair and I want to concentrate on the game."

"And another thing," Snooky said, ignoring him. "Who'd you wave at in the stands? Was it . . ."

"None of your business!" Sylvester growled. "Beat it, will you? Or do I have to throw you out?"

Heads and eyes swung around and stared down at his end of the bench. He felt his face turn bright red. Darn that Snooky for barging in and reminding him how terrible he'd played this year. Why couldn't he keep his nose out of other people's business?

223

"I'll tell you one thing, Sylvester Coddmyer the Third," said Snooky, getting up to go. "You're heading for deep trouble."

And then he was gone.

Sylvester settled back, trying to forget the pesky runt. Deep trouble? What did that mean? Maybe a star had fallen on Snooky's pointed little head!

He turned his attention to the leadoff batter, Jerry Ash, who took a swing at a high pitch.

"Strike!" called the ump.

Five pitches later, Jerry walked, bringing up Bobby Kent. For the good of the team, Sylvester thought, I hope you get on base, Bobby.

Bobby waited out the pitches, then rapped a ground skimmer down to second. Mickey fielded it, touched second base, then pegged it to first for a quick double play.

"Oh, no!" the Redbirds' fans groaned.

Sylvester was secretly ashamed that he didn't feel as bad as he probably should have for Bobby. But he was still half thinking about Snooky as he watched his pal Duane Francis fly out to deep center to end the inning.

A Gemini, Snooky had called him. So what? What had being a Gemini done for him lately? Nothing. It's what you do for yourself, he remembered Cheeko telling him. He had to take care of Number One.

That put a little pep into him as he picked up his glove and headed out to his field position. After all, he was still in the game. Coach Corbin hadn't lost faith in him. Why shouldn't he still make a few waves in this game?

• Chapter 7 •

Ken Tilton, the Wildcats' powerhouse, was up. So far he'd rapped out a single and a double. With his eagle eye and strength, he could easily pull in a triple this time at bat.

Coach Corbin motioned the outfielders to move back, and they did. Obviously, the coach wasn't taking any chances on Ken's hitting.

Rick toed the rubber, then sent a blazing pitch just inside the plate, brushing Ken off. Ken jumped back to avoid being hit as the ump called "Ball!"

The next pitch was outside. The next was inside again, but not as close to Ken as the first. Three balls and no strikes.

Was a walk better than giving Ken something

226

to swing at? Glad I'm not the pitcher, Sylvester thought.

Then, "Strike!" A streaking fastball over the inside corner.

Another "Strike!" as Rick fired again.

Ken stepped out of the box, rubbed the heavy part of his bat a couple of times, and stepped back in.

The windup. The pitch. Crack! Ken connected and sent the ball soaring out to right field.

Sylvester could see it shoot high into the sky like a tiny rocket and then start to arc down. He could tell right off that it was going over his head, so he wasted no time. He turned and ran back toward the fence as fast as his legs could carry him.

The old fear gripped him. Could he get to it in time? The fence would be in his way. He'd miss it by a mile.

But at the very last moment, just as the ball came down over his head, he leapt, his gloved hand stretched out as far as it could possibly go.

Thud! He hit the fence way up high — and caught the ball.

Pain pierced his shoulders like a bolt of lightning, but it didn't last long. Joy sprang into his heart as soon as he was back on his feet. As he heaved the ball into the infield, he could hear the crowd's roar that had started the instant he'd snagged the ball; it didn't die down for a good minute. In fact, everyone was standing up and cheering, Redbirds' and Wildcats' fans alike. They didn't get to see too many catches like that.

As Sylvester stood out in right field, arms crossed over his chest, he remembered Cheeko's advice: play tough, go for it. He was determined not to forget that.

He scanned the crowd, hoping to spot his mom and dad in their usual place. They had both said they'd try to make the game this time, but it was hard to predict with their busy work schedules. He couldn't pick them out, but he caught a glimpse of Joyce, all smiles and happy. And there was Cheeko in his usual spot.

Before he could pick anyone else out in the crowd, Leon Hollister came up to bat. He'd tripled in the first inning and flied out in the third. This time he waited for a full count, then laced a high fly ball to short center field. Bobby had plenty of time and got under it for the second out.

When the ball left Leon's bat, Sylvester had started toward it and then was relieved when he saw that it was an easy stand-up catch for Bobby. He was beginning to have doubts about fly balls. They might not all end up in his glove like the last one. His confidence began to ebb slowly.

Rod Piper was up next. After two strikes, both of them foul balls that rolled down the backstop screen, he took four straight balls and walked.

Next up was Russ Skelton, the Wildcats' tall, wiry shortstop. So far Russ had been on base each time up. Sylvester remembered that he'd walked his first time and singled the second time. Not bad for the seventh batter in the lineup, Sylvester thought.

He shook out his arms and shoulders and got

229

ready for whatever Russ might hit his way. After two pitches, the third one was hit to Trent, who scooped it up and pegged it to first. Sylvester could relax as he ran off the field.

As he passed by Cheeko, he saw his friend wave at him and give the air in front of him a short poke with his fist. Sylvester smiled, knowing that this meant to get tough. He waved back at Cheeko.

If his folks had been there, he could have introduced them to Cheeko so they would be comfortable about all those practice sessions. Once they met him and talked with him, they might even want to come to Sylvester's games and sit with him.

But first things first. The first batter hadn't left the dugout before Sylvester started worrying about what would happen if he came to bat this inning. Would he get a decent hit? Or would he disgrace himself? Even with Cheeko's coaching, he still wasn't as confident as last year when Mr. Baruth had been around.

Maybe he was too impatient. Maybe he expected too much too soon. Maybe maybe maybe.

He wiped these thoughts out of his mind as he settled down on a vacant seat in the dugout.

"C'mon, guys!" Coach Corbin said, walking back and forth and clapping his hands loudly. "We can't give up now! Hey, we're only two runs down! And they're not that good. So go out there and prove it to 'em, okay?"

"Okay!" the whole team shouted.

"Good! Okay, Eddie! Start it rollin'!"

He headed toward the third base coaching box. Eddie Exton removed his catcher's gear, put on a helmet, carefully selected a bat, and strode to the plate.

As Eddie readied himself for the first pitch, Duane Francis nudged Sylvester. "Hey, Syl, I forgot to tell you, my dad took me to a big baseball card show last Sunday."

Sylvester had a small collection of baseball cards that he'd picked up here and there. Duane was definitely in the big league as a collector and went out of his way to fill in gaps, especially with old, old cards and players you hardly ever heard about. He loved to share his finds, and Sylvester enjoyed seeing them.

"I got a whole bunch of really great old ones," Duane went on, "Red Sox, White Sox, Black Sox . . ."

"Black Sox?" Sylvester was puzzled.

"Yeah, it's a nickname they gave a bunch of Chicago guys," said Duane. "Hey, wanna take a look at them later?"

"Sure," said Sylvester. "Bring them over to my house after supper."

Sylvester turned his attention to home plate just in time to see Eddie pop out to third base. One out.

The Redbirds' fans were getting restless. "Let's get some hits!" they shouted.

Sure, thought Sylvester, easier said than done.

As Rick headed toward the plate, the Redbirds' pitcher seemed to have lost some of his energy. His shoulders were slumped and he gazed at the ground as if his eyes were about to close down.

Don't fall asleep, Rick, Sylvester felt like yelling. We need you more than ever right now.

As the innings piled up, the Wildcats' two-run lead seemed harder and harder to match, never mind pass. And as one batter followed another, a little voice inside Sylvester's head kept asking the same agonizing question: "Is the coach going to take me out?"

As long as he was in there playing, there was hope that he might come through for the team.

Rick grounded out to shortstop.

Then Jim Cowley came up, and Sylvester crossed his fingers. He usually thought superstitions were silly — black cats and broken mirrors and all that star stuff of Snooky's — but things looked so bad, he figured it was worth a try.

Jim let a strike go by, fouled the next pitch, then fanned. It was a fast, unproductive fifth inning.

"Rats!" Sylvester snorted as he uncrossed his fingers and started out of the dugout. "I knew it was baloney!"

One more inning to go. The way Bongo Daley

233

was pitching for the Wildcats, it looked as though it would be no different from the last scoreless four.

"Come on, you guys!" Coach Corbin pleaded as his team headed for their field positions. "If you can't hit 'em, at least hold 'em!"

The coach was not in a happy mood. He hated to lose.

We're doing our best, Coach, Sylvester muttered as he trotted out to right field. At least I am.

• Chapter 8 •

L es Easton, the Wildcats' short and stocky right fielder, was first man up. He watched six pitches streak by him, two strikes and four balls, to put him on base.

Next up was A. C. Compton. He walked, too.

Great, thought Sylvester, they're already winning and Rick is making it easy for them to pick up at least two more runs.

Before stepping into the batter's box, Mickey Evans swung the bat around his head a few times like an Olympic javelin ace preparing for a record throw. So far he'd managed one hit, a single, but he was always dangerous enough to pull a repeat.

He didn't. With one strike on him, he slammed the next pitch a mile high, almost directly over home plate, and Eddie Exton made the catch look easy.

Sylvester breathed a small sigh of relief. One out. Two to go.

Georgie Talman, the next batter, tried to play it smart, waiting out the pitches to the very last. But Rick remained ahead with one ball and two strikes on Georgie before he breezed one in almost a little too low to be in the strike zone. But Georgie, not wanting to risk being called out, swung. He smashed a grass-mowing grounder down to short. Trent fielded it neatly, whipped it to third, and got Les out by ten feet.

Two out. One more to go. But this one wasn't going to be easy. Bongo Daley had doubled in the first inning, and it was just bad luck that his other two outs — both fly balls — hadn't landed between the outfielders. He was powerful enough to blast one easily over the fence.

Sylvester joined his teammates in a chant of encouragement to their pitcher, at the same time backing up a few steps. Rick glanced at the runner on second base, then threw.

Bongo stepped into it, but let it go by.

"Strike!" boomed the ump.

"Way to go, Rick!" Sylvester yelled. "Mow 'im down, kid! Show 'im who's in charge!"

Act tough, sound tough, wasn't that what Cheeko had been teaching him?

The next pitch missed the plate by inches. Then Rick committed a serious error — he threw one in the dirt that skipped by Eddie and headed for the backstop screen.

"Oh, no!" Sylvester moaned, as Eddie sprang to his feet, whirled, and bolted after the wild ball. He caught it as it bounced back from the screen, then whipped it to Rick, who had come in to cover home plate.

But the runner on second had stopped on third. He'd only been off the base a short, safe distance when Rick swung around toward him. The runner on first, meanwhile, had advanced to second.

Boy, that's just great, Sylvester grumbled to himself. He could picture another run or two scoring easily, as he saw Coach Corbin walk out to the mound. After a few seconds, he patted Rick on the shoulder, then trotted slowly off the field.

Sylvester wondered whether the coach should have taken Rick out, but he gave no indication. Never show the suckers you're scared, that was another bit of Cheeko's advice.

Still standing tall on the mound, Rick again checked the runners, then delivered. The pitch was in there, and Bongo swung. Crack! It was a long, high fly to right center field.

Almost before the sound of the bat meeting the ball faded, Sylvester started running toward it as fast as he possibly could, all the while hoping it would be Bobby's ball.

Then he heard Bobby's clear, unquestionable call: "Take it, Syl! It's all yours!"

Take it? Was Bobby crazy? He didn't have a chance. No way! It was Bobby's ball, not his!

But he had to try. He picked up more speed, though where it came from he was sure he didn't know. Besides, since Bobby had dumped it on him, he *had* to do his best, even collapse in the attempt.

At the very last moment, as the ball was dropping fast in front of him, he dove at it — and grabbed it in his gloved hand.

For one split second, his mitt turned over from the impact and it felt as though the ball had wobbled out. But Sylvester recovered his wits and slid his glove forward, and showed the ball still inside, as though it had always been there.

He lay on the turf for a moment, to catch his breath, as the cheers and whistles from the fans echoed and reechoed throughout the park.

Finally, he pushed himself to his feet, rubbed some of the grass off the front of his uniform, and jogged off the field.

As he ran, he glanced at Cheeko, who was standing and cheering with the fans. Sylvester could tell that Cheeko had seen *everything* and approved the way he had "recovered" the catch.

Some of the guys shook his hand as he reached the dugout. Coach Corbin was beaming. "Another fantastic catch, Syl!"

Even Bobby Kent came up to him this time and gave him a high five. "I knew it was your ball,

Syl," he admitted. "No way I could've gotten to it. You really surprised me out there!"

"Surprised myself!" Sylvester laughed.

"Okay, last chance," cried the coach. "Let's show 'em we're not licked yet! Billy, call 'em off."

As Coach Corbin headed down to the third base coaching box, Billy Haywood called off the names of the first three batters: "Sobel! Sturgis! Coddmyer!"

Sylvester's ears perked up at the sound of his name. He'd forgotten that he'd be batting this last half of the sixth inning — the last inning and the last chance to win the game. It seemed a pretty dim possibility, practically impossible, the way things had been going.

Ted, who had flied out his first two times up, fouled off the first two pitches, putting himself into a hole right off. A swing and a miss now would mean the first out.

As Sylvester clenched his fists and watched the action at the plate, a familiar voice beside him whispered loudly, "I can't believe what you're doing out there, Sylvester. It's like you're a different person, not the Sylvester Coddmyer the Third I've known all these years!"

For a second, he panicked. Had someone seen him bobble the ball during that final catch?

The voice, now recognizable as Snooky's, went on, though, with no reference to that questionable moment.

"You were great last year, of course. And you're playing great now. But what happened in between? I mean, you were just plain lousy a week ago."

Snooky had managed to squeeze in on the bench beside Sylvester again. And there he was, asking those same, tired questions.

"I don't know, okay?" replied Sylvester. "Look, maybe I'm just on another streak. What's your problem with that? Can't a guy get lucky more than once?"

"Yeah, but . . . this is different, Sylvester. I can tell it isn't just luck." Snooky persisted, squinting over his thick glasses to examine his neighbor on the bench. "You've changed somehow. You have a different attitude. Yep, trouble. I can see trouble, Syl."

Sylvester leaned forward and stared Snooky hard in the eyes. "Snooky, will you just shut up? Mind your own business, will you? Get off my back and take your stupid stars with you. I'm fed up with you, get it? I'm fed right up to here," Sylvester said, placing his hand under his chin.

Snooky stared back, as if he were trying to read something in Sylvester's eyes. Then, without another word, he hitched up his sagging jeans and left the dugout to return to the stands.

That creep, Sylvester thought. Is he going to be on my case for the rest of my life?

He tried to thrust the little inquisitive pest out of his mind as much as possible. He leaned forward and concentrated on watching the game.

As Ted fouled off another pitch, he saw the umpire's fingers come up to reveal the count. Two balls, two strikes.

Then, a surprise — Bongo missed the plate with his next two pitches, and Ted walked.

Looking as if he hadn't a care in the world, Trent then stepped to the plate. He hadn't done that well in this game — a single and an easy grounder for an out — but he was always a threat to the opposition. And despite his nasty attitude toward him, Sylvester admired his batting ability.

"You're up next, Sylvester." Billy Haywood reminded him.

Sylvester started at the sound of his name. He blamed his forgetfulness on Snooky Malone's blathering. Somewhat flustered, he stepped out of the dugout, put on his helmet, picked out his favorite bat, and walked to the on-deck circle.

Trent waited until the count went to two balls and two strikes before he cracked a sizzling grounder between third and short for a hit. The crowd cheered as Ted advanced to second base and Trent toed the bag at first. Sylvester stepped up to the plate and narrowed his eyes at Bongo.

"Okay, Sylvester! Hit it out of the park!"

The shout broke Sylvester's concentration. It came from that pesky, but still faithful, fan, none other than Snooky Malone, who was standing up on his seat and waving his hands in the air. Others chimed in, too, and Sylvester realized he was starting to get nervous as he stood in the batter's box.

"Strike!" called the ump as Bongo breezed in the first pitch.

"Str . . ." the umpire started to say as the next pitch rolled in down the middle. But Sylvester swung at it, made the connection, and sent the ball zooming out to deep left. It curved and just missed the foul line by about a foot.

"Foul ball!" yelled the ump.

"Make the next one count, Sylvester!" cried Snooky, jumping up and down on his seat.

Sylvester obliged. He lambasted the ball to almost the same spot where he'd hit the previous pitch — except that this time it was an easy three feet to the right of the foul line pole.

Every Redbirds fan was up and cheering, giving Sylvester an ovation that could be heard in every corner of town. He spied his parents in their usual spot, applauding loudly with the others. His heart throbbed with such pride, he thought it would burst.

As he trotted around first base, he heard Russ Skelton, the shortstop, sneer. "Lucky break, Coddmyer. He threw ya' a meatball!"

Meatball, huh? Sylvester wasn't about to let him get away with that. On his way around the infield, he made a big loop and managed to give that loudmouth a nasty jab in the ribs in passing. Act tough, right? Isn't that what Cheeko would have done?

"Oof!" he heard Russ groan at the surprise poke. Sylvester just smiled and continued merrily on his way around third and then home.

Hooper Redbirds 5, Lansing Wildcats 4.

• Chapter 9 •

S ylvester could hardly believe the shouting, the cheers, the jostling, as the fans came streaming down onto the field.

"Syl! You were fabulous!" Joyce cried as she threw her arms around him. "But what happened with Russ out there?"

Oh, she noticed, he thought. So what? You have to be aggressive. That's what he'd learned from Cheeko.

Before he could explain all that, she got swept off in the crowd and was pointing him out to a bunch of her girlfriends.

Even some Wildcats fans were coming down to shake his hand. It was like a dream, a wonderful dream that had happened before, thanks to Mr.

247

Baruth, and now was happening again thanks to someone else.

And there he was. Cheeko appeared out of the blue and stood next to him, grinning from ear to ear, holding out his hand for a high five.

"Nice, that last one, really nice," Cheeko said. "You're coming along great, kid."

"I owe it to you, Cheeko," said Sylvester, slapping his outstretched palm. "Every hit of it. I sure forgot everything I learned last year, but you brought it all back and then some. You showed me how to field, how to hit again, and . . ."

"Hey, you're the guy who does the work," Cheeko cut in. "And I like the way you got that shortstop." He chuckled softly. "You're learning. Look, I gotta run. Don't forget our practice session tomorrow morning. Same place as usual, okay?"

Sylvester quickly nodded as Cheeko started to leave.

He watched Cheeko thread his way through the crowd. Suddenly he remembered something and yelled after him, "Cheeko! Wait a sec!"

But his voice was drowned out by the noise all

248

around him. Anyway, Cheeko was gone. Just like that he seemed to have vanished.

Sylvester felt the disappointment deep in the pit of his stomach. He was anxious for his parents to meet Cheeko. It would mean a lot to him if they could get to know the one who had worked with him and shown him the *real* ins and outs of baseball.

Even as he was thinking about them, his mother and father got through the crowd and embraced him. They were so excited, he couldn't tell whether they were flushed or they'd been crying. It almost brought tears to his own eyes, but he bit his lip and hugged them back.

"Rats, I wanted you to meet him," Sylvester said, "but he's gone now."

"Meet who?" Mr. Coddmyer asked. "The coach? We've met him lots of times."

"No, Cheeko," said Sylvester. "He was here, but he had to leave."

"Another elusive mentor," said Mrs. Coddmyer. "Maybe some other time, when it's not so crowded."

249

"Yeah, okay," said Sylvester lamely.

"Sylvester?"

He turned. There stood Snooky, holding out his hand.

"I'm not angry even though you were kind of mean to me," said Snooky. "And I want to congratulate you. You came through in a pinch. You did really great. No matter what's going on, I have to say that I admire you."

"Thanks, Snooky," Sylvester said, slapping the little guy's outstretched palm. "Hey, listen, I gotta go. See you around."

Snooky tugged at Sylvester's uniform shirt. "One more thing I noticed," he went on. "I saw you poke Skelton as you went by him. Isn't that kinda dirty playing?"

Sylvester thought for a quick moment, then looked him in the eyes and said, "No. Just smart."

He darted through the crowd, found his folks, and drove off with them in a pink cloud.

Back home, his father shook his head and said, "I've never seen you hit that way, Syl. I mean last year you were driving in home runs, but this year, that power is breathtaking. When did my son become such a slugger?" he joked.

Sylvester smiled back at him. "You might be in for some surprises, Dad. If you got to see more of my games . . ."

"Now that's a curve ball if ever I saw one," said Mr. Coddmyer, still in a good mood.

"No, really, you know what I mean. Anyhow, I think it's the help I've gotten from Cheeko. He pointed out a lot of things, like how I should stand at the plate, how to swing at the ball, how to be more aggressive. He said I was wimping out a little, that I had to take a really full swing."

"Well, I don't see you play that often," said Mrs. Coddmyer, "but I always thought you took a full swing."

"So did I," agreed Mr. Coddmyer. "But, look, we're no experts like Cheeko. He must have been some player himself. What team did you say he played on?"

"I never asked him," said Sylvester. "But he had

to have been in the pro's. Let's see, *C*, that could be for Cleveland, or Cincinnati, or Chicago."

"Or Cooperstown," suggested Mr. Coddmyer. "Maybe he's in the Baseball Hall of Fame!"

"A lot of choices there," said Mrs. Coddmyer. "I'll tell you one thing. From what I heard all around me today, that catch of yours in the sixth inning should be in a Hall of Fame."

"Aw, Mom, you're prejudiced," said Sylvester.

"I have an idea," said Mrs. Coddmyer. "Why don't we go out for dinner? I'm not up to cooking."

"Neither am I," said Mr. Coddmyer.

"Neither am I," echoed Sylvester.

They all laughed and headed for the car.

When they returned home, Sylvester picked up his glove and cleaned off little bits of dirt and grass that had sneaked into the crevices. He then got out the special oil he used to keep the leather soft and supple in the right places. As he worked on it, his mind wandered to his two lucky breaks. Last year there was Mr. Baruth and this year Cheeko. Mr. Baruth was gone and he'd never

252

gotten around to asking him a lot of questions. He wasn't going to let that happen with Cheeko. He was as curious as his parents to know more about him.

The phone interrupted his thoughts. "I'll get it," he shouted.

It was Duane Francis.

"Syl, you had some day!" Duane exclaimed. "Keep it up and you'll end up on a baseball card."

"Got a little way to go." Sylvester laughed. "So, are you coming over? I want to see what you got last Sunday."

"I'll be there in a jif," said Duane and hung up.

True to his word, Duane arrived at the Coddmyer house in less than ten minutes. In his hands he held a bulging shoebox, tied with an extralong shoelace.

"Come on in here," said Sylvester. He led Duane into the dining room with its big polished mahogany table. "We can spread them out on top. Just don't put anything wet or scratchy down. Mom will have a fit."

Mrs. Coddmyer called from the next room

where she was curled up with a magazine on the couch, "I heard that. And you're absolutely right!"

Mr. Coddmyer put on a CD and tuned out in his favorite chair, only half aware of the chatter in the adjacent room.

Duane opened the box, removed a stack of cards that were held together by a rubber band, and picked up the top card.

"These are the Detroit Tigers," he explained, "and this one is Ty Cobb, one of the greatest. Look at his average."

"Wow! Three sixty-seven," Sylvester read aloud. "I didn't know he played with the Philadelphia A's, too."

"That's 'cause you're not really into the old-timers, like I am," said Duane seriously. "That's where the really interesting stuff is."

"Maybe you're right," said Sylvester. "Let's take a look at some more."

Duane put Ty Cobb to one side and picked up another and read off the statistics. This was Rudy York, who hit eighteen home runs in the month of August 1937.

"Eighteen in one month!" Sylvester echoed. "Amazing!"

Duane grinned at him. "You almost did that last year, yourself. Remember? Probably would have if we played more than once a week."

Sylvester grinned broadly. How could he ever forget that season?

They went through the stack of Tigers cards and went on to the Red Sox and then the New York Yankees, one of Duane's biggest piles.

"Roger Maris!" Sylvester half-shouted as they came across that familiar face. "I know all about him. He busted Babe Ruth's home run record by one run!"

"Not officially."

"Well . . . right. He did play in more games in one season than the Babe."

"Hey, who said you don't know anything about old-timers!" Duane picked up another card. "Know who this is?"

Sylvester looked at the picture on the card and gasped.

"That looks like Mr. Baruth!" he choked.

"Hey, calm down," said Duane. "You all right?"

Sylvester nodded as he stared at the card, at the face of the big man in the striped uniform, wearing a hat with NY on it. Underneath the picture was the name "George Herman 'Babe' Ruth."

"He looks *exactly* like Mr. Baruth," Sylvester said, in a hoarse voice.

"Mr. Who?"

"Baruth," Sylvester repeated.

It did. It really did look like him.

Sylvester took the card and read the statistics on the back. He saw that George Herman "Babe" Ruth had retired from baseball in 1935 and died in 1948. That was years and years ago.

Then who . . . how . . . what . . . ?

"Who's this Mr. Baruth, anyhow?" asked Duane, curious.

"He's the guy who taught me how to hit and play the outfield last year," Sylvester answered, still puzzling over the picture.

"You never mentioned him before," said Duane. "But, boy, that name . . ."

"I know," Sylvester interrupted. "Sounds a lot like 'Babe Ruth,' doesn't it?"

"Sure does."

"But it can't be. The Babe died in 1948."

"Must be some kind of gag or something," offered Duane. "Guy looks like Babe Ruth, so everyone calls him Baruth."

"Yeah, maybe that's it," murmured Sylvester. He really didn't know what to think.

They finished off the Yankees and moved on to another stack. This was the Chicago White Sox.

Duane started with the oldest ones and, before he got very far, he passed one over to Sylvester that almost knocked his friend off his chair.

"Wait a minute!" Sylvester shouted, waving the card in front of Duane's nose. "This one looks like Cheeko!"

"Cheeko? Who's Cheeko?"

"He's the guy who's helping me *this* year!"

• Chapter 10 •

The man on the card in the White Sox uniform wore a hat just like Cheeko's with that old letter *C* on it. And he was smiling that cocky smile that was so familiar to Sylvester.

"Eddie Cicotte," Sylvester murmured quietly, reading the name under the picture. "I just can't believe it."

"It really looks like this Cheeko guy?" asked Duane.

"*Exactly* like him," said Sylvester. "And he's a southpaw!"

As Sylvester shook his head in amazement, Duane stared at the ceiling.

"You know what I think?" Duane announced. "He's another look-alike. Just like Babe Ruth and

259

that Mr. Baruth you mentioned. They're probably actors who do imitations of the Babe and Cheeko on stage or cable TV or something. And then they go on vacation to get away from all their fans, you know. So last year this Baruth guy picks this little hick town where nobody would probably recognize him. And he tells the guy playing Cheeko. Celebrities do things like that. Hey, they probably think they're just like the real thing and they can even play and coach and everything. Whatcha think?"

Sylvester didn't reply. Too much was going through his mind. Like, what about his hitting and fielding? How come he had got better so quickly? And not just a little better, but phenomenally better, like all those great catches and home runs.

"You think maybe it's some kind of ghost or something like in the movies?" asked Sylvester.

"Boy, wouldn't that be something!" said Duane.

"Wait a minute," Sylvester said. "I've got to tell my dad about this."

He went into the living room and saw that his father had nodded off in the comfortable padded chair. Sylvester knew it was just a nap and it wouldn't take much to rouse him.

"Ahem." He coughed, pretending not to notice his father's closed eyelids. "Say, Dad, could you come and take a look at something weird?"

"Sure." Mr. Coddmyer yawned, rubbing his knuckles in his eyes. "Always interested in the oddball."

In the dining room, Sylvester showed him the two cards.

"Know these guys, Dad?" he asked.

His father picked up the cards and looked at the photos. "Babe Ruth and Eddie Cicotte," he said, smiling. "Sure, I remember them well."

"You do?" Sylvester stared at him. "But you weren't even born . . ."

"No," Mr. Coddmyer said with a chuckle, "but I've read about them. Ruth was the greatest, everyone knows that. Cicotte, now, he was one of the players involved in that Black Sox scandal."

"Sure, I've heard of them," said Duane. "But how'd they get that name, anyway?"

Mr. Coddmyer put down the cards. "It's the nickname they gave some bad apples on the 1919

Chicago White Sox team. Eight of them tried to fix the outcome of the World Series that year."

"Did they go to jail?" asked Duane.

"No, but they were banished from baseball. It was just about the worst scandal that ever happened to the game."

"Wow," said Sylvester. "I can't figure it out. Babe Ruth and Eddie Cicotte, they look exactly — I mean *exactly* — like Mr. Baruth and Cheeko, the two guys I told you about. You know, helping me out last year and now this year again."

"It could be a coincidence," said Mr. Coddmyer. "It could be some actors or impersonators . . ."

"That's what I said," Duane blurted out.

"But I'm not sure I buy that," Mr. Coddmyer continued.

Neither do I, Sylvester thought. How would that explain my improvement, my home runs?

He couldn't sluff it off with easy answers. Duane wanted to believe in impersonators and his father would settle for coincidence, but Sylvester wasn't convinced of either.

Mr. Coddmyer picked up a few of the other

cards and commented about several of them. Sylvester was surprised that he knew so much about the old-timers. His father's job was keeping him so busy lately, they hadn't had much of a chance to shoot the breeze like this.

"Well, enjoy the cards, guys, and clean up when you're through," said Mr. Coddmyer. "I'm going to see what your mother finds so fascinating in her magazine, Sylvester."

He started to leave, then turned at the doorway, and said in what sounded like a casual voice, "By the way, Syl, that fellow you mentioned — Cheeko? Next time you're going to get together with him, let us know. I think your mother or I should meet him before you spend any more time with him. Okay?"

"Sure, Dad," Sylvester said.

Duane seemed to have lost interest in Cheeko by now and just wanted to go through the rest of his cards. Sylvester tried to pay attention but his mind wouldn't settle down. He kept sneaking glances at those two cards. There was no doubt that the resemblance was amazing.

• Chapter 11 •

After Duane left, Sylvester returned to the living room. His father was now wearing headphones to listen to a CD without disturbing Mrs. Coddmyer. She had her feet up on the sofa and was working away at a crossword puzzle.

"Mind if I watch TV?" he asked. His mother nodded silently. His father waved his hand, but Sylvester wasn't sure whether he was keeping time to the music or signaling to him.

He turned on the TV and clicked through the various channels. Just a bunch of reruns and talk shows. Even the sports channel had nothing but a boring old golf tournament in Japan! And it was Friday. He could stay up later since he didn't have to go to school the next day. He wondered what

Joyce Dancer was doing. He wished he'd made some kind of plan to see her that evening, even if they just went for a walk.

Every now and then, Sylvester glanced over at his father. He wanted to ask him some questions about when he was a kid and how he knew so much about baseball. Did his father play Little League baseball? Or was he into football? Basketball? Hockey? Did *his* father come to many of his games? Did *his* father have time to play ball with him? Even a game of catch? It seemed that lately Mr. Coddmyer was always too busy working or too tired from work to spend much time with Sylvester.

"I think I'll go to bed," he said, getting up and stretching his arms.

His mother glanced at the clock on the mantel, then shot a surprised look at him. "It's not even nine o'clock yet," she observed. "Are you all right, Sylvester?"

"I'm fine," he said. "I guess I'm a little more tired from playing today than I realized. I'll read a little, then hit the sack."

"Good night, dear, and sleep well," his mother said.

He leaned over and gave his mother a kiss on the cheek and then did the same to his father, just grazing an earphone. He could hear violins and trumpets. Probably Beethoven or something like that, he thought.

He went up to his room, got undressed, and crawled into bed. He didn't even try to read; he knew he wouldn't be able to concentrate. There were too many things rolling around in his head.

Were Mr. Baruth and Cheeko ghosts? Actors? Or what had his mother said . . . angels? And how come they picked him to help out? His father didn't seem too worried, just curious. He wanted to meet Cheeko. Okay, he could meet him the next morning at practice. Would Cheeko be there? Would Sylvester keep hitting home runs and making great catches? How long would it last? Would it go on until the end of the season like last year? Would Cheeko disappear just like Mr. Baruth?

He had no idea how long he was awake, thinking

all those thoughts, but the next thing he knew, there was bright sunshine streaming through his bedroom windows underneath the shades.

At breakfast, he was all set to ask his father to come watch him practice with Cheeko, but Mr. Coddmyer was nowhere in sight.

"Where's Dad?" he asked his mother.

"He took the lawn mower in for service so he could use it later this morning," she answered, sipping her black coffee. "I think he's counting on you to help him clean up the yard."

"Yeah, I can do that . . . later," Sylvester mumbled into his cereal. "Uh, Mom, are you busy right now?"

"I'm going to attack those hedges out back before they turn into the Great Wall of China," she announced firmly. "Somehow your father never manages to get around to it."

She got up and grabbed her gardening gloves, calling back as she left the kitchen, "Clean up your mess before you go anywhere, young man!"

Sylvester carefully washed his breakfast dishes

and put them in the drying rack. It was after nine o'clock. Cheeko would be waiting for him at the park.

What had his father said? He wanted to meet Cheeko. Or he wanted Mrs. Coddmyer to meet Cheeko. He didn't exactly say Sylvester couldn't even see Cheeko until then, did he? At least, it hadn't sounded that way.

Sylvester ran to the park. He'd just hit a few or field a couple of Cheeko's hits. And he'd get a chance to ask Cheeko some things, like where he lived, and what he did. Was he an actor? And what did he know about that Eddie Cicotte?

But the park was empty. Not a soul in sight. Clean as a whistle, except for a piece of paper under a stone on the pitcher's mound.

He picked it up and read the message:

"Sorry, pal, can't make it. Got a few things to take care of. See you next game."

It was signed with the letter C.

He crumpled it up and dumped it into the trash bin on his way out of the park.

Well, at least he didn't have to lie to his folks about meeting Cheeko behind their backs, after all.

He got home in time to help his father unload the lawn mower. While Sylvester hauled away hedge clippings from out back, Mr. Coddmyer put the mower to good use in front.

Later on, after they put away the mower, Mr. Coddmyer grabbed a rake and handed another to Sylvester.

"Might as well get some of these clippings," he announced.

This was the chance Sylvester was looking for.

"Dad," he said, "did you ever play ball when you were a kid? You never told me."

"I never did? That's amazing. Yes, I played . . . Little League and in high school. After that I went off to college and had to work part time to help pay for it. College was expensive, even back then," Mr. Coddmyer explained.

"Were you a pretty good player?"

"I thought so — but I didn't have the opportunity to find out. Or maybe the drive. I loved playing, even on days when I didn't see much action. It was great just being out at the park, doing the best I could. That's all anyone can do."

"Did you ever go to any games? You know, pro games?"

"A few, not many." Mr. Coddmyer paused and leaned on his rake. "I sense something behind these questions, Syl. What's up?"

Sylvester stared at the grass pile on the ground in front of him and said softly, "I guess, well, I just wish we could spend more time together, Dad."

Mr. Coddmyer came over to him and put an arm around his shoulders. "I'm sorry your mother and I have been so busy lately, Syl," he said. "It's not deliberate, you know that. Just the same old excuse, I'm afraid. Too busy making a living, not enough hours in the day. The usual, I don't have to tell you, you've heard it enough."

He rubbed his knuckles on top of Sylvester's blond hair teasingly. "Hey, I'll tell you what. The next time the Chiefs play a weekend game, we'll make a day of it." Mr. Coddmyer was referring to the Syracuse Chiefs of the International League. They played local games in a neighboring town. "Just your mother, you, and me. A swim at the lake, picnic lunch, then hours of good baseball. What do you say?"

"Sure!"

"Good. Well, looks like we've got just a bit more work to do here, so let's get to it!"

After hurrying through the raking, Sylvester rushed inside to look at the paper to see when the Chiefs' next weekend game was to be played.

"They're playing next Saturday, Dad. Do you really think Mom will be able to come along, too?"

"Come along? Where? Where are we going now?" Mrs. Coddmyer poked her head into the living room where they were looking at the paper. "I'm not going anywhere I have to look decent," she joked.

"Dad's taking us to see the Syracuse Chiefs play next Saturday. Do you have it free?" an excited Sylvester blurted out.

"Well," she considered, "I could stay home and wash my hair, balance my checkbook, look over

271

some work . . . or go to a baseball game." She paused, then smiled and said, "Just don't expect me to be the only one preparing sandwiches for the picnic lunch!"

The thought of food reminded Sylvester that he hadn't had any lunch. While he was making himself a peanut butter and banana sandwich, Joyce Dancer called.

"There's a good movie playing at the Cineplex Theater, Syl," she said. "Want to go this afternoon?"

"Sure," he said. He didn't even ask her what the movie was. It made no difference to him. He was glad to have a chance to spend some time with her.

It was a silly cops-and-robbers movie, but they had a few laughs and held hands through most of it. Afterward, they went over to the local hangout and sat slurping milk shakes.

Joyce, still laughing over the dumb movie, started to talk about one of the funny scenes that had broken her up. But Sylvester barely heard what she was saying. He was thinking about

Cheeko and wondering what he had had to do that was so important he missed practice.

After a couple of minutes, Joyce noticed he wasn't really listening. "What's the matter? I thought you liked the movie."

He forced a grin. "I did. I was just thinking about something else, that's all."

Joyce shrugged. "Oh, well, I guess I'm not as interesting as a certain guy named Cheeko."

He had a mouthful of milk shake halfway down his throat and, as he gagged, it almost came up out of his nose. Luckily, he managed to swallow it before gasping out, "How do you know about him?"

"Duane told me."

"Duane! What did he say?"

Joyce stirred her straw around the glass. "Nothing much, except you think he's terrific since he's helping you play better baseball. Maybe even a little *dirty* baseball."

"Dirty?"

"Yes, Syl, dirty. What else do you call that cheap shot you took at Russ Skelton yesterday?"

"It wasn't a cheap shot," he insisted. "Anyhow, Duane's been shooting off his mouth too much. Oh, look who just came in — that great fortune-teller, Snooky Malone."

"Who's that behind him?"

"A couple of guys on the Macon Falcons."

He looked past her shoulder at the three of them making their way down the aisle, Snooky leading the way. Duke Farrell, tall and bushy-haired, followed with an arrogant swagger. Steve Button was an inch shorter; he was broad-shouldered and wore a crew cut.

"Hey Joyce! Hey Sylvester!" Snooky exclaimed when he caught sight of them. He stopped directly in front of their booth, blocking the aisle. "How'd you like the movie?"

"You were at the movies?" Joyce asked, looking past him to the burly boys who were waiting impatiently behind Snooky.

"Uh-huh." Snooky nodded. "Mind if I join you?"

Before Sylvester or Joyce could say a word, Snooky slid into the seat next to her. Duke and Steve shot a dirty look in Syl's direction,

274

then climbed into the booth next to theirs.

"That's the dude everybody's talking about," Duke said loudly. "The kid who hit all those homers last year and finally got a few measly hits this year."

"Yeah, but ya'see, Syl-vest-er only hits 'em this year with men on base," Steve drawled. "Makes you wonder, doesn't it?"

Duke snorted. "Well, I'll tell you one thing, when we play those Redbirds on Tuesday, he ain't even going to *see* that ball, because I'm pitching. So forget about home runs, Syl-vest-er." He drawled out the name just as his pal had.

"You know who's going to hit that ball, don't you?" Steve flexed his biceps. He was sure everyone knew he was leading the league with an average close to .425.

Sylvester wheeled around in his seat and started to retort. His blood was simmering by now, but Joyce looked even angrier. She grabbed her purse and shoved Snooky out of the booth. She faced Duke and Steve, her eyes flashing.

"If you guys think I'm going to sit here and

listen to this all afternoon, guess again. I have better things to do with my Saturday!" she snapped at them. "And as for you, Sylvester, don't bother to call me until you're able to concentrate on something other than baseball, or ghosts, or planning your next cheap shot at another player, or whatever it is you're so distracted by lately!"

She stalked out of the restaurant, ignoring Duke and Steve's laughter. "Move, Snooky!" Sylvester shouted, pushing his friend out of the way.

"See you on Tuesday, Syl-vest-er!" Duke sang after him. "And be ready for a row of 0's on the scoreboard, under Hooper Redbirds!"

"We'll just see about that," Sylvester muttered. "We'll just see."

Outside, there was no sign of Joyce.

"Rats!" he snarled, kicking his sneaker against a rock. "A lot she cares about me. Well, too bad for her if she's not interested. I'm not giving up baseball just for some girl."

But somehow or other, he just didn't feel so good as he slowly walked down the street in the direction of his home.

• Chapter 12 •

T he game on Tuesday afternoon was played at the Macon Falcons' athletic field. As the Hooper Redbirds rode there on a chartered bus, next Saturday night's Chiefs game ran through Sylvester's mind. He could almost imagine himself wearing a Chiefs uniform, playing under the lights on the bright green field.

The bus pulled in at three o'clock, in just enough time for the team to change into uniforms and practice before the game started at four.

As they left the locker room and ran out to the field, Sylvester saw Duke Farrell warming up with his catcher, Greg Jackson. A mocking grin came over the cocky pitcher's face. Smile now, pal,

Sylvester thought, because you'll wear a different expression when I'm up at bat.

As soon as that thought occurred, he started to have misgivings. Suppose Duke does strike me out every time I'm up? It could happen. The whole Falcon team, the whole park, everyone would laugh me off the field.

Especially Trent Sturgis. The Hooper team's ace slugger this season hadn't been hitting all that well lately and seemed to be nursing a grudge against Sylvester.

The Redbirds were up first. Jim Cowley, at the top of the batting order, fouled off two pitches, then let four balls go by to earn himself a walk. Hmm, maybe that smartmouth Farrell isn't as hot as he pretends, Sylvester mused.

But then Ted Sobel went down in three, and Trent hit a weak grounder to short, almost resulting in a double play. Jim was out at second, but the combination of the slow bouncing ball and Trent's speed put him safely at first.

Sylvester was up next. He let out a deep breath as he left the on-deck circle and walked to the plate, wondering what would happen. He was nervous, but he couldn't let Duke see that. Stare 'im down, that's what Cheeko would do.

Swish! The pitch streaked past Sylvester's stomach for a ball. If he hadn't moved, he would have been hit. Maybe he should lean into an easy one and fake being hit, just as Cheeko had taught him. He shuddered at the thought.

"Ball two!" Again Duke zipped the ball inside the plate, forcing Sylvester to jump back several inches to avoid being hit.

He stepped out of the box, rubbed his gloved hands up and down the bat, took another deep breath, exhaled, then stepped back into the box. Sylvester fixed a hard, determined glare on the Falcons' hurler as he wound up for his next pitch.

"Strike!" yelled the ump as the ball just grazed the inside of the plate.

It seems as though Duke saved his best stuff for me, Sylvester thought. No easy pickin's here.

"Ball three!"

Again the ball came threateningly close, forcing Sylvester practically to fall back from the plate.

279

Thinking again of Cheeko's lesson, he pondered letting one of them hit him. It would be a sure way of ending the tension.

He took off his batting helmet and wiped his brow, glancing into the stands. He was happy to see Cheeko at the near end of the first base line. But Cheeko wasn't looking back at him. His eyes were fixed, almost a glassy stare, right at the mound.

Sweat made Sylvester's vision a little blurry, but for one second, he thought he saw a sort of round, familiar face, frowning at him from high up in the stands. At a distance, it looked a little like . . . like Mr. Baruth. But then the man looked down and he couldn't really tell. Sylvester shook his head and put his helmet back on.

Duke's next pitch looked as though it was going to be high and inside, the toughest spot for Sylvester to hit. But it seemed to curve at the last second and slide right down the middle. He swung at it with all his might.

Crack! It was a solid blow. Sylvester knew the

instant his bat connected with the ball that it was a goner. He'd felt that same sensation before and each time it was an over-the-fence wallop.

He watched the ball sail out to deep left field as he started to run, dropping his bat a third of the way down the base line. The Redbirds' fans cheered and whistled. He felt like doffing his hat to them as he rounded the bases, but he knew better than to show off. Getting a home run and bringing in a man on base was enough.

Again he was greeted at the plate by his happy teammates. All, that is, except Trent, who mixed in with the gang at the plate — but didn't even make a show of holding out his hand.

Stick it in your nose, Trent, Sylvester thought.

"Nice blast, Syl," said his buddy Duane.

Sylvester shrugged. "Thanks, pal," he said. "Now it's your turn."

But Duane, up next, popped out to first base. Three outs.

Hooper Redbirds 2, Macon Falcons 0.

By now, Sylvester was relaxed enough to check

281

out the crowd as he ran off to his position in right field. There, of course, was Cheeko. He actually wasn't too far from where the man who looked like Mr. Baruth had been sitting. Only that seat was now empty.

Apparently, neither his mother nor his father had made the game. Too busy with work. Oh, well, he couldn't complain too much since they were all going to the Chiefs' game this weekend.

But where was Joyce? He knew another busload of Hooper fans had followed the team. Maybe she had given up on him.

Ray Bottoms, the Falcons' shortstop, led off and pounded Terry Barnes's second pitch for a hard, shallow drive between Bobby and Sylvester for a double. This time the Falcons' fans, who out-numbered the Redbirds' fans about four to one, applauded.

Left fielder Kirk Anderson walloped a fastball down to short, which Trent scooped up and pegged to first for an out. But the next batter, Ernie Fantelli, came through with another double to score Ray.

282

"C'mon, Terry! C'mon, kid! Let's get 'em outta there!" Sylvester chimed in with the rest of the team on the field.

The cleanup hitter was Steve Button, the other unwelcome visitor who had butted in on Sylvester and Joyce after the movies. He took two hefty swings at Terry's fastball, then drove one a mile high toward the right center fence. No doubt about it — it was Sylvester's ball. He was after it, running sideways toward the fence, the second he saw it arcing in his direction.

As he neared the fence, he could tell that the ball would clear it only by inches unless he could leap high enough to make the grab.

It was almost impossible, but he tried. As he pushed off with all his might, he felt a rush underneath him, like a springboard shoved under his feet. He rose into the air and . . . plop! The ball smacked in the pocket of his glove and stuck there.

His feet landed back on earth and he quickly pegged the ball to second. Jim caught it and whipped it to third, but not in time to nab Ernie as he slid safely into the bag.

Again, there was a wild ovation from the Redbirds' fans for Sylvester's sensational catch. There was an ear-to-ear smile on Cheeko's face as he clapped along with the crowd.

Sylvester felt incredibly good. That catch ought to take a little wind out of Button's overblown ego, he thought.

Scuttling into position for the next batter, he shouted, "One more to go, Terry! Only one more!"

Robbie Axelrod, the Falcons' short, well-built third baseman, connected with a low, inside pitch that struck the left field fence for a triple, scoring Ernie. And then Tom Stringer struck out.

Redbirds 2, Falcons 2.

"Okay, Bobby, break the tie," shouted Coach Corbin. "Nail that ball!"

Bobby Kent, leading off at the top of the second inning for the Redbirds, did nail Duke's first pitch over second base for a single.

As Jerry Ash, the next batter, headed for the plate, Sylvester heard a familiar voice at a familiar spot — his elbow. "You did it again, Syl. You can do it every time you want to, can't you?"

Snooky Malone was at his side again. His face was wreathed in a broad smile.

"Do what? Who cares? Oh, never mind!" Sylvester snapped before Snooky had a chance to answer. "Buzz off, will you? What are you doing here, anyway?"

Snooky's cheerful expression faded. His face got all flushed. "Sorry, Syl," he said, apologetically. "I didn't mean to bother you. After all, I'm your friend, not your enemy."

Without another word, he stepped out of the dugout, never looking back.

Sylvester sat there, fuming. The little creep, he thought, he really sounded sorry. Maybe he was. But I don't have to sit there and take it every time he needles me, do I? I can give it as well as take it. That's what Cheeko would expect from me now.

Yeah, Cheeko had shown him a thing or two. And it was starting to pay off. He had to play tough ... and be tough, no matter what. Well, that's what he'd do from now on, even with the likes of Snooky Malone.

"What was all that about?" Duane asked, sliding into the vacant space next to his friend.

"Nothing. Just a lot of nothing," Sylvester answered.

He fixed his attention at the plate in time to see Jerry Ash lay down a bunt, sending Bobby safely to second, but getting thrown out himself.

"Bring 'im home, Eddie!" Sylvester shouted as the Redbirds' catcher stepped up to the plate, pulling on his batting gloves.

Eddie did, with a long triple to right center field. Then Terry fanned, and Jim singled, scoring Eddie. With the one man on, Ted popped up to third, ending the half inning.

Terry held the Falcons to a walk in the bottom of the inning, so no runs scored.

The Redbirds came up again with Trent leading off. His slump continued as he struck out.

Sylvester couldn't help but grin as he passed

Trent on his way to the batter's box amidst loud cheers and applause from the stands.

With a cocky stance, he ground his feet into the dirt and took the first pitch — a called strike that seemed a little inside to him, almost a brush.

The next pitch did more than brush him. It hit him.

• Chapter 13 •

Base!" yelled the ump. Then, to Duke, "Watch it, Farrell. You're putting some of 'em awfully close in there, mister. Another one like that, and you're outta here!"

About time, thought Sylvester. Boy, that sure hurt. It never felt like that when he practiced with Cheeko, when they weren't for real.

Sylvester rubbed the bruised spot where the ball had hit. His side throbbed, but he wasn't about to let anyone know how much it hurt. After all, he had brought it on himself, by leaning into the pitch slightly. And you had to act tough, he remembered.

The next batter, Duane, cracked a single over

shortstop, advancing Sylvester to second base. But neither of them got any farther. Bobby hit a line drive to the shortstop, and Jerry fanned. Three out.

As Sylvester ran to the dugout for his glove, Coach Corbin looked worried.

"Are you okay?" he asked.

"Sure, coach," Sylvester replied. "I can hardly feel it any more." But I won't forget it, he added to himself.

Ray Bottoms led off for the Falcons and lined a three-one pitch directly to Trent for the first out. Kirk Anderson fared no better, popping the first pitch back to Terry.

"One more, Terry! One-two-three!" shouted Sylvester as Ernie Fantelli stepped up to the plate.

But Terry pitched four balls, none of which crossed the plate, and Ernie had a free ticket to first base.

With little happening in the outfield, Sylvester looked around the stands and caught Cheeko's eye. Leaning back in his seat, Cheeko made a little jab with his fist that looked like a cross between an okay sign and thumbs-up. Sylvester gave him a quick wave and turned back to the action on the field.

Cleanup slugger Steve Button had just stepped to the plate and all three outfielders edged themselves back a little. Steve was ready and walloped Terry's first pitch out toward center field. It looked as if it was all Bobby's, an easy out. But just as the ball started its downward arc, Bobby tripped as though he'd stumbled into something.

It seemed miles away, but Sylvester had to try for it. From out of nowhere, he felt a rush of energy as he made his move. With lightning speed, he crossed into the center field zone, put out his glove, and grabbed the ball just inches from the turf.

There was a thunderous ovation as the Redbirds came off the field. Sylvester could hear his name being called in the midst of all the shouting.

Flopping down onto the bench, Bobby shook his head as he tried to explain what happened.

"Like, it was weird," he said. "It felt like some-one pulled the ground out from under my foot."

"Maybe it was a ghost." Ted Sobel offered this with a laugh.

Sylvester felt a little lump in his throat.

The Hooper team went down in three as they came to bat in the top of the fourth inning. In the bottom, Robbie Axelrod led off for the Falcons and made the game interesting by blasting a home run over the left field fence.

Tom Stringer kept things rolling by smashing a hard grounder down toward the shortstop position. It looked as if Trent had it, but it went through his legs for an error.

Get your tailgate down, Big Shot, Sylvester felt like yelling at him — but knew enough not to.

Ed Norman flied out to center field, but Greg Jackson smacked a triple along the third base line. That scored Tom and brought up the smartmouth pitcher, Duke Farrell.

Two runs, one out, and a man was on third.

Sylvester joined in with his teammates, shouting

toward the mound, "Hold 'em, Terry! You can do it!"

But Duke slashed a single by the pitcher to score Greg and put the Falcons ahead by one run.

Coach Corbin ran out of the dugout as the umpire raised his hands for a time out.

The coach talked with Terry for a moment, then took the ball from the downcast pitcher. He waved in Rick Wilson, who had been warming up in front of the first base seats.

After a few warm-up throws, the game resumed. Rick managed to hold Ray Bottoms to a groundout to second, and Kirk Anderson to a pop fly to first base. Three out. Redbirds 4, Falcons 5.

Ted led off in the top of the fifth with a single through the gap between first and second bases. Trent, up next, lined one over short, advancing Ted to second.

Sylvester stepped into the batter's box. A big cheer rose up from the Redbirds' fans as he thumped the fat end of his bat against the plate and waited for the pitch.

As he stared down the pitcher, he tried to forget

the sensation of being hit by the ball last time. Instead, he checked out his stance, his grip, and each pitch as it came toward him.

"Strike!"

It was inside, just grazing the plate.

"Strike two!" The second pitch was almost in the very same spot.

Then, "Ball!" Yes, but it just missed the plate by an inch. Duke was in his absolute best form.

Then, crack! Sylvester swung, connected, and drove the ball toward deep center field. It cleared the fence by five feet and cleaned the bases for three runs.

The ovation was deafening as Sylvester dropped his bat and circled the bases.

His teammates greeted him with high fives as he crossed the plate — again, all but Trent, who hung back. And, as he headed for the dugout, there was Snooky Malone jumping up and down.

"I can't help it, Sylvester," said Snooky, his voice hoarse from cheering. "You came through, just as I knew you could — and would."

Sylvester barely slapped Snooky's extended

hand before he turned away. But I have to admit that the little guy sure had guts to come over and congratulate me, after the way I've been treating him. Maybe I ought to take it easy on him, he considered.

But Snooky had vanished. Sylvester removed his batting gloves, pushed them into his pocket, and settled down in the dugout.

This game is going so great, he thought. I hope my folks are out there somewhere. Mom said she was going to try to get someone to cover for her at work. Maybe she got here in time for that home run. But I don't suppose I'd be lucky enough for Dad to go without a call on his beeper this afternoon.

Duane Francis batted a double, his second hit of the game. But Duke mowed down the next three batters and the half inning was over. Redbirds 7, Falcons 5.

The Falcons put one man on base during their turn at bat. Steve Button had fouled off three pitches and it looked as if Rick was starting to lose control and then he walked him. The next three batters went down in a row and that was it.

A caught pop fly, a single, and then a double play in the sixth and last inning ended the Redbirds' chances of collecting any more runs.

Two singles and two walks resulted in another run for the Falcons in the bottom of the inning, but that was all the scoring that took place. When the game ended, it was Redbirds 7, Falcons 6.

At the final out, an ovation resounded in the stands as the crowd swarmed down onto the field. In no time, Sylvester found himself surrounded by friends, admirers, and for the first time this season, newspaper reporters. He recognized a few faces, from the *Hooper Herald* and the *Chronicle.* They had both sent writers out to cover the game.

"Sylvester," began the reporter from the *Herald,* "I've noticed something unusual about your hitting this year. You've never gotten a hit when the bases were empty. And, when there was someone on base, you not only got a hit, it was always a home run. Any way you can explain that, well, that phenomenon?"

"Phenomenon? No, I guess I can't," replied Sylvester, honestly.

"Do you do anything different, or feel anything different, when you're in those situations?" asked the reporter for the *Chronicle*.

"I don't know. I don't think so," Sylvester mumbled. Maybe it was just coincidence, Sylvester wanted to say. Deep down, though, he wondered if it was something else. Something called Cheeko.

The reporters kept up their barrage of questions. Syl heard the steady click of cameras snapping and the whirr of camcorders getting it all on tape. He looked around to see if he could find someone else to talk to. Where was Joyce? Had she come to the game? And what about his mother and father? They were nowhere in sight.

"What about your fielding, Sylvester?" continued the woman from the *Herald,* waving a microphone toward Syl's face. He tried to push away the memory of the force he had felt propelling him into the air — and the one that had tripped up Bobby.

"Sorry," he said, his nerves getting on edge. "I have to go now." Same as last year, he thought, same big hullabaloo. It was sort of fun back then, but now . . . it doesn't seem so much like I deserve all this attention.

"Would you be surprised if a few years from now some major league team offered you a contract?" the reporter for the *Herald* persisted.

"No, I wouldn't be surprised!" Sylvester finally snapped. "Why? Because in a few years I will be good enough to play in the majors!" With that, he pushed past the surprised woman and climbed aboard the waiting bus.

He was sure he'd told them what Cheeko would have expected him to say. He wasn't as sure it came out sounding so good, though.

The bus unloaded its passengers back at the school, across from the field. Before heading home, Sylvester strolled over to the bleachers and sat down. It was nearly dark, and he hadn't noticed one occupied seat at the far end. After a few

minutes, he heard a voice come from that direction.

"I just don't know what to think of you now, Sylvester. I just don't know."

It couldn't be.

Sylvester got up and climbed over the bleachers. It was Mr. Baruth!

"Mr. Baruth! What are you doing here? When did you get back?" he asked, the words pouring out in his excitement.

"That doesn't matter," said Mr. Baruth. "I don't have time to go into all that right now. Maybe someday. What's important is what has happened to you."

"What do you mean?" asked Sylvester, chewing on his lower lip.

"Last year, I tried to help you become a better player because I saw a lot of potential there. Sort of a chip off an old block that never really got a chance."

I bet he's talking about Dad, Sylvester thought.

"And, just as important, you were a good, honest kid," Mr. Baruth went on.

"I . . . I still am," Sylvester stammered.

"Are you? Can you honestly tell me you aren't cutting corners, shaving around the edges, so to speak?"

"But . . . but Cheeko says . . ."

"Cheeko! Who cares what he says?" Mr. Baruth snapped.

"Isn't he a friend of yours? He says he knows you," Sylvester insisted.

"Knowing someone doesn't make that person your friend," said Mr. Baruth. "And it doesn't matter how someone else tells you to play the game. You're old enough to know what's right and wrong yourself. You shouldn't need any outside help."

"But what will happen if . . . if . . . ?"

"If you just play clean, the way you learned from Coach Corbin and from my few suggestions last year? Well, Sylvester, there's only one way you'll ever know."

Sylvester stared down at his shoes, his eyes smarting and the back of his throat all choked up.

When he lifted his head, Mr. Baruth was gone.

• Chapter 14 •

Hello, Joyce? It's Syl," he spoke into the telephone. "I didn't see you after the game today. What? Oh . . . well, maybe I'll talk to you later."

So she hadn't been at the game. It made her too uncomfortable to see him turning into such a bully. He couldn't even defend himself when she said that.

"I got that book you asked about," his mother called from the dining room. After dinner she liked to sit there drinking her coffee and reading the newspaper while his father carried on a commentary about the silly letters to the editor.

"Thanks, Mom," he said as he took the book up to his room. It was a history of the World Series from the very first to the one played just last year. He quickly turned to the section on 1919.

There it was, all about the Black Sox scandal. Eddie Cicotte, the pitcher, was right in there with seven others who were accused of fixing the outcome of the series by the way they hit and fielded — or didn't hit and committed fake errors. The author claimed that they had had a score to settle with the team's owner, who had treated them badly.

I don't have any score to settle with anyone, thought Sylvester. Even when I wasn't playing so hot, Coach Corbin treated me like any other player. It was my own fault, if anything, that I was in a slump.

There was a picture of the team and he picked out Eddie Cicotte. He looked just as he did on the card Duane had lent him; he'd had to promise Duane he'd guard it with his life since it was sort of rare.

It was still light out. Sylvester remembered what his father had said about wanting to meet Cheeko,

302

but that was when he was going to practice with him. Maybe it would be okay if he just went for a walk in the direction of the field while it was still light out.

He hadn't gotten three blocks from his house when he saw Cheeko coming toward him.

"Hi, Cheeko," Sylvester said, not that surprised to bump into him.

"Hi, Syl," said Cheeko. "What brings you out this time of day, or should I say night? You should be celebrating after the way you played today."

"Right," said Sylvester, "but first I want to show you this."

He reached into his pocket and brought out a baseball card.

"I borrowed it from my friend Duane, you know, our third baseman?" he said. He handed it to Cheeko, who examined it closely.

"Hey, how about that?" Cheeko cried out with gusto. "Eddie Cicotte! Chicago White Sox!"

"Then you know him?" Sylvester asked, searching Cheeko's eyes and face.

"Know him? Who doesn't?" Cheeko replied. "Everybody who knows anything about baseball has heard of him. Well, almost everybody."

There were so many questions in Sylvester's mind, he didn't know which to ask first. But he knew that he had to get some answers or they would haunt him forever.

"That picture . . . uh . . . it sort of . . . well, doesn't it," he hemmed and hawed, "doesn't it look a little . . . ?"

"Like me?" Cheeko finished, his grin spreading wider than ever.

"Yeah!" Sylvester shouted, relieved.

"Well, I'd be lying if I said that it doesn't, 'cause it does, doesn't it?"

"Sure does," nodded Sylvester.

"Look, you can walk down the street and see someone who looks like the president of the United States," Cheeko continued, "but that doesn't mean this guy is the president of the United States, does it?"

"No, but . . ."

304

"Syl, let me tell you something. There're a lot of coincidences and a lot of strange things in this world. Don't expect answers for everything."

He handed back the card and threw back his shoulders, the way he always did when he was all through practice and ready to leave.

"Are . . . are you going somewhere now?" Sylvester asked.

"It's near the end of the line for us, kid," Cheeko said, looking around.

"But I still have a lot of questions I have to ask you," Sylvester said.

"I'm a little short on answers, right now," Cheeko said abruptly. "Tell you what, I'll see you at the game next week. We'll talk afterward."

Before Sylvester could get another word out, Cheeko had turned, raced across the street, and was out of sight in an instant.

But what about Mr. Baruth? What about what he said about your not being friends? What about the Black Sox scandal?

And what about some of the strange things that kept happening at games? Bobby tripping over nothing? A pitch taking a weird turn so he could hit it? A miraculous boost so he could grab a ball going over the fence?

And, craziest of all, this business of him only hitting home runs when there were men on base?

Were those things all coincidences?

"Rats!" he shouted out loud in frustration. Would he ever get to find out?

"Sylvester!"

He whirled around. It was Snooky Malone.

"What are you doing here, Snooky? You don't live on this street."

"That's what I was going to ask you," said Snooky. "I come around the corner and there you are, standing like you're in a trance or something, and then yelling at nothing. Are you okay?"

"I'm fine, just fine," replied Sylvester.

He glanced across the street. No, Cheeko wasn't coming back.

"Looking for somebody?" Snooky asked.

306

"Nope."

He realized he still had the baseball card in his hand and started to put it back into his jacket pocket.

"What's that?" Snooky asked.

"Just one of Duane's baseball cards," said Sylvester, trying to shrug off the question.

"Can I see it? Please?"

What difference could it make? Sylvester paused, heaved a deep sigh, and said, "Okay, but don't take all night. I have to be home before the streetlights go on."

He handed Snooky the card.

"Eddie Cicotte," Snooky read. He turned it over. "Chicago White Sox. A southpaw. Hmmmm . . . never heard of him." He returned the card to Sylvester. "Why are you carrying his card?"

Sylvester shook his head. "No reason in particular," he said. "Duane, uh, left it at my house the other night. It's very valuable because Eddie Cicotte was a famous player."

"He couldn't be all that famous," Snooky said. "Like I told you, I never heard of him."

307

Sylvester took back the card and put it in his pocket.

"You know something, Snooky, there's a lot of things you never heard of. So don't expect answers for everything, okay?"

• Chapter 15 •

S ylvester was late leaving the locker room for the start of the game with the Broton Tigers. In fact, it had just about cleared out when he saw Cheeko standing in the doorway.

"Hey, buddy," said Cheeko, with his usual grin. "All set for the big one, huh?"

A win over the Tigers would guarantee the Redbirds a shot at the league championship.

"Yeah, and I'd better get out there with the guys to warm up," Sylvester replied. Too bad there wasn't time right now to ask Cheeko any of the questions that had been running through his brain for days.

"Right," agreed Cheeko. "Just don't forget what I've been telling you. You can hit the ball and

309

make the plays out in the field, even if it takes a little help now and then . . ."

"What do you mean?" asked Sylvester, almost afraid of what the answer might be.

"Never mind," Cheeko continued. "Just do what I taught you and don't be afraid to get tough. Don't let anybody walk all over you. Play hard, even a little 'tricky,' you know? Yeah, I know you do! I've seen everything you've done out there." He chuckled. "Hey, you dropped your glove."

Sylvester automatically bent down to pick up his glove. When he straightened up, Cheeko was gone.

His stomach fluttered around and around as he left the cool locker room for the warm field.

"Hey, you want to throw a few?" asked Bobby Kent as Sylvester walked by him. The last few games, Bobby had acted much friendlier. It was hard to believe that they used to be so mean to each other.

"Yeah, sure," said Sylvester, glumly.

They threw the ball back and forth a few times

310

near the first base line. Sylvester's throws were so soft that twice they barely reached Bobby.

"Hey, Syl," Bobby called. "You okay?"

"Sure, sure, I'm fine."

"You don't act it," Bobby said. "Don't look it, either."

"I'm all right," Sylvester insisted.

Bobby pegged a stinger at him. It hit the tip of his glove and bounced into the seats next to first base. Sylvester went over to retrieve it from the fan who'd reached up and grabbed the ball with a practiced flair.

It was Mr. Baruth.

"Mr. Baruth!" he exclaimed. "Boy, am I glad to see you!"

"Hi, Sylvester," said Mr. Baruth. "I'm glad I could make this game. Hope it isn't too late."

"Too late? For what?"

"To put into practice some of the things I taught you."

"About my batting? And my fielding?"

"That's part of it." Mr. Baruth smiled.

Sylvester dropped his voice. "I guess you mean,

311

like my attitude. Like what Cheeko taught me this year."

"Cheeko may have given you some pointers that have helped improve your game, but he overlooked the most important piece of advice he could have given you. Be true to yourself, Sylvester. Play the best you can but play clean and honest. You don't win any medals — or anything else — by playing dirty."

"But Mr. Baruth, didn't you, well, give me more than advice last year? Didn't you give me some extra help? That's playing dirty, too, isn't it?" Sylvester felt awkward asking him straight out like this, but the thought had been nagging at him for a while, and he was glad he had finally said something.

Mr. Baruth looked straight into Sylvester's questioning eyes and said calmly, "The only thing I did was help you realize your potential."

"Hey, Sylvester! Game's starting!" shouted Bobby. "Come on!"

Sylvester didn't have time to digest Mr. Baruth's words as he took the ball from him, tossed it toward the pitcher's mound, and trotted out to right field. Advice from Cheeko, advice from Mr. Baruth, advice from the coach, from his father, Snooky, everyone. There were almost too many words of advice to fit under his cap.

The Broton Tigers, looking sharp in their orange uniforms, were up first. Right-hander Rick Wilson, hurling for the Hooper Redbirds, had no trouble disposing of the initial two batters, Chuck Manning and "Oink" Santos.

Then Steve Cranshaw came up and blasted a triple to deep center field.

"Get 'im outta there, Rick!" Sylvester shouted as Mike Hennesey, the cleanup hitter, stepped to the plate.

Mike was short, hefty, and batted left-handed. He fouled off the first pitch, took two balls, fouled off another, then took two more balls and walked.

"C'mon, Rick! You can do it!" Sylvester yelled, his voice mixing in with the other calls from his teammates.

Lennie Chang was the Tigers' fifth batter. He took two strikes, then sent the third pitch a mile

313

high into the stratosphere. He was crossing first base when the ball descended and landed in third baseman Duane Francis's glove.

Three out.

"Okay! Cowley! Sobel! Sturgis!" scorekeeper Billy Haywood's clarion voice rang out.

Cowley, Sobel, and Sturgis, however, did nothing to help the cause. Jim struck out, Ted flied out to left field, and Trent popped up to the pitcher, flinging his bat toward the dugout with angry disgust.

"Creep!" muttered Sylvester to himself. "Keep acting like that and you'll never get a hit."

He was surprised by his own thought. Trent acted tough, real mean, and it didn't do *him* any good. How come it worked for me? Is it because I'm getting "outside help?" I wish I could just forget about all this crazy stuff and play ball!

He tossed aside the bat he'd been holding in the on-deck circle, took off his batting gloves and helmet, and ran out to his spot in right field. When the Redbirds came up again, he'd be the

314

leadoff batter. But that was something to think about later, not now.

B.K. Abbot, wearing a stubble of a mustache above his lip that made him look older than the rest of his teammates, led off the top of the second inning for the Tigers and belted a single over second baseman Jim Cowley's outstretched gloved hand. He missed it by just about an inch.

Gary Hutton walked, advancing B.K. to second, and Josh Nichols popped out to Duane. Jim Smith, up next, and batting left-handed, uncorked a shallow drive over first base that stayed in fair territory, then bounced out against the foul line beyond the first base bleachers.

Sylvester tore after it, scooped it up near the fence, and pegged it in to Jim Cowley.

But, by now, B.K. and Gary had scored, and Jim was safely on second base for a double.

From opposite sides of the first base seats, Sylvester could see two distinct faces, both smiling. Mr. Baruth was at one end and Cheeko at the other. It sure didn't look like they were friends.

315

"Nice peg, Syl," came Cheeko's voice. "Pace yourself, pal."

Mr. Baruth just beamed and said nothing.

Chuck Manning was up again. This time he drove one of Rick's fastballs through the hole between shortstop and third, scoring Jim. "Oink" Santos bounced one to shortstop, and Chuck got tapped out on the first step of a possible double play. Only his slide, going into the base directly in Jim Cowley's path, prevented the second baseman from making the play to first.

Steve Cranshaw grounded out to short, and the half inning was over. But it was a big half inning, and Sylvester wondered whether it was going to be the one that made the difference when it was over.

"Coddmyer! Francis! Kent!" shouted Billy Haywood as the Redbirds came in to start the bottom half of the inning.

Sylvester put on his gloves and helmet, picked out his favorite bat, and swung it from one shoulder to the other as he headed for the plate.

"Okay, Sylvester!" Coach Corbin shouted from

316

the third base coaching box. "Start it off! You know what to do, kid!"

Sylvester looked over at the coach and caught a glimpse of the fans in the seats behind him. There were two people shouting and waving who really stood out — his mother and father. Mr. Coddmyer was giving him the high sign while Mrs. Coddmyer put her fingers to her lips and blew him a big kiss. And there, a few seats behind them, was Joyce. So she was willing to give him another chance.

He felt great. It was so good seeing all of them.

Swish! "Strike!" yelled the ump as Jim Smith breezed the first pitch past him.

He'd been wondering whether Joyce had come to the game. He hadn't really had a chance to check out the crowd until then.

"Strike two!" cried the ump.

Sylvester stepped out of the batting box, rubbed his gloved hands up and down the handle of the bat, and stepped in again. Two strikes, huh? Smith would probably waste the next one.

He didn't. It was right down the middle.

Sylvester swung and froze as the pitch landed

317

kerthunk in the catcher's mitt.

The Redbirds' fans groaned. The Tigers' fans cheered.

"That's okay, Syl," said Duane as he passed by Sylvester on his way to the plate. "You'll get another shot."

But a strikeout? Sylvester kept his head bowed all the way to the dugout.

What was wrong with him? There was probably an easy answer if he could just concentrate. That was it! He hadn't been concentrating. He'd let his mind wander and that was the only reason he struck out. He didn't have to hit them all out of the park, but he did have to pay attention if he was going to get anywhere.

Now that's a real lesson, he thought as he put his mind to what was happening at the plate.

Duane had let the first two pitches go by, then connected with a high one that he knocked to right center field for a double. Then Bobby Kent belted a line drive through the gap between first and second for a single, scoring Duane.

Jerry Ash and Eddie Exton could do nothing,

318

and the inning was over. Broton Tigers 3, Hooper Redbirds 1.

Sylvester scooped up his glove and trotted out to right field. He tried to avoid Cheeko by not looking directly at him, but his glance swept in that area of the stands. There was Cheeko, standing next to Mr. Baruth. It looked as though they were arguing. At least, Cheeko seemed to be angry about something. Mr. Baruth just stood there, shaking his head.

As the fans got settled down for the next play, Sylvester set his mind to the action at the plate. Left-handed batter Mike Hennesey led off with a high fly to Jerry for the first out. Rick fanned Lennie Chang, walked B.K. Abbot with four straight pitches, then fanned Gary Hutton. Three out.

Rick himself led off the bottom of the third for the Redbirds, and Sylvester wondered if he'd have a chance to bat. He was fifth in the rotation. Considering the success Jim Smith was having on the mound, his chances were slim.

They became even slimmer as Rick bounced out to shortstop.

Then the top of the batting order was up again, and Jim Cowley started some action with a single over short. Ted Sobel lambasted one to left field that looked as if it might go over the fence. It didn't, but it struck that barrier and bounced back. The Tigers' Gary Hutton grabbed it and pegged it in. The throw held Jim on third and Ted on second with a double.

Well, there sure are men on base now. If they're still on when I bat, what will I do? Sylvester felt a weak tremor inside him. Will I hit a home run? Or will I strike out again?

Trent waited out the count, walked, and now the bases were loaded.

Sylvester got up from his crouch in the on-deck circle.

Cheers exploded from the Redbirds' fans as he stepped to the plate, pulled down on his helmet, and waited for Jim Smith to pitch to him.

Then, for a long moment, the crowd was silent, so silent Sylvester could hear the pounding of his heart.

• Chapter 16 •

He tried to concentrate. What difference did it make whether it was a strikeout or a home run, as long as he did the best he could? That rang a bell! That's what his dad had said, and what Mr. Baruth had always told him. And Coach Corbin. Even Joyce said so. In fact, the only one who had never said that was Cheeko!

Jim Smith's first three pitches were all curves, none of which went over the plate.

Then he blazed in a fastball. "Strike!" called the ump as Sylvester let it go by.

The next pitch was a fastball, too, but this one was grazing the outside corner when Sylvester's bat connected with it. The sound was like a rifle shot, and the ball like a white bullet as it streaked out to deep left center field ... and over the fence.

The crowd was on its feet as the applause echoed and reechoed throughout the park. Sylvester dropped his bat and ran down the first base line, removing his batting gloves and sticking them into his pocket as he did so. He shot a glance at the stands, eager to see the proud faces of Mr. Baruth and Cheeko. But they were nowhere in sight.

The Redbirds surrounded him at the plate, jumping up and down as they exchanged high fives with him and with each other.

"Told you," Duane said, grinning.

Sylvester grinned back.

But that was it for the Redbirds that half inning. Neither Duane nor Bobby was able to continue the hitting streak.

Broton Tigers 3, Hooper Redbirds 5.

Josh Nichols led off for the Tigers in the top of the fourth. Short and squatty, he looked at Rick and waved the bat like a war club. Crack! A sharp hit over Jim Cowley's head for a single.

It was a good start. Jim Smith lashed out another single, advancing Josh all the way around to third. Then Chuck Manning came up and cleared the bases with a triple, tying up the score.

"Oh, no!" Sylvester moaned. Peering over at Chuck on third base, he could just see his grand-slam home run going down the drain.

But none of the next three Tigers was able to do anything to bring the runner home. The inning ended with the score still tied, 5–5.

Sylvester trotted off the field, reached the dug-out, and settled down. Again, there was a chance he might come up to bat. He couldn't imagine what might happen, but he didn't feel those strange rumblings in his stomach anymore. In fact, he was pretty sure he could handle things no matter what crossed the plate when it was his turn at bat. After all, he had come through last time — and without any "extra help."

It was a quick half inning as the Redbirds failed to put a single man on base. The Tigers came off the field with no traces of exertion.

Their leadoff batter, Lennie Chang, flied out to left field. That brought up B.K. Abbot, who doubled to right center.

Another out, and then an error by Duane, created a good scoring situation for the Tigers as Jim Smith, with two hits already to his credit, came up to the plate.

But Jim laced a grounder to second, resulting in the third out, and the Redbirds came off the field to start the bottom of the fifth inning.

Second baseman Jim Cowley walked on four pitches. It looked as though the Tigers' pitcher was a little tired after just batting and trying to beat out the throw to first. He didn't seem able to get one over.

That changed when Ted Sobel came to bat. The first pitch was straight over the heart of the plate. Ted walloped it into right center for a double. Coach Corbin arm-spun Jim in to home as Chuck Manning pegged in the ball. Jim barely made it as he hit the dirt and slid safely across the plate. Tigers 5, Redbirds 6.

Trent was up next. Sylvester put on his helmet, picked up his bat, and knelt in the on-deck circle. With only one out, there was no doubt he'd come up to bat again. But the old pressure, the question of whether it would be a home run or nothing, no longer mattered. He was comfortable with the fact that doing his best was all anyone could ask of him.

"Syl! You're up!" a voice shouted. It was Billy Haywood.

He hadn't even noticed what happened at the plate: Trent had just struck out in three straight pitches.

He jumped to his feet and passed Trent, who was walking back to the dugout with a disgusted look on his face.

"That's okay, Trent," Sylvester said without any sarcasm. "Can't do it all the time. You'll get 'em back."

Just for a second, Trent glanced at him, as if surprised to hear a kind word from Sylvester. But he continued, silently, toward the dugout.

Sylvester observed that Ted was still on second. He stepped to the plate and focused on the pitcher's mound. He got ready for the first pitch.

"Strike!" Jim Smith's curve ball just grazed the outside corner of the plate.

The next pitch was in there, and Sylvester swung. Crack! A long high drive to center field! It looked good!

The Redbirds' fans sprang to their feet, cheering and applauding, as Sylvester dropped his bat and headed for first base.

He ran slowly as he watched the soaring ball reach its apex and start arcing down. From just the corner of his eye, he saw that Chuck Manning had his back close to the center field fence, his glove hand held high in the air.

A moment later the applause changed to sighs and moans of disappointment. The ball descended *not* on the other side of the fence, but into Chuck Manning's waiting glove.

• Chapter 17 •

F or one second, Sylvester wanted to crawl
under the turf and just disappear. But then,
he shrugged off the feeling. At least he had given
it his best shot. He lifted his head and started to
run back toward the dugout.

And then the strangest thing of all happened. A
cheer started in the stands. He could have
sworn it was that squeaky, pesky voice of Snooky
Malone's that he heard first.

"Coddmyer! Coddmyer! Coddmyer!"

It was picked up by a few others, then some
more, then more, until a huge crowd was shouting
his name all at once and clapping rhythmically.

It lasted less than a minute, but it was something he never forgot. Even though he hadn't hit

a home run, hadn't even gotten a hit, the fans were still on his side. They appreciated what he had done. They hadn't forgotten.

Even the guys in the dugout were on their feet.

Rick: "It was real close. Too bad, Syl."

Eddie: "Couldn't get any closer without going over. Tough luck, Syl."

Jerry Ash: "Bum break, pal. You'll get 'em next time."

Sylvester was so flustered, he was at a loss for words. "Let's just hold them," he managed to sputter.

Good news came for his pal Duane, who was at bat. He hit a clean single to short right, scoring Ted. Bobby then grounded to retire the side. Three out. Tigers 5, Redbirds 7.

Chuck Manning led off with a walk to start the top of the sixth inning. "Oink" advanced him to third with a single, his first hit of the game. And then Rick walked Steve Cranshaw to load the bases.

Rats, thought Sylvester. The bases loaded, no outs, and their best hitter is up. So far, Mike

Hennesey, the Tigers' cleanup hitter, had walked and gone down twice. He was still a threat that couldn't be underestimated.

He popped up to third and Duane snagged it. One out.

Lennie Chang swung at and missed three in a row. Two outs.

And then, B.K. Abbot stepped up to the plate, looking really strong. With his reputation as a long-ball hitter, the outfield backed up a few steps.

On Rick's first pitch, he blasted a fly that was just short of right center field. But it was a judgment call whether it was Bobby's or Sylvester's ball. It would be a hard catch for either of them, and both had to go for it.

The two outfielders raced in that direction, neither sure who would shout first, or whether they would collide in the attempt.

As time and space grew short, amid the uproar from the stands, a voice on the field cried, "Sylvester, it's yours! Go for it, buddy!"

It was Trent!

Bobby swerved out of the way and Sylvester

330

made a horizontal leap that would have ended in a belly flop if he were diving into a swimming pool. But his glove was turned in the right direction, and he grabbed the ball in the webbing just before it touched down.

The game was over. The Redbirds won, 7–5, and Sylvester started to run off the field to the sound of the cheers and applause that rang from the stands. Before he could get as far as the infield, he was swept up by his teammates. Trent threw an arm around his shoulders and gave him a friendly punch. "Way to go, slugger," he said, and his smile was genuine.

The swarm of fans pouring down from the stands surrounded him, but he was able to pull away to spend a few minutes with the special people in his life before boarding the bus. His mother and father could hardly speak, they were so hoarse from shouting.

"We're definitely going out to dinner tonight," his mother croaked.

"Yes." His father agreed. "And you get to pick the restaurant."

Sylvester grabbed someone standing near him and winked at the girl hovering a few steps away.

"Okay, but can I bring a couple of friends? I'd like Snooky and Joyce to come," he said.

His father laughed. "The more the merrier!"

"Okay, then, one more," he said as his eyes scanned the crowd. "If he hasn't disappeared, I'd like to ask him to join us."

"Him? Who?" Mrs. Coddmyer asked.

"Mr. Baruth," said Sylvester. "I guess he's gone. I wonder if I'll ever see him again."

Snooky piped up, "According to your stars, you're still in for a few surprises, Sylvester."

Sylvester threw up his arms, shook his head, and boarded the bus.

BASEBALL PALS

To my brothers

Fred
Mike
Tony
John
Rudy

and

Pop

BASEBALL PALS

by Matt Christopher

Illustrated by Margaret Sanfilippo

1

JIMMIE TODD brushed away a lock of brown hair from his forehead. He pounded his fist into his baseball glove and scowled at Johnny Lukon.

"Why can't I pitch?" he said. "I'm captain. We just voted on it, didn't we? And can't a captain play whatever position he wants to?"

"But you're no pitcher," said Johnny. He was a long-legged boy with brown eyes and fire-red hair. He was wearing a brand-new first-base mitt. "Why don't you let Paul pitch? He's a lefty, and lefties make good pitchers."

"Sure," said Alan Warzcak, sitting on

337

one of the legs of the batting cage. He was small but could run faster and hit better than most boys his age. "You never pitched before. Let Paul pitch. He's taller than you and he has a good curve."

Jimmie clamped his teeth over his lower lip. His eyes darted fire. He thought of a lot of things he could call Johnny Lukon and Alan Warzcak. But he didn't. His younger brother, blue-eyed, sandy-haired Ervie, was standing beside him. He didn't want Ervie to go home and tell his mother he'd been quarreling with the boys on the ball diamond.

"I can pitch, too," Jimmie said stubbornly. "I've been practicing ever since it got warm weather."

Ervie's big blue eyes rolled around to him. Jimmie's ears reddened. Ervie was sort of chubby. He wore blue overalls that dragged at the heels of his shoes. He hardly ever said anything. His eyes always did the talking. Every time Jimmie told a fib those eyes would look up at him, and Jimmie would feel guilty.

"Well, almost ever since then," Jimmie corrected himself.

The blue eyes rolled away. Ervie never even smiled.

"If we want a team in the Grasshoppers League, we'd better make up our minds now what positions we're going to play," said Jimmie. "I'll pitch. Johnny Lukon will play first base."

Then he turned to his close friend, Paul Karoski. Paul was the nicest kid he had ever known. He never said much. He never argued. He was the tallest one around, too. He was a good pitcher, although Jimmie thought that Paul would

339

make a better first baseman. But now that Johnny Lukon had a first-base mitt, there was only the outfield for Paul to play.

"I know what you could play, Paul," Jimmie said, his eyes sparkling. "You can play the outfield, can't you?"

Paul shrugged. "Yes. I suppose so."

Jimmie's brows arched. "Will you?" he pleaded. "You can play center. That's where most of the flies are hit."

If he made Paul believe that playing center field was as important as pitching, maybe Paul wouldn't mind the change.

"If you say so," Paul said.

Jimmie's face brightened. He looked at Johnny, Alan, and the faces of the other players standing around. His expression clearly said, "I told you so, didn't I?"

He felt good. Everything was settled now. He was going to pitch. All winter

long he'd been thinking about it, while he read a book on big-league pitchers. He used to think a pitcher had to be tall and able to throw a ball faster than anyone else on the team. But that wasn't so. The book had told about pitchers who weren't very tall and were still great hurlers. It had told about pitchers who weren't the fastest throwers on their teams, but were smart and could throw hooks that struck men out like anything.

That was the kind of pitcher he wanted to be. Smart, and throw a lot of hooks. Jimmie smiled happily. He looked at Ervie, who was standing beside him with his hands in his pockets. But he couldn't tell whether Ervie was happy or not.

Something about him made Jimmie lose his smile. Something about the way Ervie was looking at Paul Karoski.

2

JIMMIE took a deep breath. He turned away from Ervie and tried not to be bothered by him. He wished he could leave Ervie home, then he wouldn't be afraid to tell the boys anything. With Ervie around, he had to be careful what he said and what he did.

His eyes roved over the faces again. They settled on a boy a little taller and fatter than Ervie. His face was moon-shaped. His nose was like an old-fashioned shoe button.

"Hey, Tiny! Are you going to catch for us this year?"

343

Tiny Zimmer shook his head. "No. I'm going to play with the Red Rockets"

"The Red Rockets?" Jimmie's forehead knotted into a frown. "Why? Don't you want to play with us?"

Tiny shrugged. "They asked me last week. They've already given me a jersey."

"Well, how do you like that?" Jimmie said, disgusted with the little fat boy. "What are you doing here if you're playing with the Red Rockets?"

Tiny shrugged again. "I came with Paul."

Jimmie glared at him. Tiny wasn't a good player, but he had nerve to stand behind the plate. Jimmie couldn't think of anybody else to take Tiny's place. Nobody had ever asked for the position. It was a tough one to play. Besides, Tiny was the only boy who owned a catcher's mitt.

Jimmie kicked the short-cropped grass with the toe of his sneakers. "A fine start this is! How are we going to play in the Grasshoppers League if we don't have a catcher?"

The Grasshoppers League was starting soon. In order to join, a team had to have at least nine men. Their names had to be in on a certain date. If the names weren't in, the team's chance to enter was lost.

Jimmie wet his lips. He looked at Ervie. If only Ervie was four or five years older, he thought, then he could catch.

"Well, are we going to have a team in the league, or not?" Jimmie snapped. "We need a catcher. Who's going to catch?"

"I'll catch," a soft, deep voice spoke up from the rear of the group.

345

Jimmie rose on his toes. "Mose Solomon? Do you own a catcher's mask and a mitt, Mose?"

"My big brother does. But he'll let me take them. He bought a new outfit."

Jimmie breathed a sigh of relief. "Will you go after them, Mose? Then we can play a game."

"Okay!" Mose ran off.

Most of the kids had their gloves with them. So did Jimmie. He had also brought a ball and bat, hoping there would be enough players to choose up sides.

"What are we calling our team?" Wishy Walters asked. "The Planets?"

"Sure. The same as last year," Jimmie said. He was anxious to play ball. He wanted to get on the mound and pitch. He wanted to prove to those boys who wouldn't believe he could pitch that he

346

was as good as Paul Karoski — or even better. "Let's choose up sides!" he said.

Johnny Lukon chose with him. Jimmie tossed his bat to Johnny, who caught it near the middle. Then, hand over hand, the two boys worked to the top of the handle. Johnny won first choice.

"Paul," he said.

"Mose," Jimmie said.

The two teams were picked at last. There weren't enough players, so Jimmie asked Ervie if he'd like to play.

"Sure," said Ervie.

"Okay. You play right field." Jimmie pointed to where he meant.

"I know," murmured Ervie quietly.

Jimmie and Johnny chose for last raps. Jimmie won. Mose Solomon arrived with a mask and catcher's mitt. The batting cage was pulled out of the way and the game began. Jimmie was glad Mose was catching. It would be almost like a real game.

The lead-off man stepped to the plate. Jimmie put his right foot on the rubber and wound up. He threw one fast toward the plate. It was a foot outside. The batter let it go.

"Put it over!" somebody yelled.

He threw another wild pitch. Then one was close to the inside corner, but the batter didn't swing at it.

"What're you waiting for?" Jimmie cried.

"Put 'em over the plate!" Johnny Lukon wailed.

He was ready to pitch when Wishy said, "Jimmie! Here comes Mr. Nichols! Ask him to umpire."

"Good idea! Mr. Nichols!" Jimmie

shouted across the field. "Oh, Mr. Nichols! Will you umpire for us?"

Mr. Nichols was a tall, dark-haired man with a quick, happy smile. He always came to the park to watch the kids play.

He waved a greeting. "Sure, Jimmie," he said. "I'll be glad to."

He stepped behind the pitcher's mound and the game resumed.

Jimmie pitched.

"Ball one!" said Mr. Nichols.

Jimmie pitched again.

"Ball two!" said Mr. Nichols.

Jimmie grew worried. Why couldn't he throw that ball over the plate? The home base looked like a big, flat dish up there. It should be easy to throw the ball over.

But Jimmie walked that man, and he walked the next.

349

"Take it easy," Mr. Nichols advised him. "Don't throw so hard."

Maybe that was the trouble, Jimmie thought. He threw easier. Smack! The ball sailed over second base! A run scored. The runner on first stopped on third. The hitter stopped on second. A two-bagger!

Jimmie's heart sank. This wasn't the way it should be. He had plenty of speed. He had a hook. Those batters weren't supposed to hit his pitches.

At last Johnny's team made three outs. The score was 4 to 0, and the first inning was only half over!

Jimmie's side scored two runs.

The second inning was a repetition of the first. Johnny's team was knocking Jimmie's pitches all over the lot. Before three outs were made, four more runs had scored.

Jimmie came to bat. He stepped into one of Paul's fast balls for a line drive over short. The ball sailed deep into the outfield. Jimmie raced around the bases and stopped on third. A smile tugged at the corners of his mouth. That hit had felt good and solid. It made up a little for those bad throws and the men he had walked.

Someday he would be a good pitcher, he thought. He'd throw the ball wherever he wanted to. High, low, inside — anywhere. All he needed was practice.

3

"MR. NICHOLS," Johnny Lukon said, "we want to play in the Grasshoppers League, but we need a manager. Would you be our manager, Mr. Nichols?"

Mr. Nichols smiled. His gray eyes twinkled as if he had just been honored by something very important.

"You sure you want me to be your manager?" he asked.

"Yes. We talked about it. Would you manage us, please, Mr. Nichols?"

Mr. Nichols chuckled. "Okay. I'd be glad to. I know most of the boys who run

353

the Grasshoppers League, and we will get our team entered as soon as possible."

He looked at the hot, anxious faces around him. "Now, do you have a captain?"

Jimmie stepped forward. "I'm the captain," he said.

"Okay. Suppose you come to my house tonight, Jimmie, and give me the names of your players so that I'll know who's on our team?"

"Yes, sir."

"What about bats and gloves? Does everybody have them?"

"Most of us have."

"What about balls?" Billy Hutt asked.

"Those are furnished by the league," Mr. Nichols said. He glanced at the mask and mitt in Mose Solomon's hands. "Are those yours, Mose?"

"Yes."

"Good. Can you boys be here again the same time tomorrow? We'll go through fielding and batting practices."

"Sure!" the boys said happily.

Jimmie felt a tug at his sleeve. He turned.

"I want to go home," Ervie said.

"Oh, please, Ervie," said Jimmie. "Not yet. We have plenty of time."

"I'm hungry," Ervie said.

"Hungry?" Disgust flashed in Jimmie's eyes. "Is that all you want to do? Eat?"

Ervie blinked his eyes. "I think we should go home. It's late."

"You go home if you want to," Jimmie replied gruffly. "I'm staying here."

Ervie peered up at him. There was hurt in his eyes. Jimmie turned his back to him, hoping Ervie would go home. But

356

when he looked around, Ervie was still there, gazing at him with those haunting blue eyes.

"Look, Ervie," he pleaded, "I'm captain of the Planets. I'm supposed to stay here. I can't go before the others go. Can't you understand?"

Ervie didn't answer. He just blinked his eyes again.

"Listen, Ervie," Jimmie said in a low voice, "I want to practice pitching. The best place is here on the diamond. I need the practice. You want us to be ready when the league starts, don't you? You want us to have a good team, don't you?"

"Yes," said Ervie.

"Then will you stay a while longer?"

"No," said Ervie. "I want to go home. I'm hungry."

4

JIMMIE walked ahead of Ervie. He was disgusted. He didn't look back once until he reached the corner. Ervie was about twenty feet behind him.

"You walk too fast," said Ervie, puffing.

When they reached the corner, Jimmie took Ervie's hand. He felt bad because he had been mean to Ervie. "Maybe you're right, Ervie," he said. "Maybe it is late. Let's hurry."

They entered the kitchen. Jimmie smelled the cooked potatoes and ham and his mouth watered. His stomach felt empty now, too.

Mrs. Todd turned from the kitchen stove. Her shiny black hair hung in soft waves. She was wearing a blue dress with white polka dots.

"Well," she said, "look what the wind blew in. My two baseball players!" A smile flickered in her eyes. "It seems, though, that someone's memory isn't as good now that baseball season is here."

Jimmie was puzzled. "What do you mean, Mom?"

She pointed at the clock on the wall. "Do you see what time it is?"

Jimmie looked. "It's five minutes to five."

"Yes. Can you remember what time I asked you boys to come home?"

"Four o'clock. But nobody had a watch, Mom," Jimmie added hastily.

His eyes met Ervie's, and his face turned red. He had lied again. He had not wanted to come home. He had wanted to stay. If Ervie hadn't insisted on coming home, he would have been at the field yet.

He prayed Ervie wouldn't tell on him. Ervie didn't.

Mrs. Todd ruffled Jimmie's hair. "Well, I suppose that none of you baseball players would carry a watch with you. Daddy is home and supper is about ready. Wash yourselves, while I set the table."

After supper Jimmie asked his mother if he could go to Paul Karoski's house. She consented.

Paul was in the back yard, playing pitch and catch with someone. When Jimmie reached the corner of the house he saw that the other boy was Tiny Zimmer.

"Hi," Jimmie greeted.

361

"Hi," Tiny said. He was crouched be-hind a piece of wood that was supposed to be home plate. He took one glance at Jimmie, then turned his attention back to Paul.

Paul didn't say anything. He was too interested in winding up and keeping his eyes on the target that Tiny had made with his glove. Paul's left hand went back over his shoulder, then came around fast. The ball snapped from his fingers and sped toward the mitt. Plop!

"Thataboy, Paul," Tiny said. "Right over the outside corner."

Jimmie watched Paul throw awhile. But Paul didn't look at him once, as if he weren't even there.

Paul looked pretty good, Jimmie thought. But he should play first base, or the outfield. The Planets didn't need two

362

pitchers. Jimmie would be the only one they needed.

Wishy Walters came up behind Jimmie. He watched for a while too, then said, "Want to come to my house, Jimmie? I have a hard rubber ball. We can play a few games."

"I might as well," said Jimmie.

Wishy's house was a block down the street. It was a brick building with a wide porch in front. Mr. and Mrs. Walters were sitting on the porch. Jimmie spoke to them. They asked how his mother and father were. Then Wishy got his rubber ball.

"I'll be Cleveland," Wishy said.

"I'll be the Detroit Tigers," Jimmie said.

They went to the side of the building, then threw fingers to see who would "bat" first. Wishy won. He stood close to the house and Jimmie about six feet behind

363

him. Wishy would throw the ball against the house. When it bounced back Jimmie would try to catch it. If he caught it, it would mean an out. If he missed it, it would mean an error and a "man" would get on first base. If the ball went past him and he didn't touch it, it would mean a hit.

Wishy was ahead 10 to 6 by the third inning. Jimmie didn't care. He wasn't interested in the game, now. He was thinking about Paul. Paul was his best friend, yet Paul had hardly looked at him when he was there a few minutes ago.

Was Paul mad at him? Was he sore because Jimmie wanted to pitch? But he did say he'd play the outfield, didn't he? Didn't he mean it? Did he still want to pitch?

But I want to pitch, Jimmie told himself. We're only going to play one game a

364

week. There won't be enough games for two pitchers. Can't Paul understand that?

There were footsteps behind him. Jimmie turned. Tiny Zimmer was coming down the cemented alleyway, a big grin on his moon-shaped face.

"Hi, fellas," he said.

"Hi, Tiny," Jimmie murmured. "Where's Paul?"

"Home." The grin on Tiny's face widened. "I have some news for you guys. Paul isn't going to play with the Planets. He's going to play with us. The Red Rockets."

5

JIMMIE went home. He kicked a stone in the driveway. He banged the toe of his shoe against the first step that led to the porch. Why did Paul have to play with the Red Rockets? Why?

He went inside. His mother was in the kitchen, mending a pair of Ervie's pants.

"What's the matter, Jimmie?" she asked.

"Nothing," said Jimmie. He went into the living room. Ervie was playing with his toy stagecoach on the thick rug.

"Hi, Jimmie," he greeted. "Will you play with me?"

"Not now."

Jimmie turned away and headed for his room. He could feel Ervie's eyes on his back.

He sat on his bed and thought about Paul Karoski. Paul and he were such great buddies. They were like brothers. They had always played together, ever since they were old enough to walk. Sure, they would get mad at each other once in a

while. Who didn't? But it never lasted long.

How could Paul do that? Jimmie thought. How could Paul turn his back on him, and on the Planets, to play on another team?

Jimmie swallowed an ache in his throat. He pulled a handkerchief from his pocket and wiped his eyes.

"What's wrong, Jimmie?" a voice said softly behind him.

Ervie had come in so quietly Jimmie had not heard him.

"Nothing," he said. He went to his desk, and yanked out a drawer. He took out two sheets of heavy yellow paper and a box of crayons.

He tried to think of something to draw. But his mind was filled with thoughts of Paul. Without Paul the Planets would

368

not amount to anything. He could hit. He could run. And if anything ever happened to Jimmie, he could pitch.

Well, thought Jimmie angrily, let him pitch for the Red Rockets! I don't care!

He pulled the drawer out again and shoved the paper and box of crayons back into it. Then he rose and put an arm around Ervie's shoulder.

"Come on, Ervie," he said. "I'll play with you."

6

THE PLANETS couldn't practice the next afternoon. It rained off and on and the field was too wet. Thursday morning though, the sun came out nice and shiny. By afternoon the field was dry.

The team gathered at the field. They played catch for a while. Some of the boys talked about Paul.

"Why did he quit?" one of them asked.

"I don't know."

"He's going to pitch for the Red Rockets, that's why."

"The Red Rockets? He belongs to us, doesn't he?"

"He doesn't have to. He can belong to any team he wants to."

Jimmie pretended he didn't hear them. He wished that they would stop talking about Paul. After all, he was their pitcher. Once he got going, he'd be even better than Paul. Just wait and see.

Mr. Nichols arrived. He was wearing a blue baseball cap and a sweat shirt. He looked like a real manager now.

"Hi, boys!" His gray eyes sparkled as he looked at the faces. "Where's Paul Karoski?" he asked.

"He joined the Red Rockets," Wishy said. "We're going to miss him. He was a good player."

"He was the best pitcher we had," Johnny Lukon said.

"We don't need a good pitcher," Wishy said. "Jimmie can pitch as well as

371

anybody. What we need are hitters."

Jimmie looked at Wishy and felt a little better that somebody was on his side.

"Well, Jimmie Todd can be our pitcher," Mr. Nichols said. "I think that after some practice he'll be just as good as Paul Karoski. Let's hope he'll be better!"

Some of the boys laughed. Jimmie felt like smiling, himself.

Yet he wished that Paul was playing with them. It wasn't right that Paul should play with another team. He belonged here — with the Planets.

"Let's have batting practice," Mr. Nichols suggested. "Jimmie, take these three balls and get on the mound. Some of you boys pull that batting cage closer to the plate."

The cage was moved up.

"Johnny, Alan, and Billy," Mr. Nichols

said, "you three can start to bat. Hit five and lay one down. Okay, Jimmie! Throw 'em in there!"

Jimmie stood on the rubber, made his windup, and threw the ball. Mr. Nichols, standing behind the batting cage, watched him. The pitch was wide. Johnny let it go by.

"Outside!" Mr. Nichols said.

Jimmie picked up another ball, wound up, and threw.

"Too high!" Mr. Nichols said.

The next pitch hit the dirt in front of the plate.

The manager gathered up the three balls and tossed them back to Jimmie. "Come on, Jimmie, boy. Take your time. Get 'em over."

Jimmie was careful with the next pitch. He didn't throw it hard. It went over the

373

plate. Johnny swung at it and the ball sailed out to left field. The next pitch was low, but it came in easy, and Johnny swung again. He missed. "Come on! Throw 'em in here, will you?" Johnny cried.

"I wish Paul was pitching for us," Alan Warzcak murmured softly, but loud enough for Jimmie to hear. "He puts 'em all over."

"I know," Billy Hutt said. "We used to have fine batting practice when he was pitching!"

"All right, boys. Enough of that," Mr. Nichols cautioned. "Come on, Jimmie. Take your time, boy. You'll get 'em in there."

But Jimmie couldn't get them in there. After a while, Mr. Nichols went out to the mound himself and pitched.

7

THEY practiced all the next week. First they had batting practice, then Mr. Nichols would hit balls to the infielders and outfielders. While Mr. Nichols did that, Jimmie practiced pitching.

He had learned to throw a drop. He was proud of it. Now, if he could only get his fast throws over the plate . . .

At the Friday afternoon practice Mr. Nichols called the boys together.

"I've scheduled a game with the Pirates for tomorrow afternoon," he said. "Everybody be here at one-thirty. I'll try to get a couple more games before the league starts so that we won't plunge into it cold."

Jimmie was up bright and early Saturday morning. After breakfast he went to Mose Solomon's house. Mose's mother came to the door and said that Mose was still in bed.

"Who's that, Ma?" Mose's voice came from somewhere upstairs.

"Jimmie Todd!" she called back. She smiled at Jimmie. "I guess he wasn't asleep. Just lying there. You want to come in and wait for him?"

"Thank you," said Jimmie.

After Mose washed, dressed, and ate his breakfast, he brought his mitt and played catch with Jimmie.

"Give me a target," Jimmie said.

Mose held his mitt in front of his left shoulder until Jimmie could put a ball in that spot. Then he'd change it to his right shoulder and then in front of his chest. The ball seemed to go everywhere but where Mose held the mitt.

"Come on, Jimmie. Come on," Mose said encouragingly.

"I'm trying!" cried Jimmie.

After a while he became tired. "Let's quit," he said. "I must pitch this afternoon."

As the hour of the game drew near, Jimmie's stomach tightened into knots. He wanted so much to be a pitcher, but he wasn't doing too well. If he only had control . . .

He walked a man in the first inning. The next man singled, sending the runner to third. Jimmie stood on the rubber and looked at the two fingers Mose held below his mitt. Mose was signaling for a curve ball.

Jimmie's hands trembled. No one was out, and already two men were on. One was in scoring position. Everybody was looking at Jimmie. They were waiting to see what he could do.

"He'll walk you!" a voice shouted from

the grandstand. "Just stand there with your bat on your shoulder, Mike!"

His heart thumped in his chest. Perspiration covered his face. There seemed to be too much going on. People were shouting. . . . Mose was giving him a target. . . . The infielders were talking it up. . . . Two men were on bases. . . . He tried to think about everything at once.

He wound up. The runner on third took a big lead. Jimmie stopped his windup, whipped the ball to third. The boy ran back. Alan Warzcak tagged him before his foot touched the bag.

"Balk!" shouted the umpire, who stood behind Jimmie.

Jimmie was startled. He looked at Mr. Nichols, sitting in the dugout. Mr. Nichols nodded.

"You can't throw a ball to a base once

you've started to wind up," the umpire said. "Never wind up with men on base. They can steal on you. Okay, kid!" he said to the runner on third. "Take the base!" He turned to the runner on first. "Go to second!"

Mr. Nichols trotted out to the mound. He put an arm around Jimmie's shoulder. "You're all nerved up, Jimmie. Relax. Take it easy. This is just a scrub game. About that windup and throw when a runner's on base — do you understand it now?"

"Yes," Jimmie murmured.

"Okay." Mr. Nichols patted him on the shoulder, and grinned. "Just let 'em hit it."

The Pirates scored three runs in the first inning. The Planets tied it in the second. The third inning went by scoreless. In the fourth Jimmie walked two men in a row and the next man hit a homer that put the

Pirates way ahead again. The Pirates made two more runs in the fifth, and there the game ended. Score — 8 to 3.

"Don't worry," Mr. Nichols said as the boys gathered their bats and gloves and headed sadly for home. "We have a good team. Once Jimmie finds that plate, nobody will beat us."

Jimmie kept his eyes straight ahead. I'll find it, he thought. I have to find it, or we might as well not join the league.

8

THE PLANETS played a game Tuesday afternoon against the Mohawks. Jimmie felt a little more confident before the game began. He had practiced a lot. His control was improving. Mr. Nichols said so himself.

The first two innings went by without a man reaching first base. Lou Rodell, the Planets' shortstop, hit a grounder to short in the top of the third inning. The Mohawks' shortstop caught it and threw it over the first baseman's head. Lou ran to second on the play.

Jimmie stepped to the plate. He batted

fifth in the batting order. He pulled his cap down tight on his head, gripped his bat near the end of the handle, and dug his toes into the dirt.

The ball came in. It was low. Jimmie let it go by.

"Ball!" cried the umpire.

The catcher threw the ball back to the pitcher. Jimmie waited again. The pitcher stretched his hands high, brought them down. He looked over his shoulder at the runner on second, then threw the ball toward the plate.

It came in chest-high. It looked like a strike. Jimmie stepped into it. He swung. Crack! The ball sailed toward left center field. Lou scored. Jimmie rounded second, then third.

"Go! Go!" yelled Mr. Nichols, who was coaching third.

Jimmie ran like a deer. He crossed the plate for a home run!

"Thataboy, Jimmie!" Wishy Walters shouted. "Win your own ball game!"

The homer made Jimmie feel good. They were ahead now — 2 to 0. If they could just hold that lead . . .

Kippy Lake flied out to center. Wishy struck out. George Bardino popped a fly to the pitcher. Three outs in six pitched balls. Boy, that was quick, thought Jimmie.

The Planets ran out on the field.

Jimmie pitched. "Ball!" said the umpire.

"Ball two!"

"Strike!"

"Ball three!"

"Ball four! Take your base!"

Jimmie trembled. He couldn't walk any more men. He couldn't. . . .

He stretched, pitched. The batter held out his bat. He bunted the ball down the third base line. Jimmie raced after it. He picked it up, made a motion to throw to second. Too late there! He heaved it to first.

"Out!" yelled the base umpire.

But throwing out the man didn't help Jimmie's control. He became wilder and wilder. He walked in runs. When he came to bat he didn't feel like hitting. He wished the ball game was over. He wished they would call it off.

Mr. Nichols talked with the Mohawks' manager during the fourth inning. Then he came to the dugout and said:

"This is the last inning, boys. At the rate we're going, we'll be playing all day."

The Mohawks won, 14 to 4.

Jimmie walked home with Ervie. The

rest of the team paired off by themselves.

"You lost, didn't you?" Ervie said.

"Yes," said Jimmie. "The Mohawks swamped us. But we'll win the next one," he added quickly. "You wait and see."

He thought of Paul Karoski. If Paul played with the Planets, things would be different. He'd feel more like playing if Paul was on the team.

He missed Paul a lot. He missed Paul's nice, quiet manners. He missed Paul's coming over to watch television with him. Paul used to come almost every day, and Jimmie would go to visit him, too. Even Mrs. Todd missed him. Every once in a while she asked about him.

"Do you think the Planets are good enough to play in the Grasshoppers League, Jimmie?" Ervie asked in his easy, quiet way.

Jimmie locked at him, startled. "Why? Don't you think so, Ervie?"

Ervie was younger than he. He couldn't know very much about it. But deep in his heart Jimmie knew that whatever Ervie said meant a lot to him.

"No," Ervie replied. "I don't. The Planets aren't going to win any games. They don't have a good — I mean —" Ervie paused.

"They don't have a good what, Ervie?" Jimmie said, and held his breath.

Ervie's eyes met his squarely. "They don't have a good pitcher, that's why!"

9

THE following Friday, at the supper table, Mr. Todd said, "I'm going fishing in the morning. How'd you like to come along, Jimmie?"

Jimmie's heart leaped. "Sure! Where are we going, Dad?"

"To Spring Lake. The boys at the shop say the pikes are really biting."

Jimmie clapped his hands. "Oh, boy! We haven't fished in weeks, have we, Dad?"

"Last time was about a month ago," Mr. Todd smiled.

They were up at five o'clock the next

morning. Mrs. Todd made a basket of sandwiches, a quart thermos of coffee for Dad, and a pint thermos of milk for Jimmie.

"Why don't you come along, Mom?" Jimmie asked.

"What — and leave Ervie home?" She smiled, and pulled his ear. "No, never mind. We'll plan a picnic soon for the whole family. I'm not much of a fisherman, anyway."

Mr. Todd rented a boat at a place called Kam's Boat Landing. The boat was equipped with a motor. He and Jimmie put their fishing gear into the boat and chugged out to where the lake was smooth as glass and deep.

They baited their hooks with minnows that Mr. Todd had bought at the landing. Jimmie baited his own hook. His father had taught him how to do it. Then they cast their lines into the water and sat there and waited for the fish to bite.

Seagulls flew in the still air around them. A crow cawed in the distance. Once in a while the sun peeked through a crack in the gray clouds.

Jimmie grew restless. They had sat here all morning and they hadn't caught a fish yet.

"What happened to all the fish those men were talking about, Dad?" he asked.

His father grinned. "I don't know. They must have seen us coming, and swum off. What's the matter? Getting tired?"

"Well — kind of."

"Have a sandwich," his father suggested.

Jimmie took a sandwich out of the basket and poured himself a glass of milk. He liked this part of it. It was fun to eat out here in the boat. His father ate, too, but steadily watched his line.

Another half hour dragged by.

Jimmie straightened his back, stretched his arms, and yawned. "We're not going to catch any fish, Dad," he said. "Let's go home."

"Now, hold your horses," said Mr. Todd. "We're not going home yet. Let's try another spot."

They tried another spot. It didn't seem any better.

"I'm getting tired, Dad," Jimmie murmured.

"Yes, I know. And impatient, too."

Just then the red and white bobber on Jimmie's line plunged down into the water! Jimmie gripped the rod.

"I caught one, Dad! I caught one!" he cried excitedly.

He wound the reel, and felt the fish fight on the end of the line. He wondered what it was. It felt like a big one.

Finally, a long wriggling fish leaped from the water.

"A pike!" Mr. Todd shouted. "And a beauty, at that!"

Mr. Todd grabbed the leader, removed the pike from the hook, and dropped it, still wriggling, into the creel.

"See?" he said. "Isn't this catch worth all that time you spent waiting?"

Jimmie's heart throbbed. He grinned happily. "It sure is!" he said.

"Patience," Mr. Todd said. "It's an important thing in fishing. It's the same in baseball, or anything else. When you want something you have to keep at it. But you can't be in a hurry. Suppose I had become disgusted earlier the way you did and wanted to quit? We would've gone home with nothing. That would be a fine way to greet Mom, wouldn't it?"

Jimmie smiled. "I guess you're right, Dad," he said.

10

THEY had fish for supper. Mr. Todd had caught two, right after Jimmie had caught his, so there was plenty to go around.

Early in the evening Jimmie began to think about Paul again. Lots of times on Saturday nights Paul would come and watch television with him. Sometimes his mother and father would come, too. Now it was more than two weeks since Paul had been here.

It was Tiny Zimmer's fault, Jimmie told himself. Tiny was the one who had asked Paul to play with the Red Rockets.

396

Suddenly, Jimmie had an idea. Maybe if Mr. and Mrs. Karoski came, Paul would come, too!

He went to his mother.

"Mom, why don't you invite Mr. and Mrs. Karoski over? It's Saturday night, and they haven't been over in a long time."

"I thought about that, too." His mother smiled. "I'll call them on the telephone right now."

The telephone was in the living room. She dialed a number.

"Hello? Mrs. Karoski? This is Mrs. Todd. How are you?"

They talked a bit. Finally Mrs. Todd invited Mrs. Karoski and her husband over for the evening.

"Tell them to bring Paul, too!" Jimmie whispered.

"Bring Paul with you," Mrs. Todd said.

She hung up, smiling. "They'll be glad to come!" she said.

Forty-five minutes later Mr. and Mrs. Karoski came. But Paul wasn't with them.

"Where's Paul?" Jimmie asked Mr. Karoski.

Mr. Karoski was a middle-aged man with a mustache and horn-rimmed glasses. He shrugged his shoulders. "He's home. He didn't want to come."

"Why not?"

Mrs. Karoski answered. "I don't know. He just didn't want to come. I don't understand that boy. Sometimes he won't say anything."

"I know why," a small voice said.

Jimmie looked at Ervie. Something that felt like wire clamped around his chest.

Ervie looked up at Mrs. Karoski. His blue eyes seemed bigger than ever. "He's

mad at Jimmie," he said. "Paul wants to pitch, and Jimmie wants to pitch. They both want to pitch for the Planets."

Jimmie bit his lip. His face flushed.

"Oh, *you*, Ervie!" he cried loudly, and ran out of the room.

11

THE whole Todd family went to church Sunday morning. Mrs. Todd cooked steak, mashed potatoes, carrots, peas, and corn. She cooked onions with the steak, too, but neither Jimmie nor Ervie liked onions.

Jimmie helped his mother with the dishes. Then the family drove to the park.

It was a nice day. The golden sun splashed its warmth over the green grass, trees, and everywhere. The park was crowded with families. Children laughed. Mothers wheeled baby carriages.

Mr. Todd parked the car. Everybody

piled out. They walked on the grass that felt like a carpet under their feet. They stopped and talked with friends.

Then they walked up a small hill. Here and there rosebushes and geraniums decorated the park. Chestnut trees loomed into the sky. Gray squirrels jerked their tails as they hopped over the grass.

"Look, Mom!" Ervie cried. "Squirrels!"

Cries and yells echoed from beyond the hill.

"Sounds like a baseball game," Mr. Todd said.

They reached the top of the hill. A ball game was going on in the field beyond.

Jimmie saw that boys of his own age were playing. He recognized some of the boys from his team. Then he saw who was pitching and he stopped in his tracks and shoved his hands hard into his pockets.

"What do you want to watch that game for? It's just a scrub game," he said.

"Paul Karoski is pitching," Mr. Todd said. "Let's just watch a few minutes."

They went closer to the field. They stopped beside other people who were watching. Jimmie remained behind. He didn't want any of the boys to see him. They might ask him to play, and he didn't want to. Not with Paul there. Paul was sore at him. He'd probably quit if Jimmie played.

Paul went through his windup. His left arm went back. His right leg lifted. Then his arm came around and the ball snapped from his fingers. It sped toward the plate like a bullet. The batter swung.

"Strike three!" the umpire shouted.

Mr. Todd chuckled. "Say! Paul looks good, doesn't he? He has beautiful form

for a kid. That boy will make a great pitcher some day."

The words stung Jimmie. They hurt more because his father had said them.

"One of these days I'll be as good as he is," he said stiffly. "I can throw faster than he can now. All I need is control."

His father looked at him. "Oh? You told me you were pitching, but you didn't tell me you were that good."

Jimmie's face colored. "Well, that's what Mr. Nichols said."

He met Ervie's eyes. His face grew hot and sweat shone on his forehead. He had said the wrong thing again. He could tell by the look Ervie gave him.

"Let's go," he said. "I'm getting tired standing here."

His father patted him on the shoulder. "Okay, Jimmie. We'll go."

12

ON MONDAY morning Jimmie sat on the steps of the back porch. He was alone. Ervie was somewhere in the house, playing by himself.

Jimmie had never been so unhappy in all his life. Just because he wanted to pitch, he thought. What was so wonderful about pitching, anyway?

If he had let Paul pitch for the Planets, everything would be all right. They would have a good team, and he and Paul would still be pals.

At last he went into the house and brought out a tennis ball. He stood in the driveway, threw the ball against the wall of his house, and caught it on a bounce. He did this for a while, then he yelled for Ervie.

"Ervie! Will you come out?"

A few minutes later Ervie came out of the house. "Did you want me, Jimmie?"

"Yes. Will you get my bat and hit some grounders to me?"

"Sure!" Ervie said, and scampered back into the house. He came out with Jimmie's yellow bat. Jimmie handed him the tennis ball.

"You stay here," he advised Ervie. "I'll get down by the fence. Just hit 'em on the ground."

Jimmie trotted to the fence at the edge of the lawn. Ervie tossed the ball up with his left hand, then tried to hit it with the bat. The ball dropped to the ground before he could swing the bat around.

"Come on, Ervie! You can hit it! It's easy!"

Ervie tried again. The same thing happened. At last he did hit it, but the ball dribbled so slowly that it stopped before it was halfway to Jimmie.

Jimmie shook his head in disgust.

A boy walked by the end of the driveway. Jimmie caught a glimpse of him before he got behind the next building.

"Wishy!" he shouted. "Wishy Walters!"

Wishy poked his head around the corner and waved. "Hi, Jimmie!"

"Come here!" Jimmie motioned.

Wishy came forward. His heels clicked on the cement driveway.

"Would you like to hit me some grounders?" asked Jimmie.

"Grounders?" Wishy's forehead puckered in a frown. "You're a pitcher. Why do you want me to hit you grounders?"

Jimmie thought a moment. He didn't know whether to tell Wishy. But Wishy was a good boy. He could trust Wishy with a secret.

"If I can get Paul back on the Planets, I'll play an infield position," Jimmie said. "I don't think I'll ever be a pitcher, Wishy."

"Oh, sure, you will," said Wishy. "All you need is control. You have a lot of speed, Jimmie."

"But time is going fast, Wishy. The day when we play our first league game will be here before we know it. And we're not ready. We've lost every practice game we've played."

"But we've only played two," argued Wishy. "Anyway, Paul won't play with us now. He's going to stick with the Red Rockets."

Jimmie paled. "How do you know?"

"He told me," said Wishy. "And when Paul says something, he means it."

Jimmie stared at the ground. "But — he was my best friend. He'll play with us if I tell him he can pitch. I'm sure he will." The thought of it excited him. "Come on, Wishy. Hit me grounders!"

"Okay," said Wishy. "If you want me to."

Wishy tossed the ball up just as Ervie had. But he hit it. Jimmie caught the ball on a hop. He threw it back to Wishy, who caught it, and hit it back to him. At first he hit it easy, then harder. The tennis ball would bounce across the lawn like a wild rabbit. Sometimes Jimmie missed it. But most of the time he caught it.

He began to like it.

"Wait!" he said. "I'll get my baseball and glove!"

This was more like the real thing. A couple of times Wishy hit the ball over

the fence and Jimmie sent Ervie after it.

Finally Jimmie had to sit down.

"Boy, I'm tired!" he said. He sprawled out on the lawn. His chest heaved.

When he caught his breath he sat up. "Will you come over after supper, Wishy?"

Wishy nodded. "Sure."

"Thataboy!" smiled Jimmie.

13

THE PLANETS had batting practice that afternoon. Jimmie pitched to four men. He didn't do any better than he had before, so Mr. Nichols asked Johnny Lukon to pitch to the batters. Johnny was good at it. A lot better than Jimmie.

"I don't know what I'm going to do with you," Mr. Nichols said as Jimmie waited for his turn to bat. "I thought your control was improving, but I guess it isn't. You have speed, and a nice curve. If you had control, you'd be the best pitcher in the league."

413

Jimmie didn't say anything. What Mr. Nichols had just told him didn't make him feel bad. He wasn't worried, or hurt.

His turn to bat came. He swung at the first four pitches without missing. The fifth throw was high and he missed it a mile. He knew he shouldn't have swung at it. But he felt as if he could hit anything today.

After the boys hit, Mr. Nichols had the infielders practice. Jimmie sat on the bench and watched them. He knew the routine. The third baseman would catch the ball and throw it to first. The first baseman would throw it home. Home to third again, and back around the horn.

He watched Lou Rodell at short. Lou seemed to be afraid of grounders. He would back up a lot. Jimmie noticed that Mr. Nichols didn't hit the ball too hard to him.

After infield practice was over, Mr. Nichols called the boys together.

"I've arranged another game with the Pirates," he said. "They didn't beat us as bad as the Mohawks did. The game will be played here tomorrow afternoon at two o'clock. Tell your folks to come if they'd like to."

Jimmie didn't tell his mother and father about the game. He didn't want them to see him pitch. Anyway, his father couldn't go. He had to work. Jimmie was glad of that.

The game began. This time the Pirates had last raps. Johnny Lukon led off with a single. Alan flied out. Then Billy Hutt hit a grounder past third for a two-bagger. Johnny stopped on third as the fielder threw in to cover home.

Lou grounded through second, scoring Johnny and Billy. Jimmie came to bat. He let a knee-high pitch go by.

"Strike one!" said the umpire.

The next two pitches were balls. Then another strike.

Jimmie pulled his cap down tight, braced his feet in the dirt, and waited for the next pitch. The ball sped in, chest-high and over the heart of the plate.

Jimmie blasted it. It sailed high into center field. The fielder ran back, caught it, and threw it in!

"Get back! Get back!" yelled the coach on first to Lou.

The Pirates' second baseman caught the throw-in from center field and snapped the ball to first. It reached there before Lou could tag up.

"Out!" shouted the umpire.

Three outs. The Planets took the field.

The first batter grounded out to third. The ball was hit solid. That was just luck he hit straight at Alan, Jimmie thought. Jimmie would have walked the next hitter, but the batter swung at bad throws and struck out. The third man flied out to center.

"Nice going, Jimmie!" Lou yelled.

"Nice pitching, Jimmie!" Alan said.

After that things weren't so good. Jimmie walked a man in the second inning, and in the third he hit a man on the shoul-

der. He began to worry. The Pirates started to hit him hard. When they didn't hit, Jimmie helped them by walking their men.

In the fourth, Mr. Nichols went out to the mound. He called Johnny from first.

"I think Jimmie is wild because he's worried he might hit another batter," Mr. Nichols said. "You two boys switch positions for the next two innings. We're only playing five. Okay?"

"Okay," Jimmie said.

He didn't care. Matter of fact, he was glad.

He liked first base. He moved into position and mixed his cries with the other infielders'.

"Come on, Paul!" he shouted. "Come on, Paul!"

His throat caught. He looked around hurriedly. He hoped nobody had heard him yell Paul's name instead of Johnny's.

14

DURING practice the next day, Jimmie went up to the manager. "Are all the names of our players in yet, Mr. Nichols?" he asked.

"Not yet. I'll have to have them in before Thursday."

"Thursday?" Jimmie's brows puckered. "Is that when we play our first Grasshoppers League game?"

Mr. Nichols nodded. "That's right! Better work hard on your control, Jimmie. Winning that first game is important!"

"I know," murmured Jimmie.

After practice, Jimmie didn't go home

with the others. He asked Wishy Walters to stay with him.

"I want you to hit me some grounders, Wishy," he said. "Will you?"

"Sure," said Wishy.

"Hit 'em hard as you can!" Jimmie said, and ran out to shortstop position.

Wishy hit five grounders to him. Jimmie caught them all. Then Mr. Nichols, who had been watching, picked up Wishy's glove and went to first base. He watched Jimmie run behind the grounders and catch them as if it was easy. Jimmie saw Mr. Nichols on first and pegged the balls to him. His throws were good. They seldom were directly over the bag, but they were close enough. Once in a while he made Mr. Nichols stretch for one, but not often.

Finally, Mr. Nichols exclaimed, "Say!

You look sharp out there! How long have you been playing infield?"

"I played infield last year," Jimmie said. "The last few days I've been practicing at home."

"Oh, you have?" Mr. Nichols seemed surprised. "What about pitching?"

Jimmie didn't answer right away. He thought a moment, then said, "I'll tell you about that tomorrow, Mr. Nichols. I have to find out something first."

15

THE next morning Jimmie and Ervie went to Paul Karoski's house. It was eleven o'clock. Paul should be home, Jimmie thought. He wanted Ervie along because even though Ervie was a little guy he was somebody. Jimmie didn't want to go alone to see Paul.

He knocked on the front door. His heart beat so loud he could hear it.

The knob turned. The door opened. Mrs. Karoski stood there, her hair in a bun, a comb pressed into it. Her nose wrinkled up as she smiled.

"Jimmie and Ervie Todd!" she cried. "How are you?"

"We're fine, Mrs. Karoski," Jimmie replied. "Is Paul home?"

"Paul?" Mrs. Karoski's smile faded. "Isn't he at your house?"

Jimmie shook his head. "No. Isn't he home?"

Mrs. Karoski lifted her shoulders. "No! Maybe he went to play with somebody else. I don't understand what happened to that boy. Doesn't he play with you any more?"

Jimmie looked away. "Well — I've been busy practicing baseball. I guess he has, too."

She looked at him curiously. "Don't you play for the same team?"

"No. Paul plays with the Red Rockets. I play with the Planets. That's —

426

that's what I wanted to see him about."

Mrs. Karoski shrugged. "Well, I don't know where he is. If he comes home soon, I will tell him you want him."

"All right, Mrs. Karoski. Thank you." Jimmie took Ervie's hand. "Let's go to the park," he said. "Maybe he's there."

The park was four blocks away. They walked around the swimming pool, then up the hill to the baseball diamond. Nobody was playing ball. Only two or three kids were around.

"He's not here," Jimmie said. "Let's go to Tiny Zimmer's house. Maybe he's playing catch with Tiny."

But Tiny said he hadn't seen Paul all morning. Why didn't they try some of the other boys' houses? They went to Wishy's house, then to Johnny Lukon's, then to Billy Hutt's. They tried every house they thought Paul might possibly go to — but nobody had seen Paul.

"I wonder where he could be, Ervie," Jimmie said worriedly. "Let's go home. Maybe while we were gone he came to our house to see me!"

They hurried home.

"Was anybody here to see me, Mom?" Jimmie asked anxiously.

Mrs. Todd shook her head. "No. But where have you been? Aren't you going to eat dinner?"

"I'm not hungry, Mom," he said, his heart sinking in despair. "We were looking for Paul Karoski ever since eleven o'clock. He's not home, and he's not at any of the boys' houses we've been to. I think he's lost, Mom."

"Lost in the city? Don't worry. He must be somewhere around. Relax, and eat something. It's after one o'clock."

They crunched on toast and cereal and drank a glass of milk each, then went outside again.

Wishy Walters was coming up the walk.

"Hi, Wishy," said Jimmie. "Have you seen Paul Karoski today?"

Wishy thought a moment. "Yes. I saw him this morning."

"You did?" Jimmie's heart cartwheeled. "Where? When?"

"About ten o'clock. He was getting into a car."

"Whose car?"

Wishy shrugged. "I don't know. I wasn't close enough to see."

Jimmie breathed fast. "What color was it? Maybe that'll help."

Wishy thought again. "Brown. No — blue."

"Blue? You sure?"

"Yes. I'm sure. Blue."

"Blue. Blue." Jimmie repeated the word over and over again, trying to think of someone who owned a blue car.

It dawned on him. "Don Perkos!" he shouted. "Don has a blue car! And Don is Paul's cousin! I bet it was his car!"

He ran to the street corner as fast as his legs could carry him.

"Jimmie!" Ervie yelled. "Wait for me!"

"No! You stay there! I'm going to find out if that was Don's car!"

When the light turned green he ran across the street and down the two blocks where the Perkos family lived. He stopped in front of the large front door, half out of breath.

Mrs. Perkos answered his knock. She

was a tall, thin lady with very dark skin. She looked at Jimmy curiously.

"Mrs. Perkos," Jimmie gasped, "do you know where Don is?"

"Sure," she said. "He went to the lake."

"Which lake?"

She tilted her shoulders. "I don't know. He just told me he was driving to the lake. There are so many lakes around, I don't know which one. I'm sorry."

Jimmie's throat knotted. "Okay. Thank you, Mrs. Perkos."

He walked to Paul's house. "I think that Paul went with Don Perkos, his cousin," Jimmie said to Mrs. Karoski. "I saw Mrs. Perkos. She said that Don drove to the lake, but doesn't know which lake. And Wishy Walters told me he saw Paul get into a blue car. Don has a blue car. That's why I think Paul —"

431

Mrs. Karoski's eyes filled with tears, and her lips quivered. "Why didn't he tell me where he was going? Why didn't he tell me?" she cried.

Just then a car drove up to the curb. Jimmie turned quickly, hoping to see a blue car.

But it wasn't blue. It was gray.

16

JIMMIE recognized the boy in the front seat. His heart jumped. "It's Paul!" he said.

He leaped down the steps and across the walk. Paul climbed out of the car. He glanced at Jimmie, then looked up at his mother. A smile lighted his face.

"Hi, Mom!" he said.

"Paul!" Mrs. Karoski opened her arms and hugged Paul tightly to her. "Where were you? Four hours you've been gone! Why didn't you tell me you were going some place?"

"It's my fault, Aunt Josie," Don Perkos

433

said. He looked about eighteen. He was neatly dressed, but his black hair was mussed and there was a smudge of grease on his pants. "I was driving to Orange Lake," he explained. "I saw Paul on the street and asked him to come along. I just wanted to drive down and back again. It wouldn't have taken us more than half an hour. That's why I told him he didn't have to run to the house to tell you."

"So what happened?" Mrs. Karoski asked. Tears no longer filled her eyes.

Don shrugged. "We reached the lake, and the car stopped. It wouldn't start again. I wanted to call home, but I couldn't find a telephone. I'm awful sorry, Aunt Josie. I guess I should've had Paul tell you."

Mrs. Karoski said happily, "That's all right. As long as I have my boy back. Next

time I think he'd better tell his mother."
She kissed Paul's forehead, then held his
face between her hands.

"Hungry?" she asked.

"Yes."

"You should be." Mrs. Karoski motioned to Don. "Come inside and bring
your friend. There is food for all of you."
She paused. "Where is your car now?"

"At the lake. Thanks for asking us to
eat, Aunt Josie. But I'm going to see Mom
a minute, then get a mechanic to look at
my car."

"All right. I hope it's not too expensive
to fix."

Don climbed back into the gray car.
The young man behind the wheel shifted
into gear and they drove off.

Jimmie looked toward the house. Mrs.
Karoski was walking in with Paul.

"Hey, Paul!" Jimmie cried. "Just a minute!"

Paul and his mother turned around at the same time. An apologetic look came over Mrs. Karoski's face. "I'm so sorry!" she said. "I forgot you, Jimmie! Come on in!"

"No, thanks, Mrs. Karoski. I just want to ask Paul something." He looked at Paul. "If you want to pitch for the Planets, you can."

For a second Paul looked him straight in the eye. "I'm pitching for the Red Rockets," he said sharply, and walked into the house.

17

JIMMIE went home. He felt as if he had lost something.

Ervie was playing with his toys in the back yard. "Did somebody find Paul?" he asked.

"Yes," Jimmie said quietly. "He just got home."

"Did you see him?"

"Yes. He doesn't want to play with us. He's going to stay with the Rockets."

He could hardly say those last words.

"Play with me, will you, Jimmie?" Ervie pleaded.

"Okay. I'll play with you." Anything,

438

Jimmie thought, to forget about Paul.

Ervie had his trucks and steam shovel out. Jimmie operated the steam shovel. He loaded the bucket with sand from a little sand pile, then dumped it into a truck. Ervie pushed the truck across the lawn and dumped it where he had made a road.

Pretty soon Jimmie heard footsteps in the alley. He looked over his shoulder.

"Hi, Mose!" He smiled. "Bring your glove?"

"No." Mose paused in the driveway. "Somebody wants to see you out here, Jimmie."

Jimmie stepped to the edge of the grass. "Who?" he said.

Mose didn't tell him. "Come on," he said. "He's out front."

Jimmie ran to find out who wanted to

see him. He heard Ervie running behind him. At the end of the alley stood Johnny Lukon, Wishy Walters, Billy Hutt, and a couple of other members of the Planets.

In front of them stood — Paul Karoski!

"Hi, Jimmie." Paul smiled.

"Hi, Paul!" Jimmie stared. He could hardly believe his eyes. It seemed a year since Paul had spoken a word to him. A year since Paul had been to see him about anything. "Did — did you want to see me, Paul?"

Paul nodded. "I've changed my mind. I would like to pitch for the Planets," he said.

Jimmie took his hand. "Oh, Paul, I'm so glad! Did you tell all the boys? Is it all right with them?"

"Sure it's all right," said Wishy. "When I went to see Paul, he told me you were

440

there and asked him. I tried to tell him to come back, too, but he wouldn't listen. So then I brought these guys to his house and we all talked to him."

Jimmie noticed that Ervie was standing beside him, listening to every word, too.

"Paul said the team didn't need two pitchers," Wishy went on. "You wanted to pitch and he wanted to pitch, so when the Red Rockets asked him he said yes. He felt bad not pitching with us, especially when we lost those games. But he didn't want to tell you — you said you could pitch, and it would look as if he thought you couldn't."

Jimmie choked back an ache in his throat. A chubby hand slipped into his. He gripped it tightly. He was glad Ervie was here. Ervie always made him feel funny when he'd tell a fib to somebody, but at a time like this Ervie was like a strong pillar he could lean on.

"I know," Jimmie said. "I thought I could pitch. I didn't care what anybody else thought. Johnny tried to tell me. Alan tried to. Even my brother Ervie here tried to. But I wouldn't listen." He took a deep breath. "I had to find out for myself. I'll never make a pitcher, Paul. Never. I'm glad you came back."

"I knew he'd come back," Ervie said, his blue eyes sparkling. "I knew it all the time!"

The boys laughed.

"I'd better call up Mr. Nichols," said Jimmie. "Our first game is Thursday, and the names have to be in before then."

"Better call up Steve Beeler, too. He's the Red Rockets' manager," said Johnny Lukon. "Paul's name can't be on two ros-

443

ters, or he won't be able to play on either team!"

"That's right!" said Jimmie.

He ran into the house. He telephoned Mr. Nichols and asked him to put Paul Karoski's name on the roster. Mr. Nichols sounded very happy to hear that Paul had changed his mind.

Then Jimmie hesitated. Maybe it would be better if Mr. Nichols telephoned Steve Beeler, he thought.

Jimmie asked him.

"Yes," said Mr. Nichols. "I will do that, Jimmie!"

"Do you think he will mind, Mr. Nichols?"

"You mean about releasing Paul if he has his name on the list?"

"Yes."

"I don't think so. I'll call him. Stay by

444

your phone. I'll let you know as soon as I talk with him."

"Okay, Mr. Nichols."

Jimmie hung up. He sat by the phone, his heart hammering in his chest. If Mr. Beeler would not release Paul, then his hopes would disappear like smoke. The Planets would finish the season in last place.

The phone rang. He picked it up.

"Jimmie? Mr. Nichols again. It's all settled. Paul is now officially a member of the Planets."

18

PAUL stretched, looked over his shoulder at the man on first, then threw. The ball sped toward the plate. The batter swung. Crack! A hot grounder sizzled across the grass toward short.

Jimmie charged it. He caught the ball on a hop, threw it to second. Kippy caught it, touched the bag, then whipped it to first.

A double play!

"Thataway to play that ball, Jimmie! The way to go, Jimmie!"

Jimmie grinned as the ball sailed around the horn. He hadn't had so much fun since last year. This was the position for him. He didn't have to throw the ball over the heart of the bag all the time, either. Johnny Lukon's long arms and legs helped him stretch out far enough to catch almost any ball Jimmie threw to him.

It was the first Grasshoppers League game. The Planets were playing the Mohawks. It was the fourth inning and the Planets were leading, 6 to 3. Jimmie remembered the game which the Mohawks had won, 14 to 4. Boy! What a difference it made with Paul on the mound!

Paul liked it with the Planets, too. You could see he was happy the way he stood on the mound, the way he pitched, the way he praised the guys when they hit.

The Mohawks came to bat in the fifth inning. It was their last raps. Their last chance to beat the Planets.

447

Paul wound up, threw. Crack! The ball bounded down short. Jimmie waited for the hop, came up with his glove. But the ball wasn't in it!

His heart sank. He looked behind him. The ball had gone through his legs to the outfield!

A groan lifted from the crowd.

Billy Hutt threw the ball in. Jimmie caught it, glanced at the runner on first, then carried the ball halfway to Paul.

"I'm sorry, Paul," he said, as he tossed it to the lefthander. "I should have had that."

Paul grinned. "Get the next one," he said.

The next batter bunted. The Planets were caught by surprise. Nobody had expected a bunt. The whole infield was playing deep. Everybody was safe.

"Come on, Paul! Come on, kid! Get 'em out of there!" The chatter began.

Men were on first and second. There were no outs. Paul toed the rubber, looked at the runners, then pitched.

"Ball one!"

The crowd grew tense. Why did I have to miss that ball? moaned Jimmie. This would never have happened.

Paul pitched. A line drive to short! Jimmie caught it. He tagged the first runner before the player could get back to second.

"Out!" shrilled the umpire.

Then Jimmie whipped the ball to first to get the second runner before he could tag up. It was close!

The umpire's hands flattened out. "Safe!" he shouted.

Paul struck the next man out.

449

A loud, air-splitting roar burst from the grandstand. Jimmie ran in toward the mound where Paul was waiting for him, a big happy smile on his face.

"Thataboy, Jimmie! You saved me on that play! That was neat!"

Jimmie was so happy he could shout. Nothing better could have happened to him than making that double play.

The other players came and patted them on the back.

"Thataway, Jimmie!"

"Nice pitching, Paul!"

"I guess we have the team now, don't we!"

A slow smile spread over Jimmie's face.

Winning the game was all right, he thought. But even more important was having Paul back on the team.

Catcher with a Glass Arm

To
Rudy and Kitty

Catcher with a Glass Arm

by Matt Christopher

Illustrated by

FOSTER CADDELL

1

"BALL two!"

Jody had to reach almost out of the catcher's box for that pitch. He looked at the runner on first. The Tigers' man was jumping back and forth, teasing Jody to throw the ball.

Jody didn't know what to do. If he threw to second base, he might throw wild. He had a poor peg. If he threw to first, the runner might dash for second.

"Throw it here!" yelled Moonie Myers angrily.

Jody tossed the ball to Moonie, who

457

was waiting for it about six feet in front of the pitcher's mound. That settled his problem for a while.

Moonie toed the rubber, looked at the man on first, then pitched.

"Strike two!"

That pitch breezed in knee-high, about an inch from the outside corner. Jody caught it smack in the pocket of his mitt. It stung a little.

Then Jody saw the runner on first take off like a shot for second base. Sweat broke out on his face. Even before he threw he knew that the ball would not reach second. He could catch any pitch near the plate, but he could not throw a ball within twenty feet of a target.

Jody saw Rabbit Foote run from his shortstop position to cover the bag. Jody heaved the ball. It arced over Moonie's

458

head like a fat balloon and struck the grass short and to the left of Rabbit.

Rabbit caught the hop. By the time he tried to make the play, the runner was already on the base.

The Tigers' bench let out a lusty cheer. They had plenty to cheer about, too. This was the last of the fourth inning and they were leading 5–4. Now there was a man on second and no outs. They had a good chance to fatten that score.

Rabbit tossed the ball to a disgusted Moonie Myers and trotted back to his position. He was small but quick-footed as the animal for which he was nicknamed. He had a lot of spark, too. He showed it now as he started a chatter that spread like wildfire among the other infielders.

Jody joined in, but it was hard to yell through an aching throat. It was his fault that a man was on second base, just as it was his fault that the Tigers had got two runs in the second inning. At that time he had thrown wild again to second, and two men had scored . . . ! He had expected Coach Jack Fisher to put in somebody else to catch. But there was no other catcher.

Moonie breezed in the next pitch. *Whiff!* One out.

The next hitter flied out to left field. Then Jody caught a high pop fly, and the inning was over.

Jody breathed a sigh of relief. He took off his catching gear, put on a protective helmet and picked up a bat. He was leading off this inning. Boy, he'd like to hit that ball this time. A hit would make up for that bad throw to second.

461

"Batter up!" cried the umpire.

Jody stepped to the plate. He was a left-handed hitter, already with a single and a walk to his credit. He let the first pitch go by, then swung at the next. The bat connected with the ball solidly. The white pill flashed over second, and Jody rounded first for a clean double.

The fans cheered, and the knot that had lodged in Jody's stomach disappeared. That was what a good hit did for you. It was like medicine. It made you feel all well again.

Right fielder Roddie Nelson let a pitch go by that was straight down the heart of the plate.

Another pitch breezed in, curving across the outside corner. Roddie swung. Missed!

Jody, leading off the bag, turned and trotted back. He tried to remember when

462

Roddie had got his last hit. He just couldn't. This was their second League game, and Roddie had not yet touched first base. Roddie was just hopeless, that's all.

The pitch. "Ball one!" Roddie almost swung at that one.

The pitch again. It looked good. Roddie swung. *Crack!* It was a beautiful sound. Real solid. Jody saw the ball flash like a meteor over his head and he knew it carried a label on it. A home-run label.

The ball sailed over the left-field fence for Roddie's first hit of the year — a two-run homer.

The fans had never cheered so loudly. Roddie came in, crossing the plate behind Jody. He was so happy he couldn't say a word. Jody was the first to shake his hand and congratulate him.

"Nice socko, Roddie!"

There were no more hits that inning. Now the score was 6–5 in the Dolphins' favor.

Moonie worked hard on the first batter and struck him out. Then a single through short changed things quickly. The runner was the Tigers' lead-off man, a speedster on the base paths.

He took a small lead as Moonie climbed upon the mound.

"Steal, Peter!" a Tigers player yelled from the bench. "That catcher can't throw! He's got a glass arm!"

Jody winced. *A glass arm.* Nobody had ever said that about him before.

2

MOONIE stretched, looked at the man on first. Quickly he turned and snapped the ball to first baseman Birdie Davis. The runner scooted back safely.

Birdie returned the ball to Moonie. Once again Moonie went through his stretch. Again came the cry from the Tigers' bench:

"Steal, Peter!"

The pitch came in, slightly high and outside. Jody caught it. He saw the runner racing for second, head lowered and arms pumping hard. Jody heaved the ball, making sure he didn't throw too hard for fear the ball might sail over Rabbit Foote's head.

Instead — the ball fell short! Rabbit missed the hop and the ball bounced out to the outfield. The runner raced on, to third. He stayed there as center fielder Arnie Smith made a perfect peg in to Moonie.

"I told you he had a glass arm, Peter!" yelled that same voice from the Tigers' bench.

Jody tried to ignore the cry. But he couldn't. The words *glass arm* stormed through his mind like an echo.

Moonie toed the rubber and threw in a low inside pitch that was probably harder than any he had thrown. Jody never thought that the batter would bite at it.

But the batter did. He hit a dribbler toward the mound. Moonie picked it up and tossed it to first for the put-out.

Two outs. The runner was still on third.

One more out, thought Jody . . . just one more, and this rough inning will be over.

Crack! A line drive over Moonie's head! The runner scored and the hitter held up at first.

The game was tied up now, 6–6. Jody pressed his lips firmly together, yanked on his chest protector, and returned to his spot behind the plate.

The pitch . . . A hit to short! Rabbit picked it up, threw to second. . . . *Out!*

Jody whipped off his mask and walked to the bench. He didn't look at anyone, but he heard someone from behind the backstop screen say, "Don't let it bother you, Jody. You'll get that ball up there."

On the bench Coach Jack Fisher patted Jody on the knee. "You seem to be afraid to throw that ball, pal. Heave it hard. Let it fly."

Jody shook his head. There was nothing he could say.

Now Mike Brink, pinch-hitting for Arnie Smith, started the ball rolling. He singled through second, and scored on a double by Johnny Bartho. That was all the Dolphins put across that half-inning, but it was enough. The Tigers couldn't do a thing at their turn at bat, and the game went to the Dolphins, 7–6.

Jody removed his catching gear and put it into the canvas bag. He had started walking toward the gate when a tall, thin man with a crew cut and dark-rimmed glasses approached him.

"Good game, Jody. You did a great job behind that plate."

"Thank you," said Jody, trying to smile. "Guess I can't throw worth beans, though."

"Don't worry. You have a strong arm. I can tell. You're just afraid to use all that power." He smiled and Jody smiled with him.

"Want to come home with us?" the man invited.

Jody didn't know whom he meant by "us." He had never seen the man before. "No, thanks," he said. "I don't live very far from here. I can walk home."

"Okay. See you at the next game."

"Good-by," said Jody.

The man walked toward Coach Fisher

and a group of boys who were helping him load up the canvas bag. Jody turned and stepped through the gate.

"Meowrrrr!"

Jody grinned. "Hi, Midnight," he greeted. "Come to meet me, did you?"

The black cat rubbed up against Jody's leg and Jody bent down to pet it. Midnight was really a wonderful pet. He tagged after Jody almost everywhere Jody went. And Jody loved him. He probably loved Midnight as much as he did baseball.

He found Rabbit and Birdie waiting for him too, and they all walked home together.

Rabbit talked a blue streak most of the time, hardly giving Birdie or Jody a chance to squeeze in a word. But that was Rabbit for you. Jody liked him a lot.

Then Rabbit said, "Gets me why you can't throw that ball to second, Jody. Boy! Would I like to have tagged that one kid. He runs like a streak, but we'd have had him if you'd thrown the ball at the bag."

"I know," admitted Jody. "But I can't. That's all there is to it. I just can't."

He suddenly remembered what a Tigers player had said — glass arm.

"Moonie was real sore," said Birdie. "Maybe he won't pitch any more."

Jody's mouth dropped. "Why not?"

Birdie shrugged. "Oh. You know how he is."

Jody pressed his lips together. Yes, he knew how Moonie was. But it was *him* Moonie was sore at.

471

3

THE SUN was blazing overhead just before noon Saturday as the blue car zipped along Route 4. In the front seat were Mom and Dad Sinclair. In back were Jody, his sister Diane, Rabbit Foote and, of course, Midnight. They were going on a picnic.

It wasn't going to be just an ordinary picnic, though. Dad had plans. As a matter of fact, it was his idea to have Rabbit come along.

Jody didn't know what those plans could be. Dad had suggested that they

472

bring along a bat, baseball and some baseball gloves. That was strange since Dad, a real golf bug, had his bag of clubs in the trunk with the foodstuffs.

Lincoln Park was thirteen miles away from home. It was a beautiful green spot with hills protecting it on all sides. There were picnic tables sheltered underneath trees and along the hillsides. There was a large swimming pool already dotted with swimmers. There was a softball diamond, and plenty of room to drive a baseball a mile.

There were already golfers practicing on long and short putts. That was what Dad liked to do, too.

Dad parked the car. Jody and Rabbit found a vacant table nearby.

Dad asked, "Do you kids want to go swimming until dinner is ready?"

"Okay by me," said Rabbit.

The boys ran to the bathhouse with their trunks. At their heels raced Midnight, his black tail high in the air. The boys got into their trunks and then dived off a low diving board into the cool, clean pool.

It was almost half an hour later when Diane came after them. From the edge of the pool she cupped her hands to her mouth and shouted:

"Jody! Rabbit! Come and get i-i-i-it! You, too, Midnight!" she added.

The boys climbed out of the pool and walked to the picnic table, water dripping off their bodies. Diane tossed each a towel and they dried themselves as best as they could. Then they sat and ate. After that they were too filled to swim any more. Anyway, they knew they shouldn't so soon after eating. They went to the bathhouse and dressed.

"Bet Dad will be out there with his golf clubs," said Jody as they started out the door.

"He's out there, but not with his golf clubs," observed Rabbit. "He has the bat, ball and gloves. Guess he wants to give us a workout, Jody."

"We're going to have some throwing practice," said Dad. "Rabbit, take this glove and get down there about where second base would be. Jody, put on your mitt. I'll get halfway between, about where the pitcher's box would be. I want to see you throw that ball, Jody. In those games I've seen I can tell that you're hold-ing back. You're not throwing that ball at all as you should."

So that was it, thought Jody. *And I never even thought he cared how I threw!*

Dad laid the bat aside and threw the baseball to Jody. "Okay. Throw it back to me," he said.

Jody threw it easily. Too easily. It struck the ground two feet in front of his father.

"Throw them up here, Jody!" said Dad, holding his glove against his chest.

Jody tried again. Still low.

"You're straining too hard, Jody," said Dad. "Snap your wrist. Like this."

Jody watched his Dad move his wrist back and forth as if it worked on a hinge. Then he tried to do the same thing. He succeeded, and a pleased smile came to his lips.

He threw the ball to his Dad. It floated through the air like a balloon.

"Why are you afraid to throw that ball?" cried Dad. "Why?" He was almost angry.

Jody shrugged. "I don't know." He really didn't. He *wanted* to throw the ball hard. He *wanted* to snap it as his Dad did. But he couldn't.

"All right," said Dad. "Throw it to second."

Jody reared back and pegged the ball over his Dad's head. It hit the ground and bounced twice before it reached Rabbit.

Dad didn't like that at all. He shook his head from side to side.

"Try it again, Jody. Keep your feet straight, and don't move them. Bring that ball back over your shoulder and then snap it like a whip."

477

Jody tried it. He threw the ball fairly straight, but it was low. It went directly at Dad and he caught it.

"That's the idea," said Dad. "But aim at Rabbit."

Jody aimed at Rabbit, but Rabbit wasn't where he threw the ball. Dad had him try again and again, making Jody practice short throws to him, and long throws to Rabbit. Once in a while Jody threw the ball exactly where he was supposed to. But most of the time he didn't.

"Oh, Jody!" cried Dad finally. "*How* can I teach you? I *know* you can throw a ball harder than that."

Dad's face was red. You could tell he was angry. He was sweating, too. They had been out here at least an hour.

"Put the stuff back into the car," Dad

478

said. "We'll have to leave soon, anyway. There's a storm coming."

He walked with giant strides across the park, leaving the boys to gather the bat, ball and gloves. Jody watched his back. A lump formed in his throat and stuck there. *He's disappointed in me. But what can I do? I've tried as hard as I can.*

A wind came up suddenly. It whipped the tops of trees and shook leaves loose from their branches. Everything and everybody were in the car when the first big drops of rain splashed against the windshield. Midnight huddled like a black ball on Jody's lap, purring. Dad started the car and drove it hurriedly out of the park.

The rain fell thicker and harder. Black

clouds swirled and twisted in the sky. Forks of lightning pierced the clouds.

Dad slowed the speed of the car. The windshield wipers were whipping back and forth, but the rain came down so hard that the wipers were hardly doing any good.

"I'll park off the road as soon as I find a place," said Dad. "This is certainly bad, but it won't last."

Suddenly a great blinding flash lit up the half-darkened sky. Everything seemed to turn white for one instant. Then a terrible sound filled the air.

Just ahead of them Jody saw a telephone pole break in the middle and collapse across the road!

"Dad! Watch it!" he screamed, and hugged Midnight tightly against him.

From the rear seat Mom and Diane let

out a frightened cry. Dad shoved in the brake pedal. The car stopped quickly. Luckily he was driving slowly. But Jody heard a *bump* beside him. He turned and stared at Rabbit lying with his head back against the seat. His eyes were closed, and a red welt stuck out on his forehead!

"Rabbit!" Jody cried, and shook his friend by the arm. "Rabbit!"

Rabbit didn't move.

Jody turned wide, horrified eyes at his Dad.

"Dad," he whispered, "is he dead?"

4

DAD leaned across Jody's lap. He lifted Rabbit's head.

"Rabbit!" he said, rubbing the boy's cheeks with his hands. "Wake up, son."

Rabbit's eyes blinked open. He moaned and lifted a hand to the bump on his forehead.

Jody took a deep breath and smiled with relief. "Boy! You had me scared!"

"Sorry, Rabbit," said Dad. "You smacked your head against the dashboard when I slammed on the brakes. I'll wet my handkerchief. You can hold it

483

against the bruise to help stop the pain."

He opened the window on his side and held out his handkerchief in the rain. When it was real wet, he squeezed most of the water out of it, folded it several times, and put it against the bruise on Rabbit's head.

"There you are," said Dad. "Now just hold it there awhile."

Jody looked at his friend with an ache in his heart. That was only a bump, but Rabbit's face looked very pale. He didn't look well at all.

"Are we in a pickle!" murmured Dad.

Jody looked at him, then looked outside. Black wires were hanging over the roof of the car, wires from the telephone pole that was blocking their path in front of them.

"Guess we're stuck," said Jody.

"Thank God we didn't get hit by that pole," said Mom. "Looks as if we'll just have to sit here until the rain stops and somebody removes those wires."

"Your deduction is quite correct, Martha," replied Dad.

The black clouds twisted and spiraled away, and the rain stopped almost as quickly as it had begun.

"I'm going out a minute," said Rabbit, and opened the door.

"Rabbit!" Dad shouted. "No! Close that door and keep it closed!"

Rabbit slammed the door and turned a white face and wide, terrified eyes to Jody's father.

"I'm sorry, Mr. Sinclair," murmured Rabbit. "I almost forgot. Those wires are alive. Lying on the car like that, they could kill a person."

Dad smiled and patted Rabbit on the knee. "That's right, Rabbit. By stepping outside and touching this car you would have grounded yourself and been electrocuted."

"I know," said Rabbit. "I just wasn't thinking, I guess."

A few minutes later a car came alongside them and stopped. It was the first car they had seen since the telephone pole had been struck. A man and woman were in the car.

"Has anybody gone to get help for you?" yelled the man.

"No," replied Dad. "We'll be very much obliged if you'll report this to the police or the telephone company, sir."

"We'll do that," said the man, and drove off.

In less than ten minutes, a large green truck with tools and equipment piled on it drove up. Four men got out. They were telephone men. You could tell by their green uniforms and helmets. One approached Dad.

"Everybody all right, sir?" he asked.

"Quite all right, except for one young passenger," said Dad. "He banged his head against the dashboard when I hit the brakes."

The man shook his head. "Sorry to hear that, but it could've been worse. The lines are dead now. You can move on while we hold up the wires."

"Thank you very much," said Dad.

The four men held the wires up off the car, and Dad drove away, waving back to them.

"Well," said Mom, "that was an experi-

ence I'll never forget as long as I live."

"Me, too," said Diane.

Jody didn't say anything. He was thinking about Rabbit. How badly was he hurt? Would he be able to play in Wednesday's game? Without Rabbit playing shortstop, the team would hardly have a chance against the Gophers. And, if Rabbit didn't play, the whole team would blame Jody.

I wish it was I who got hurt — not Rabbit, thought Jody.

5

WHEN the game rolled around Wednesday evening against the Gophers, Rabbit Foote was not in the lineup. His head was still swollen. The doctor had said that he had better not play baseball for a week at least.

Jody was nearly sick all day thinking about it. He blamed Dad a little, too, at first. But then, it wasn't Dad's fault that a storm had come up and a bolt of lightning had struck the telephone pole and knocked it down. That was an accident.

Dad was really sorry that Rabbit had

490

got hurt. He seemed to feel as responsible as Jody did.

After the teams had their batting and infield practices, the Gophers took the field.

The Dolphins started well that first inning. With two away, Arnie Smith singled and Johnny Bartho singled. But the Gophers snuffed out the Dolphins' chance of scoring by catching Joe Bell's grounder and throwing him out. Joe was playing short in place of Rabbit.

The Gophers came to bat and scored a run. In the second inning the Dolphins picked up two.

Nothing serious happened again until the bottom of the third. The Gophers got hot. With one man out, they began to powder Moonie's pitches as if it were batting-practice time. To make matters worse, Jody threw twice to third, in an effort to nab a runner, and both times the ball hit the ground far in front of third baseman Duane West. Duane and Moonie yelled their heads off at him. Jody could even hear Dad shouting from the bleachers.

"Come on, Jody! Throw the ball *up!*"

But all the yelling in the world would not have done any good. Nobody knew that but Jody.

When, finally, the inning ended, the Gophers had put across four runs. Moonie came in shaking his head. He had his lips clamped together, and his eyes didn't lift once to the players around him. You could tell that he was taking most of the blame.

Moonie hated errors or bad plays, no

matter who made them. Jody wished Moonie wouldn't be like that. Baseball wasn't much fun with a guy who acted that way on the team, no matter if he did pitch a good game most of the time.

It was Moonie himself who started things off with a bang in the top of the fourth. He socked a triple against the left-field fence, and then scored on Duane's single. Frank York flied out. Arnie put life back into the team by knocking out a double. Left fielder Johnny Bartho, who was Moonie's best pal, singled. Joe Bell, after hitting four fouls, finally banged out a single, too.

Hunk Peters, the tall right-hander for the Gophers, must have become tired throwing all those pitches. He walked Birdie Davis on four straight balls. You would think that the coach would send Hunk to the showers, but he didn't.

Then Jody grounded out, and Roddie struck out, and the big inning was over. Score: Dolphins 6; Gophers 5.

The Gophers didn't lose heart. With two outs, they began to hit again. Moonie looked as if the world were going to collapse on his shoulders. He yelled at Jody for not throwing the ball high enough to second, when a runner stole. He yelled at Joe Bell for throwing wild to home. He kicked the rubber when the batters knocked out base hits.

And then Coach Fisher climbed out of the dugout, called "Time!" and walked out to the mound. Jody stood behind the plate, waiting.

The coach put an arm around Moonie's shoulders and talked to him. The pitcher looked up at him and then looked away again, shaking his head unhappily. The coach kept talking to him. Then a smile appeared on Moonie's face. When the coach walked off the field the fans cheered, and even Jody smiled.

Moonie didn't yell any more. Nor did the Gophers get any more hits. But they had already scored two runs, putting them one ahead of the Dolphins.

Moonie led off in the fifth inning. He received a big hand as he stepped to the plate. Hunk walked him, and then struck out Duane.

Mike Brink pinch-hit for Frank, and singled through the pitcher's box. Moonie went to second. Arnie walked, Johnny Bartho struck out, and Joe Bell came

495

through with another single that scored Moonie.

It was Joe's third hit of the game. The crowd gave him a tremendous cheer, for Joe was usually poor at the plate as well as in the field.

"How do you like that?" said Coach Fisher, grinning broadly. "That boy's playing like a big leaguer today."

Birdie flied out, ending the inning.

The score was tied, 7-all. But again the Gophers came through, scoring to break the tie.

Jody led off in the top of the sixth. This was the Dolphins' last chance.

Jody tapped the tip of the bat against the plate and waited for the pitch he wanted.

"Strike!" The ball just grazed the inside corner.

Another pitch. Jody stepped toward it, lifting his bat.

No. Too high . . . "Ball!"

Hunk scraped some dirt into the hole in front of the rubber. Then he stepped on the rubber and made his windup.

He breezed the ball in. It sailed toward the plate like a white streak — a little high, and inside. Jody stepped into it again. Just as it approached the plate, the ball curved in. Jody tried to duck.

Smack! The ball struck the front right side of his helmet, glanced off, and Jody fell. With the helmet on, he hardly felt any pain. But stars blinked like lightning bugs in front of his eyes.

He heard feet pounding on the ground. And then a voice crying, "Oh, no!"

6

JODY sat there awhile, his eyes closed. Someone yanked off his helmet and put a cool hand against his head.

"I'm sorry, Jody! I didn't mean it!"

Jody recognized Hunk's voice.

The stars stopped blinking, and Jody opened his eyes. Hunk was kneeling in front of him, his brown eyes wide with worry. Beside him was Coach Fisher.

"Feel better, Jody?"

"Yes. I feel okay." The coach helped him to his feet.

"I'll have a runner for you," said the coach.

But Jody put the helmet back on and trotted to first. "I'll be all right, Coach," he said. "I can run."

"Are you sure?" Coach Fisher looked at him anxiously.

Jody grinned. "I'm sure," he said.

Then he saw that the manager of the Gophers was removing Hunk Peters from the game and was putting in a left-hander. The southpaw warmed up for a while; then the game resumed.

The Dolphins' fans yelled loud and hard for Roddie Nelson to get a hit. They needed a run to tie the score, two runs to put them ahead.

A ball was called, and then a strike. Now Roddie got ready for the pitch he wanted. The ball breezed in, chest-high. Roddie swung. *Crack!* The ball arced out to short right field. The Gophers' second baseman and right fielder both raced after it. Jody stopped about a third of the way to second, waiting to see if the ball would be caught.

"I got it!" yelled the second baseman, running hard.

He had his gloved hand stretched out to receive the ball. He caught it and whirled to throw to first. Jody sped back in time.

The crowd cheered the Gophers' second baseman. Even the Dolphins' fans applauded him. It was a great catch.

Moonie came to the plate. Once again the fans greeted him with applause. He took a called strike, then belted a sizzling grounder to second. The second baseman

501

bobbled the ball, and both Jody and Moonie were safe.

Lead-off man Duane West came up next. The two runs the Dolphins needed to get back into the lead were on first and second.

The Gophers' left-hander stepped to the mound, checked the runners, then threw. He had speed and pretty good control. He threw four pitches — one ball, and the rest strikes. Duane went down swinging.

Two outs.

Mike Brink took a called strike, then fouled two pitches in a row. The southpaw threw his next pitches low and inside. Mike waited; then the count was three and two.

"This is it, Mike!" Coach Fisher yelled. "Make it be in there!"

The ball breezed in, knee-high. Mike swung. *Crack!* A hot grounder to short. The shortstop caught the hop, tossed the ball to third, and Jody was out.

The game was over. The Gophers were the winners: 8–7.

Rabbit was back in the game Thursday. The Dolphins were playing the Tigers again, the last game of the first series.

Rabbit had healed well. The welt had disappeared from his head. And he was doing fine at short, too. By the third inning he had handled five grounders without an error and had assisted with five put-outs.

As for Jody, he wasn't doing *anything* right. Two men had already stolen second on him. One had even stolen third. On that play Jody had almost thrown the man out, but *almost* wasn't good enough.

However, it was at the plate that something strange had really happened to Jody.

The first time up, he had swung at the first pitch and popped out. Nobody knew how he really felt then. He was glad he didn't have to spend a longer time at the plate.

Now he was up again. Johnny Bartho was on third, and Joe Bell on second. The Tigers were leading, 3–2.

Jim Gregg, the Tigers' tall, wiry right-hander, hurled in the first pitch. It came in belt-high. Jody watched it, and all at once he thought it was streaking at him. He got scared and jumped back from the plate.

"Strike!" yelled the umpire.

The next pitch was slightly higher and just as close. Again Jody jumped back.

"Strike two!" yelled the umpire.

The Tigers' players started to laugh and make fun of him. His teammates shouted at him to swing. "Come on, Jody! You can hit him!" yelled Coach Fisher from his third-base coaching box.

Jody stepped out of the batter's box a moment, rubbed dust on his hands, then stepped back in again. Sweat stood out on his forehead and rolled in tiny rivers down his face.

"Stick in there, Jody, boy!" a voice said from the grandstand. "Don't be afraid of them!"

Jody remembered that voice. It belonged to the man who had been so friendly toward him during those first few games.

In came the pitch. It was knee-high. It was going to groove the middle of the plate. Jody could see that — *yet his right foot stepped back away from the plate as he swung. He missed the ball by a foot!*

That made the third out. Jody saw Johnny Bartho kick the third-base sack as he turned and headed for left field.

Jody tossed his bat aside and began putting on his shin guards. His hands shook. He had trouble fastening the buckles. Coach Fisher came over and helped him.

"What happened, Jody?" he asked quietly. "You looked scared up there."

"I know," said Jody.

"No sense being scared. Just stay in there. Forget what happened the other day. Make up your mind you're going to hit that ball. You've hit it before — you'll hit it again."

506

In the sixth Jody was up again. The score was 4–2 in the Tigers' favor. Birdie Davis was on first.

Jody waited out the pitcher. He got three balls on him, then a strike. *I wish he walks me, I wish he walks me,* Jody was telling himself.

"Strike two!" yelled the umpire.

Three and two. This would be it. He had to watch this next pitch closely.

The ball came in. It looked good, almost even with the letters on his jersey. Then all at once it seemed to come at his head. He ducked back, almost losing his balance.

"Yeaaa!" yelled the umpire. "You're out!"

Jody clamped his lips lightly for a moment, then walked away.

When the game was over the score was

the same, 4–2. As the teams walked off the field, Jody kept his eyes lowered so that he wouldn't have to look at anyone.

Suddenly he heard someone say, "Jody! Wait! I'd like to see you a minute!"

7

JODY turned and saw the tall, thin man who had become one of his best fans.

"Hi, Jody," the man greeted. "See that you have more troubles now, haven't you?"

"Guess so," said Jody, and began rubbing the toe of his right shoe into the grass.

"Two problems," said the man. "That's pretty rough going. Not throwing well and being afraid of a pitched ball are two of the worst things a ballplayer could wish for himself."

"I know," said Jody. "Guess I'll never be any different."

The man chuckled. "That's where you're wrong. You see, you do have a strong arm. You're just afraid to throw hard — you think you'll throw the ball *too* far. That's wrong thinking.

"Your new problem is worse. You can't be afraid of a pitched ball, because then you'll *never* hit. But you have hit, before — and very well, too. That bang you got on the head the other day scared you. You must forget that. That's why ball-players wear helmets nowadays. When I played ball, we didn't even think of helmets. So — don't be afraid any more. How about it?"

Jody smiled. "Okay."

The man walked away.

"Who is that?" Jody asked Roddie, who had stopped to wait for him. "He comes to most of our games."

"Jim somebody," said Roddie. "He's friend of Coach Fisher's. What was he saying to you?"

Jody told him as they went on their way home.

As days went by so did ball games. Jody showed improvement in his ball throwing, but not in his hitting. In two games he had poked out only one hit, and that was a blooper over second. Coach Fisher moved him from seventh to last place in the batting order. In the last two games the coach took him out in the fourth inning and had Rabbit Foote catch.

One day during practice Jim drove up

alongside the ball park and came onto the field. He sat in the stands and watched the Dolphins practice.

Jody caught his eye and smiled. Jim smiled back and waved.

At bat, Jody remembered what Jim had advised him about not being afraid of a pitched ball, because the helmet would protect him; that's why he wore it.

He recalled that bang on the head from a pitched ball. He forgot if it had hurt or not. Guess it wasn't the pain he was afraid of, anyway. He was just afraid of being hit, that's all. He *tried* not to be. But when he stood at the plate he just couldn't help it. He couldn't help it now. He stepped "into the bucket" each time the ball came in instead of stepping straight forward. He was hitting the ball, but not at all as he used to before he had been hit on the head.

"Hey, Jack!" Jim yelled suddenly from the stands. "How about letting me throw in a few?"

"Sure, Jim," said the coach. "Come on."

"Stay there, Jody!" cried Jim. "Let me throw to you."

Jim came in and put on the glove Coach Fisher handed him. He warmed up first, then began throwing to Jody.

With each pitch Jody's right foot moved back. He was pulling himself back, too.

"Stay in there, Jody," said Jim. "I won't hit you."

Almost all the pitches were over the plate. Jim certainly had marvelous control. Jody tried hard to step straight ahead when he swung. Each time he felt a strong urge inside him to pull away from the pitch. It was as if something were *making* him do that.

He hit a couple of grounders, missed a few pitches, and lined one over first. Then he bunted one down the third-base line.

Jim grinned at him. "You're coming around fine, Jody!" he said.

After practice was over, Jim talked to Coach Fisher a few moments. Jody saw the coach nod.

"Jody, Frank, Duane and Birdie" — Coach Fisher snapped off the names — "stick around! Jim wants to work with you awhile!"

The other boys left — all except Johnny Bartho and Moonie Myers, who sat on the bench to watch.

Jody wondered what Jim intended to do. In a moment he found out. Jim or-

516

dered each player to his regular position, then had them throw the ball to each other. That was all they did. They just threw. He had Jody do the most throwing, making him throw hard to first, second and third.

Jody's first throws were weak. Gradually he improved. Sometimes his throws were over the baseman's head. But he was doing much better than he had done in any game.

"This gets me," Jody heard Moonie grumble from the bench. "What's he spending all his time on Sinclair for? He's just wasting his time for nothing!"

"That's just what I was thinking," said Johnny. "Come on. Let's go home."

8

EARLY Friday morning Jody and Midnight left the house and walked down the street. They were going to the lake about two miles away, to sit on Flatiron Rock and watch the ducks for a while, and then come back.

Suddenly a voice yelled out: "Jody! Wait a minute!"

Jody turned. Coming around the corner of the street he had just passed was Johnny Bartho. Johnny had started toward him at a run.

Jody waited, a little bit puzzled. Johnny was seldom without Moonie.

Johnny pulled up alongside him, scuffing his shoes so that he made Midnight jump with fright. He was carrying a flashlight.

"Hi," he said. "Where are you going?"

"To Flatiron Rock," replied Jody. "Midnight and I go there once in a while."

"You *and Midnight?*" Johnny looked down at the cat. "I've heard of guys being good friends with dogs, but never with cats."

"You get them trained, they're as smart as dogs," said Jody.

He started walking again, and Midnight began trotting beside him. If Johnny wanted to come along, okay. But he wasn't going to ask him. He could still remember

Johnny and Moonie talking about him at the games and practices, and none of it was any good.

"I asked Moonie if he'd want to go to Indian Cave today, but he can't," Johnny said. "You ever been there?"

"Of course," said Jody. "Many times." He shrugged. "Well — three or four times, I guess."

"Ever been *inside?*"

"Well, no," said Jody. "Never inside. Never *far* inside, I mean." He looked curiously at Johnny. "Why? Is that where you're going? Is that why you have that flashlight?"

Johnny smiled. "Yes. Let's you and I go, shall we? It's not far from here, and we can go inside and explore. I found two arrowheads in there once. Moonie found one, too. Of course, we had to go in a long ways. You're not scared, are you?"

"No," Jody said. "I'll go with you. What's there to be scared of?"

They walked a quarter of a mile down the road to a wooden bridge. They stepped off the road and slid down the steep bank to the edge of a creek.

The boys walked up alongside the creek, Midnight following close behind. They reached falls that were about ten feet high and two feet wide. They climbed the rocky ledge that was like steps beside it. They reached the top. Here the creek was wide but the water was very shallow.

The cave was a big hole in the hillside to the left.

"Here we are!" said Johnny. "Watch

that crack in the floor. There's water in it."

They rested for a while on a large rock. Then Johnny turned on his flashlight and started to walk deeper into the cave. A chill crawled along Jody's spine as he followed at Johnny's heels.

"Meow!" said Midnight. He hesitated awhile, then trotted in after them.

"Look at that," said Johnny.

He was shining the flashlight against the wall. Into the flat surface of a huge rock were carved pictures of a tepee and of an Indian chief. Jody wondered how long those had been there. Maybe scientists knew, he thought. Or those men who studied Indian lore.

They walked farther in. I wonder how far he's going, Jody thought.

"Scared?" asked Johnny.

"No," said Jody. "Why should I be scared?"

He was scared, but he wasn't going to let Johnny know it. Not for one second.

Suddenly his left foot slipped on a slimy rock. He fell to his knee and let out a cry. Johnny turned, flashed the light on him, then on the rock beside him.

Jody's heart flipped. Not a foot away from him was a pool of water. The water was about four feet below the floor of the cave. It looked deep and dangerous. Jody shuddered as he rose slowly to his feet.

"I'm sorry," said Johnny. "I knew the pool was here somewhere, but I didn't see it either. We'll go to the falls, then turn back."

Jody soon heard the hum coming from farther inside the cave. They walked on for another fifty feet, the hum of the falls growing louder all the time. And then Johnny shone the flashlight straight ahead, and Jody saw the falls. The water looked like a huge white curtain. He couldn't see the bottom of it. From where they stood all they could see was the spray that leaped up, and all they could hear was its thundering noise.

The whole thing was creepy. Jody felt goose-bumps on his arms.

They started back, walking side by side now. Johnny talked almost all the way back, telling about the Indians and how they had fought the pioneers, and about Daniel Boone and Davy Crockett.

At last Jody saw the round hole of day-light ahead. A little while later they were out of the cave.

"Aren't you glad you came with me?" smiled Johnny.

"Sure am," replied Jody, smiling back. "Sometime I'm going again."

Just then he saw Midnight scooting back into the cave.

"Midnight!" yelled Jody. "Come back here!"

"He's chasing a rat or something," said Johnny. "I saw it run ahead in front of him. Don't worry. He'll be back."

They waited. After a few minutes Midnight didn't come back and Jody became worried. Was it really a rat Midnight had chased, or was it something else?

"I'm going in after him," he said.

"Well, I'm not," said Johnny. "I don't have any love for cats. Here. Take my flashlight. I'll wait for you out here."

Jody took the flashlight and went into

the cave. "Midnight!" he called. "Midnight! Come here, pal!"

Midnight didn't come.

Jody walked farther into the cave. Every few seconds he would call out Midnight's name. At last he heard an answer: *"Meow! Meow!"*

"Midnight!" Jody cried. "Midnight! Come here!"

Still Midnight did not come. But Jody kept hearing him.

And then Jody started running forward. He knew what had happened.

He reached the pool, shone the flashlight into it. There was Midnight, unable to get out. And there was another animal. It looked like a rat, but Jody wasn't sure.

"Midnight!" Jody scolded. "See what happens when you run away from me?"

He got on his knees and reached down.

He stretched his arms as far as he could, but he couldn't reach far enough.

"Midnight!" sobbed Jody. Tears burned in his throat. "I can't reach you!"

9

JODY pushed himself to his knees. A lump filled his throat. He swallowed, but the lump remained.

Midnight sure had gotten into a mess this time! But it wasn't all his fault. He liked to chase mice and other animals that were smaller than he was. This time he had gone too far.

How was Jody going to get his cat out of that pool? There was a wall all around it. The water flowed in through a deep narrow crack in the rock floor, and it flowed out through a deep narrow crack.

529

It was impossible for Midnight to crawl out by himself. He tried, but he kept sliding back into the water.

What was worse, Jody could not get him out either.

I can't leave him there! Jody thought. *I can't let him drown! But how am I going to get him out? If I ran back for a net he'd be drowned by the time I got back!*

A net? Suddenly the thought gave him another idea. His sweater!

His hands trembled as he laid the flashlight on the dry rock-floor beside him and hurriedly slipped off his sweater. Then, while he held the flashlight in one hand, he leaned over the edge of the pool again and held the sweater down with his other hand.

"Come here, Midnight," he pleaded

softly. "Come here, pal. Grab hold of my sweater."

Midnight was still swimming around, his black fur matted against him like a shiny coat.

Jody kept calling to him to grab hold of the sweater. Midnight did not seem to hear him. Or maybe he didn't understand.

"Midnight, listen to me. Put your claws into my sweater. It's the only way, Midnight. The only way. Please!"

Midnight was clawing at the wall at Jody's left. He fell back and tried again, a little closer to Jody this time. Again he fell back, his head going under the water so that for a moment he was completely out of sight. Once more his head popped up and he began swimming hard to keep afloat.

"Midnight! Here, pal!" Jody flashed the light onto the sweater.

Midnight looked at the sweater. He swam toward it, sank one claw into it. Then he sank another claw into it. Jody felt the sweater stretch. He grabbed a stronger hold of it and slowly began to pull it up, with Midnight clinging on.

"Just a little more, Midnight!" he whispered. "Hang on a little more!"

A moment later he put his left arm around his cat and lifted him into his arms.

"Midnight! My pal!" he cried. He hugged the cat tenderly to him while his heart spilled over with joy. "Come on! Let's get out of here!"

He carried Midnight out with him.

When he reached the outside Jody returned the flashlight to Johnny and began drying off Midnight with his sweater. Johnny's eyes were like marbles as he looked at the cat.

"What happened to him?" he asked.

"Chased a rat right into the pool," said Jody.

Johnny looked at the front of Jody's shirt and pants. "You're soaked," he said. "Did you have to pull him out?"

"I tried, but I couldn't reach him," Jody said. "Then I pulled him out with my sweater."

Johnny stared at him. He didn't say anything for a long time, even when Jody started down the hillside, Midnight trailing at his heels.

On their way into the village they met Moonie, Duane and Frank. The boys

534

wanted to know where Jody and Johnny had been, and Johnny told them. Then he told them about Jody's cat chasing a rat or something into the cave and right into the pool, and how Jody saved the cat by pulling it out with his sweater.

The boys laughed. They thought it was funny. Jody didn't want to hear any more about it, and started to walk away.

"Why did you have to laugh?" Johnny Bartho snapped angrily. "Would you have thought of using your sweater to save a cat? I probably would have let it drown. You probably would have, too!"

Jody turned and stared at Johnny. He couldn't believe that it was Johnny Bartho talking like that about him and Midnight. Johnny Bartho, Moonie Myers's best friend . . . !

"Cats!" jeered Moonie. "I wouldn't give a nickel for one!"

Jody flushed. He looked directly into Moonie's eyes.

"I'm glad you said that, Moonie. You don't deserve a cat. You don't deserve any kind of pet!"

Jody spun and walked hurriedly away. He felt good that he had told Moonie off.

There was batting practice at 5:30. Coach Fisher was throwing. His pitches were not always down the groove — some of them were wide, some were inside. Jody was batting. He took a cautious step back with his right foot from each pitch.

"Stay in there, Jody," said the coach. "You're putting that right foot in the bucket."

"Sure he is!" said Moonie loudly from near first base where he was playing catch with Johnny Bartho. "He's scared! Why don't you get up closer and toss the ball underhand to him, Coach? Maybe he'd hit it then!"

Jody's face turned a deep red.

This was the first time Moonie had spoken to him since this morning. He knew Moonie was sore. Moonie had not liked it when Jody had told him that he did not deserve a pet.

Jody also figured that Moonie was jealous because Johnny Bartho had taken him and Midnight into Indian Cave. Now Moonie was trying to get even. He wanted to shame Jody in front of Coach Fisher and everyone else.

But Coach Fisher was looking hard at

Moonie. "One more wisecrack like that, Moonie," he said, "and you'll turn in your uniform. Never let me hear you talk like that again." He turned back to Jody. "Okay, Jody. Stick in there. Step into the pitch, not away from it. You'll gain your confidence again. Don't worry."

He stepped on the mound and threw. Jody held his jaws firmly together as he watched the ball come in. He tried to forget about Moonie and think only of Coach Fisher's words: *Step into the pitch, not away from it.*

He did just that. The ball came close, but as it started by him he saw that there was still plenty of space between it and him. He was sure it would cut the inside corner of the plate for a strike if he didn't swing.

He swung. *Crack!* The bat met the

538

ball solidly and sailed over first baseman Birdie Davis's head for a clean hit.

"Thataboy, Jody!" said the coach. "Just step into it. That's all you have to do."

10

OLD-TIMERS' DAY! The day when men who used to play baseball, but were too old to play any more, got two teams together and played each other. The money that was donated would be for bats, balls and other needed equipment for the little leaguers.

It was July 28, Saturday afternoon. The weather was ideal for baseball. The field was in excellent shape. Several men, including Jody's father and Coach Fisher, had been working on it this morning.

"Make sure every stone is cleared away,

540

no matter how little it is," Coach Fisher had said, laughing. "We can't take a chance on bad hops!"

The bleachers were filled with fans. Many brought their own lawn chairs on which they could sit to watch the game comfortably. A stand was set up near left field for ice-cold pop and hot dogs.

All the league teams were assembled at the game. They sat wherever they wanted to. Most of the Dolphins' team were sitting on the top seat of the bleachers behind first base. Jody was sitting next to Rabbit Foote, grinning happily. He hadn't seen Dad play baseball since that first Old-Timers' Day game three years ago. And that was so long ago he could hardly remember it.

He tried to pick out as many of the players as he could. He recognized Rab-

541

bit's father and Terry McClane's. But that was all. He didn't know any of the other boys' fathers. He saw Jim, too. Wonder what position he played?

Names were given to the teams. One was the Reds, the other the Blues. Jody's father played on the Reds' team.

The game started, and the crowd began yelling. Mr. Sinclair was on first. His uniform fit him like a glove. Especially his pants. But that wasn't unusual. The uniforms were tight on most of the bigger men.

The first man up punched a looping single over second and the crowd cheered. The second batter tried to lay down a bunt, but fouled. Then he hit a high bouncing grounder to short. The shortstop caught the hop, threw it to second

542

for the force-out, and the second baseman snapped it to first. A double play!

Mr. Sinclair really had stretched far out for the throw, and Jody smiled. Dad really didn't look bad there at all!

The third hitter clouted the pitch far out to center. The center fielder misjudged the ball and the hitter got two bases. He could have gone to third, but he was a big man, gray-haired, and he looked too tired to run any farther.

The crowd laughed and applauded him.

The next hitter was left-handed. He belted a grounder down to first. Mr. Sinclair caught it, made the put-out himself, and half an inning was over.

Jody saw Jim run out to center field. The way he runs I bet he could cover a lot of ground even now, thought Jody.

The Reds came to bat. A single and an

error gave them a chance to score. Rabbit Foote's father was third hitter and he clouted the pitch for a double. He was short and fast — just like his son Rabbit — and if the second runner had not stopped on third Mr. Foote would have gone on to third himself.

Two more runs came in and Mr. Sinclair came to the plate. He let a strike go by, then belted a long fly to left. It was mighty high. But the left fielder moved under it and caught it.

"Nice hit, anyway, Dad!" yelled Jody.

Jody was anxious to see Jim hit. He seemed to know a great deal about baseball. By the size of him, he might even drive one over that left-field fence. But Jim didn't get up to bat until the next inning.

There were men on second and third when he came to the plate.

"Come on, Jim!" the fans yelled. "Knock those men in!"

The pitcher stepped on the mound, checked the runners, and delivered. The ball came in, chest-high. Jim, a right-hander, made a motion to swing. Then he moved back from the plate.

"Strike!" said the umpire.

"Come on, Jim!" one of his teammates yelled. "Stay in there! It won't hit you!"

The second pitch came in. Jim stepped back with his left foot again.

The crowd laughed. Rabbit Foote and some of the players laughed, too. Jody didn't. He just sat there staring at Jim.

The umpire called the next two pitches balls. The next was a strike. Jim swung at

it and missed it by a foot. You could tell he was afraid of the pitch.

I can hardly believe it! thought Jody. *And he's the one who keeps telling me not to be afraid!*

"Rabbit," said Jody, "everyone calls him Jim. What's his last name?"

Rabbit looked at him. "You don't know?"

"No, I don't," said Jody.

Rabbit jerked his thumb at the boy beside him. Jody leaned forward and looked at Moonie Myers — Moonie, whose face was red as a beet, and who was the only boy on the top seat besides Jody who wasn't laughing.

"That's Mr. Myers," said Rabbit. "Moonie's father."

11

J ODY was stunned. Moonie's father
. . . No wonder he came to all the
games! No wonder he always had a car-
load of kids with him. Jody had never
really thought much about who he was.
He had just figured that he was a good
Dolphins' fan.

"Strike three!"

Mr. Myers went down swinging. It was
an awkward swing, as if he had decided
to cut at the ball at the very last moment.

The crowd roared. A lot of the fans
poked fun at him. It was happy fun. No-

body was serious. But still, the way Mr. Myers turned away from the plate and walked to the dugout, anybody could tell he was far from happy.

Jody took another look at Moonie. Moonie was sitting like a statue. He was staring straight ahead, his arms crossed. A couple of other kids looked at him, too. But Moonie didn't move a muscle.

Two innings went by and Mr. Myers was up again. There was a man on first base, and no outs.

"Let's get two!" Jody's father yelled as he stood in front of the first-base bag, holding the runner on.

The first pitch breezed in, and Mr. Myers moved back from it.

"Strike!"

The fans laughed and poked fun at Mr. Myers again. Jody looked at the faces around him. Some of them looked sorry for Mr. Myers. But most of them just thought it was very funny that Mr. Myers was afraid of the pitches.

"*Stay in there, Jim! Hit it!*"

The folks sitting in front of Jody looked around at him and smiled. Rabbit grinned at him, too, and poked him lightly in the ribs. His face turned red a little. He really hadn't meant to yell out like that.

He saw Mr. Myers dig his toes into the dirt, tap the bat against the plate and then hold it above his shoulder. The pitch came in and Mr. Myers didn't move his feet an inch.

Two more pitches whipped in and Mr. Myers just stood there watching them.

"What're you waiting for, Jim?" somebody yelled. "Get that bat off your shoulder!"

550

"Hit it, Mr. Myers!" Jody whispered to himself. "Hit it! Show 'em you're not afraid!"

The pitch came in. Mr. Myers moved his foot forward and swung. *Crack!* The ball sailed out like a shot over the second baseman's head for a clean hit. The runner on first went around to third. Mr. Myers made his turn at first, then went back to the bag, a happy, proud smile on his face.

The fans cheered. It was the loudest noise they had made since the game had started. Jody, Rabbit and all the kids on the top row stood up and clapped thunderously. All . . . except Moonie.

"Come on, Moonie!" cried Rabbit. "Give your dad a hand! That was a beautiful hit!"

Moonie's face colored. His eyes blinked

a couple of times and then a smile burst over his face. He stood up and began to clap as hard as he could.

"Thataboy, Dad!" he shouted. "Thataboy!"

The game ended with the Blues winning, 7–6.

The boys walked out of the ball park and began to talk about Mr. Myers's being afraid of a pitched ball and about that nice single he had hit.

"He's just like you, Jody," Frank York said. "Maybe that's why he always tries to help you when you bat. You've been awful scared of those pitches, too, ever since you got beaned."

Jody nodded. "Could be," he said.

"Did your dad get beaned sometime

when he was playing baseball, Moonie?"
Frank asked.

Moonie shrugged. "I don't know. If he
did, he never told me."

They kept talking about their fathers.
Jody learned some things he had never
known before: that some of them had
played with teams in the International
League, which was just one jump below
the major leagues. His own dad had
played semi-pro.

They were approaching Jody's house
when he heard a dog barking loudly
nearby. The boys stopped talking and
looked for the dog.

"There he is," Johnny Bartho pointed.
"At the bottom of that pole."

They saw a German police dog standing at the foot of the electric-light pole in

front of Jody's house. He was looking up at something on the pole and barking his head off.

Jody looked up to see what he was barking at. A cry started in his throat, then stuck there.

Sitting on the very top of the pole was Midnight!

12

THE GERMAN police dog belonged to the Slater family, who lived two blocks away. He was kept in their yard most of the time, but sometimes he would leave and roam the neighborhood. His name was Firpo.

"Firpo!" Jody shouted. "Get away from here! Go on home!"

The big dog merely looked at him, then kept barking at Midnight.

Johnny Bartho picked up a large stone and threw it at the dog. It missed Firpo by inches.

556

"Don't!" said Jody. "You might hurt him. I'll get him away from here."

Cautiously, he started toward the big police dog.

"Careful, Jody," warned Rabbit. "He might bite."

"He's not dangerous," said Jody. "I've been close to him before."

Slowly he walked up to the dog, talking softly all the while. "Come here, Firpo. Come here, boy."

Firpo stopped barking and looked at him. As Jody approached him Firpo stepped away. He barked a few more times, but now his bark was only half as loud as it was before.

"Come here, Firpo," said Jody quietly. "Let me take you home."

Firpo stopped moving and began to wag his long tail. His ears stood up

557

straight and his tongue hung out of his opened mouth. He was looking directly at Jody and he didn't seem dangerous at all. Jody took hold of his collar and gently led him down the street.

Behind him he heard the boys laughing. "Well, how do you like that?" said Johnny. "Who said Jody Sinclair hasn't got nerve?"

Jody took Firpo home, then ran all the way back. Midnight was still on top of the pole. He was like a fluffy black ball. Only his head and his shining eyes moved.

"We tried to call him," said Moonie, "but he won't budge."

Jody looked up. There were six wires on the crossbars of the pole, just a couple of feet under Midnight. Dangerous wires that could mean death. Jody was reminded of the trip back from Lincoln Park when they were trapped by the same kind of electric wires. The thought made him shudder.

"Jody," Johnny Bartho said suddenly, "Moonie's dad works for the telephone company. He has climbers. He can bring Midnight down. Can't he, Moonie?"

Moonie shrugged. "He doesn't climb poles any more."

"But he can still get a pair, can't he?" Johnny said.

Jody wiped sweat from his brow. "Maybe he wouldn't want to climb that high up," he said. "And those wires. They're real dangerous. Maybe he wouldn't want to take a chance."

"Oh, sure, he will," said Johnny. "I'll go ask him. Okay, Moonie?"

Moonie stood there a moment, chewing on his lower lip and thinking. "I'll go," he said then.

Just then Jody's dad and mother stepped out of the house. Mr. Sinclair's hair was uncombed, and he was wearing only his pants and a T-shirt. Jody knew he must have just finished taking a shower.

"What's going on, boys?" he asked.

"Midnight's on top of the pole, Dad," Jody said. "Firpo chased him up there. Moonie was just going to call his dad to bring some climbers."

Mr. Sinclair came off the porch and looked up the pole at Midnight. "Can you beat that?" he said.

"*Meow!*" said Midnight.

"That's a job for the SPCA," suggested Mr. Sinclair. "They have experts who handle jobs like this. No need to bother Jim.

Anyway," he chuckled, "after that hit he got he wouldn't feel like climbing an electric-light pole!"

"That's right! The SPCA!" said Jody. "I'd forgot all about them!"

Mr. Sinclair put in a call to the Society for the Prevention of Cruelty to Animals. Within an hour a man drove into the driveway in a pickup truck. The boys pointed to Midnight, sitting on top of the pole. They watched the man put on his climbers and a long pair of gloves and climb up the pole. Nobody made a sound as the man put his gloved hand around Midnight, clutched him by the back of his neck and lifted him off the pole.

Midnight let out a loud *"Meowr!"* and started to claw at the air with his paws. But the man had him well under control.

He climbed down the pole with Midnight. When he reached the ground, he handed Midnight to Jody and Jody hugged him fiercely.

Jody thanked the man, who smiled and left. Mom and Dad went back into the house. Johnny Bartho and the other boys departed, too. Only Jody and Moonie remained.

"Moonie," Jody said, "I want to thank you, anyway, for wanting to go after your father."

Moonie shrugged. "That's okay, Jody. I think he would have been glad to rescue Midnight for you. He likes you a lot."

"I know," said Jody. "I like him, too."

"Jody, how about playing catch?"

"Okay. I'll go in and get a ball and a couple of gloves."

He brought out his own glove and the

one Dad had. They started in playing catch.

The very first ball Jody pitched was a looping throw that barely reached Moonie.

"Oh, come on, Jody. Throw 'em up, will you?"

Jody tried again, and again Moonie had to rush forward a few steps to catch the ball before it hit the ground.

"I don't know, Jody," said Moonie, shaking his head. "I don't think you'll ever be able to throw."

Jody had forgotten all about his poor throwing. Now that he was reminded of it, he became worried all over again.

He had twice the problem Mr. Myers had! Mr. Myers was only afraid of a pitched ball. He, Jody, was afraid of a pitched ball — *and* he couldn't throw.

13

"THROW that ball! Hit me on the head with it! What are you afraid of? Hurting my hand?"

It was Jim Myers talking. He was on the mound, Jody was behind the plate, and Moonie was on second. Jody didn't have his catching equipment on. All they were doing was throwing the ball. Jim would hurl it to Jody, and Jody would either throw it back to him or to Moonie.

He was doing better than he had all season. The ball snapped from his hand like a shot. He was throwing accurately,

565

too, right at Jim Myers's head. And, when he pegged it to Moonie, the ball whipped through the air directly into Moonie's glove almost every time.

After a half an hour of this throwing practice, Jim and the boys pulled the batting cage up behind the plate. Then Jim Myers had Jody put on a helmet and pick up a bat.

"Stay in that box and don't move," said Jim Myers. "Watch some of those balls go by. Look them over as well as you can." He grinned. "Remember what you yelled to me at the Old-Timers game? 'Stay in there!' you said. Well, I stood in there. Now let me see *you* do it. . . . Okay, son. Pitch 'em in."

Moonie pitched them in. Jody stood in the batting box, his bat held high over his shoulder. He watched the first ball come in and goose pimples popped out on his arms. But he stood there, and the ball zipped by and hit the batting cage. Moonie pitched in a dozen balls. Twice Jody was tempted to dodge back. But the ball breezed by him, missing him by almost a foot.

"Fine!" said Jim Myers. "Okay, now. Let's see you hit it, Jody. Just take a short step forward."

A half a dozen neighborhood kids were in the outfield. They all had gloves. Jody began swinging, taking a short step forward as Jim Myers had advised him to do. Gradually he began to hit the ball. Gradually he began to feel more comfortable at the plate. He kept hitting until he was tired, then he pitched to Moonie for a while.

"Okay," said Jim Myers. "We'll do this

every day between practices and games. Can you be here tomorrow evening, Jody?"

Jody thought a little. "We play the Bears tomorrow," he said.

"Okay. Make it be the next day, then," grinned Jim Myers.

Jody smiled. "Okay!" he said.

He felt good. Mr. Myers was sure a great guy! Imagine him taking such an interest in a boy that he was willing to sacrifice a lot of his time just to make this boy be a better thrower and hitter.

On August 2, just before the Moose game, Coach Jack Fisher called his team together.

"We have one more game to play after today's," he said. "If we win today, we'll have a good chance to be in the play-off.

We've been doing quite well all season, considering that most of you boys have played little before."

He cleared his throat and looked at Jody. "Jody, we'll start Rabbit at catching today. You've been starting to hit again, but the Moose have some good hitters who are fast on bases. They'll take advantage of you every time they get on. You are throwing better than you did at the start of the season. Don't get me wrong. But against these boys you must do even better. I think, with Rabbit catching, they won't dare to run as much."

"Who's playing short?" Moonie asked.

"Joe Bell," said the coach.

"Isn't Jody going to play at all?"

"Not today."

Jody looked across at Moonie. Their eyes locked. Then Jody looked down at the ground. He thought about all the hours he had spent practicing batting and throwing. He had improved a lot. He was sure of it. It wasn't fair that Coach Fisher wasn't letting him play today.

"Infielders, hustle out there. Rabbit, warm up Moonie. We have only a few minutes left."

14

MOONIE took his time on the mound. He pitched hard and had the Moose swinging and missing. He mowed down the first two with strikeouts. He was a little wild on the third hitter, and walked him. Then the Moose cleanup man, Mel Devlin, stepped to the plate and the Moose fans began giving him support from the bleachers.

Mel was tall and thin. He held up his bat as if it were a toothpick. He had five home runs this year so far. One of them had been against Moonie during the early part of the season.

From the bench, Jody watched eagerly. He remembered those pitches Mel had hit. They had been high ones, right across the letters of his shirt.

Keep them low, Moonie, Jody thought. *Right around his knees.*

Moonie toed the rubber and pitched. The pitch was high — *straight across the letters of Mel's shirt.* Mel swung with all his might. *Crack!* The bat met the ball solidly. The white pill streaked like a missile to left field.

But it was curving! It was going . . .

"Foul!" cried the umpire.

The Moose fans groaned.

The Dolphin fans cried, "Just one long strike, Moonie, ol' boy!"

Jody's heart thudded. Man, that was

close. *Come on, Moonie! Keep them low!*

Moonie kept working hard on Mel. He gave no more high ones. But neither did he throw him another strike. Mel got a free ticket to first base.

Moonie had trouble with the next batter. The hitter fouled three pitches in a row. Then Moonie curved him, and the batter swished out.

"Nice going, Moonie," said the coach. "Three strikeouts that first inning. Keep it up. You're doing fine."

The Dolphins didn't get a hit during their turn at bat. The Moose came back and threatened again. They got a man on. A sacrifice bunt put him on second. A long fly to right field was caught, but the runner tagged up and made it safely to third.

Two outs. The Dolphins' infield played deep. Moonie stretched, delivered, and a grounder was hit to short. Joe Bell charged in after it. He fumbled it! The ball skittered behind him. He picked it up, fired it to first.

Safe! And the runner scored.

The next hitter popped to first and the side was retired.

The innings moved quickly. The Moose put two more runs across in the top of the third. In the bottom of the fourth Roddie tripled and Duane drove him in with a hard single over second base.

Moonie then stepped to the plate and pounded a smashing drive to right center field. Duane raced to second, to third, and then tried to score.

"Hit it!" Frank York, who was next batter, yelled at him.

Duane slid. The throw from deep second base was almost perfect. The catcher caught the ball, put it on Duane, and the umpire yelled, "Out!"

Moonie took his turn at second and then returned and stayed there.

"Let's keep it going!" yelled Coach Fisher. "Swing at 'em, Frankie!"

Frankie waited for the pitch he wanted. He swung. A single! Moonie came all the way in to score, making it two runs for the Dolphins.

Then Arnie struck out to end the rally.

Score: Moose 3; Dolphins 2.

The Moose lead-off man pulled a surprise. He dragged the first pitch, bunting it down the third-base line. Duane ran in, tried to field the bunt, and slid. He got up disgustedly, tossed the ball to Moonie, and returned to his position. Only now he played in close, on the grass, in case the batter tried a sacrifice bunt.

The batter did! But he bunted the ball down the first-base line. It looked as if he, too, would get a hit out of it.

Birdie, also playing in close, charged in after the bunt. He fielded it, turned and whipped the ball to Moonie, who was running to cover first.

Out!

The Dolphins' fans cheered. "Nice play, Birdie!"

"That's the way to play heads-up ball, Moonie!"

One out, man on second.

Moonie stepped on the rubber. He took a quick look over his shoulder at the man leading off second, then delivered. *Crack!* A hard blow just over Frank York's head. Frank leaped. The ball barely grazed his glove. The runner on second made it to third and then bolted for home.

Roddie scooped up the ball in right field and heaved it. It was a good throw. It struck the ground twenty feet in front of home plate and bounced up into Rabbit's waiting mitt.

The runner hit the dirt and slid across the plate just as Rabbit put the ball on him. It was close. Very close.

But the umpire's hands were spread out flat. And very clearly he shouted: "Safe!"

That was it for the Moose that inning. Now they led 4–2, and Jody didn't think the Dolphins had a chance. He was getting tired sitting on the bench, too. And worried. Would Coach Fisher ever let him catch again this year?

Birdie walked, and Johnny Bartho doubled, sending Birdie around to third.

Joe Bell, who was due for a hit, was up next. Coach Fisher gave him the squeeze signal. Joe tried twice to bunt and both times fouled the pitches. On the next pitch he struck out.

Rabbit tossed aside one of the two bats he was holding and started for the plate.

"Rabbit, wait! Jody, hit in place of Rabbit!"

Jody looked up, surprised. Had he heard right? Had the coach spoken to him?

"Come on, Jody!" said the coach. "Let's hustle!"

"Yes, sir!" murmured Jody, and sprang out of the dugout.

15

JODY moved as if he were in a dream. He picked out his favorite bat and swung it back and forth a few times to limber his muscles. Then he stepped to the plate.

"Strike!" The first pitch was near his knees and he backed up a little.

"Stay in there, Jody, boy!" someone yelled in the bleachers. "Be a hitter!"

His heart warmed. He knew whose voice that was. *I'm not afraid*, he thought. *I'm not.*

Another pitch. "Ball!"

Then it came in, letters-high. Curving in toward him. He pulled back his bat and swung with everything he had.

Crack! The blow could be heard all round the field.

The ball sailed out to deep right field — over the fielder's head! It looked as if it would go over the fence. It didn't. It struck the grass in front of it, bounced up against the fence, and the fielder caught it. By the time he pegged it in, Birdie and Johnny had scored, and Jody was resting on third base.

"Beautiful hit, Jody!" yelled the coach. He ran forward and slapped him happily on the back. "You really blasted that one, fella!"

"Thanks," said Jody, breathing hard.

Roddie came up, socked a one-one pitch toward center field. It was a real

580

high fly. Jody held up at third until the fielder caught the ball. Then he raced in as hard as he could, scoring easily.

Duane grounded out, and the rally was over. Three runs, and Jody had knocked in two of them himself and had scored the third. He felt just fine.

And that curve he had hit — he knew he'd never be afraid of a pitched ball any more.

The Moose came to bat for the last time. They were a beaten bunch. Moonie mowed down the first two hitters and the third popped out to Jody.

The Dolphins won, 5–4.

They had won their chance to compete in the play-off game.

They beat the Gophers on Tuesday to clinch second place with ten wins and five losses. On Wednesday the Tigers walloped the Bobcats to win first-place honors with twelve wins and only three losses.

The standings:

	WON	LOST	GAMES BEHIND
Tigers	12	3	—
Dolphins	10	5	2
Bobcats	8	7	4
Bears	6	9	6
Moose	5	10	7
Gophers	4	11	8

Now the two teams were to play each other for the championship. Coach Fisher was keeping Rabbit Foote behind the plate. Rabbit was doing all right. In the Gophers game he had thrown out two men who might have scored if they had stolen second safely. Coach had had Jody pinch-hit, though, and he had hit safely.

It was Jody's arm the coach was afraid

582

of. He couldn't trust Jody to throw that ball hard and straight when he really had to.

The Tigers started things rolling immediately. They began hitting Terry Mc-Clane, scoring two runs in the first and then two more in the second. The Dolphins got a run in the bottom of the second to make the score 4–1.

Then Terry bore down. He threw the ball across the corners, and the third inning went by without the Tigers' scoring.

Johnny blasted a long drive in the bottom of the third and scored on Joe Bell's single. The Tigers held them from scoring more that inning.

Then, in the top of the fourth, with Tigers on first and second, a terrible thing happened.

Rabbit's right thumb was split open by a foul tip.

Time was called and Coach Fisher looked at the thumb. It was a nasty cut.

"Just patch it up, Coach," Rabbit said. "I can still play."

"I'll patch it up," replied the coach, "but you're not going to play." He looked around. His eyes spotted Jody. "Jody, help get those things off Rabbit and put them on yourself. Hurry it up."

Jody unbuckled the shin guards and buckled them on his own legs. Then Rabbit tossed him the chest protector and the mask.

"Good luck, Jody," he said

"Thanks," said Jody.

Coach Fisher took Rabbit to the dugout, opened the first aid kit and took care of Rabbit's thumb. On the field Jody was catching Terry. He threw the ball twice into the dirt, then tried harder and threw the others perfectly. After eight pitches the umpire called time in and the game resumed.

"Okay, boys!" the Tigers' fans began to yell. "Now's your chance! You can steal this catcher blind! That glass arm of his can't throw out a turtle!"

"Come on, boy! Come on, Terry! Slam it in here!" Jody rattled on like this. He hoped it would smother those awful things the opponents were yelling about him.

He caught Terry's first pitch, rising quickly to throw to third if he had to. But the runners remained on their bases.

"Come on! Steal!" someone in the bleachers yelled. "Let's see you steal on him!"

That voice! It wasn't the same one that

had yelled the first time. That one wasn't familiar. This one was. It belonged to Mr. Myers. But why should Mr. Myers . . . ?

The pitch came in. From the corners of his eyes Jody could see the runners take off.

"Throw 'im out, Jody! Throw 'im out!"

Jody pegged the ball hard to third. The ball shot like a white meteor. Duane caught it, pulled it down, and touched the runner sliding in.

"Out!" yelled the base umpire.

The Dolphins' fans screamed happily.

Jody could hear Mr. Myers laughing in the bleachers.

There was no more base-stealing that inning. And no more runs for the Tigers. The Dolphins began blasting the ball and put across two runs to tie the score 4-all before the Tigers stopped them.

586

The Tigers came up in the fifth, the top of their batting order ready to gnaw the Dolphins to bits.

The first man walked, and once again the cry rose for the runner to steal.

"He can't throw to second! That glass arm broke when he threw to third!"

That was the Tigers' fan yelling.

"Sure! Try out that arm! See what happens!"

And that was Mr. Myers.

It was like a game those two men had up there in the bleachers, one sitting on the Tigers' side, the other on the Dolphins'.

The ball came in. The batter shifted his position in the batting box. He was going to bunt.

He met the ball squarely. It struck the ground in front of the plate, hopped twice, and Jody pounced on it. He picked it up, pegged it hard to second. Frank York caught it, stepped on the bag, and whipped the ball to first.

Twice the base umpire jerked up his thumb.

A double play!

"There you are!" yelled Mr. Myers. "There's your glass arm!"

The Dolphins' fans cheered, clapped and stamped their feet on the bleachers' seats. The Tigers' fans only stared and shook their heads unbelievingly.

The next batter whiffed.

Jody was first batter for the Dolphins. Loud applause filled the stands as he stepped to the plate. He felt good. Real good.

He took a called strike, then knocked out a clothesline single over first. Roddie bunted him to second. Then Duane socked one into the opposite field for two bases. Jody scored. Terry singled, too. Duane was called out at home after a strong peg from the outfield. Frank popped out, and the inning was over.

The Tigers got men on, but they couldn't bring them in. The Dolphins won, 5–4.

Coach Fisher and all the rest of the Dolphins team crowded around Jody. They slapped him on the back and shook his hand and all talked at the same time.

When things quieted down a little, the coach said, "Nice game, Jody. You certainly came through when we needed you the most."

"Thanks, Coach," said Jody. "How's Rabbit's thumb?"

589

"Oh, it'll be all right." The coach grinned. "I patched it up fine."

Mr. Myers stepped forward and stretched out his hand.

"May I have the honor?" He smiled. "Guess you proved what that arm is *really* made of, didn't you, Jody?"

Jody took Mr. Myers's hand and smiled back. "I guess so, Mr. Myers," he said.

"It's iron, Dad," Moonie said, laughing. "It's never been glass!"

Challenge at Second Base

To Fred and Gloria

Challenge at Second Base

by Matt Christopher
Illustrated by Marcy Ramsey

··· *1*

The white runabout hopped and skipped over the rough water like a rabbit chased by a fox. Not far away a bird glided down, touched the water with its bill, and swooped away.

Stan, sitting on the rear seat behind his brother Phil, felt the bumps. Suddenly his eyes opened wide and he straightened as if somebody had prodded him in the back.

Wasn't this Monday? The day the baseball suits were given out?

Stan's heart flipped. Yes, it was!

"Look at me!" he cried out loud. "Playing around in the middle of Lake Mohawk! Phil!"

he yelled into the wind to the boat's pilot. "Phil, what time is it?"

Phil looked at his wrist watch. "Five minutes of five!" he answered over his shoulder.

"Holy catfish!" shouted Stan. "They were passing out the suits at four-thirty! I have to get home and get out of my trunks, Phil!"

"You won't right away!" replied Phil. "Look ahead of us and to our left! Somebody's in trouble!"

"But, Phil!" Stan protested. "I've got to —"

"Not till we help out that guy first!" said Phil sternly.

Stan squinted past the sharp bow of the boat, to the left of Phil's head. He saw something white in the water, but could not make out what it was. He stood up, angry at himself for having let the time go by unnoticed.

"It's a sailboat!" he yelled. "Somebody's waving at us!"

The sailboat was lying on its side, its white

598

sail flapping in the water. A person was clinging to it, waving frantically.

Phil gunned the motor and turned the
wheel. A short scream burst from Stan as he
lost his balance and started to fall. For a brief
moment he was looking straight down at the
deep green water. His face was hardly more
than two feet away from it. Then his hands
gripped the edge of the boat and he held on
tightly.

Seconds later he was sitting down, his heart
pounding.

Quickly, Phil approached the tipped sailboat. He cut the motor and the boat lost
speed.

Stan was able to read the name on the
boat, even though it was upside down. *Mary
Lou*.

"It's Jeb Newman's boat!" Stan cried.
"That's Jeb!"

"Hi, guys!" greeted the boy in the water.
He was grinning as if a tipped sailboat were

a common occurrence with him. "Thanks for the rescue!"

"We'll help you put her back up!" said Phil.

Jeb was wearing swim trunks. Stan expected to see Gary with him. Gary was Jeb's younger brother, a strong prospect for second base on the Falcons' team. That was all right, except that Stan wanted to play second base, too.

Phil let the motor idle as he drifted close to the sailboat. Stan dived in, and he and Jeb swam to the other side of the boat. While Phil lifted the mast, Stan and Jeb pushed against the side of the boat until it was back up in position.

Jeb climbed into it, the water inside the boat up to his shins. Then Phil helped pull Stan back into the motorboat.

"A gust of wind caught me off my guard while I was turning," explained Jeb. "Guess

I'm still an amateur." He unhooked a pail and began bailing out the water.

"How come you're not at the ball park?" he asked Stan. "You're playing with the Falcons, aren't you?"

"I forgot about it," said Stan, and looked anxiously at his brother. "Maybe we can still make it, Phil."

"See you around, Jeb!" yelled Phil, and once more gunned the motor.

The sudden burst of noise frightened a flock of birds flying low near them. Stan was afraid he had little chance beating out Gary at second base. After all, why shouldn't Gary be good? Jeb was working him out a lot — going to the field with him when nobody else was there and hitting grounders to him for hours.

If Phil would help Stan like that, Stan would be good, too. Phil, though, acted as if he didn't care whether Stan played or not.

Stan shook his head. He just couldn't figure out Phil anymore. Last year Phil had played professional baseball with Harport. This year he didn't play at all, except pitch and catch with Stan. And Stan practically would have to twist his arm to get him to do that.

"I'm afraid we'll be late, Stan," said Phil.

"I'm afraid, too," replied Stan sadly.

··· 2

Phil drove Stan directly to the baseball field. The place was as empty as an open sea.

"Guess I don't get a suit." Stan's voice caught a little.

"Don't lose all your hopes," replied Phil. "The coach is probably holding one for you."

"I doubt it," said Stan. "Coach Bartlett is real strict about these things. He said that if a boy didn't have a good reason for not showing up at practice, he wasn't interested in playing. He was keeping out somebody else who was."

"But you have a good reason for not being

603

here this afternoon," said Phil. "It was my fault."

Stan didn't answer.

On the way home in the car, Stan got to thinking about Phil. From the brief conversation he had between Mom and Dad, he knew that Phil hadn't done too well with Harport. Even so, he could have signed a contract with them this year, but he had refused. Stan didn't know exactly why Phil had refused. If Stan were in that position he certainly would not have!

"Why didn't you play with Harport this year, Phil?" Stan asked. "Did you want more money?"

"What?" Phil seemed to be daydreaming. "Oh! No. No, it wasn't money," he said finally.

"Then what was it?"

Phil looked at Stan. He seemed a little embarrassed. "You won't mind if I don't want to talk about it, will you, little buddy?"

Stan shrugged. "No. If you don't want to."

He couldn't understand it at all. What other reason was it if it wasn't money?

Well, Stan had his own worries now. Without a suit he couldn't play for the Falcons in the league. What was he going to do now? Most of his pals would make the team. He was sure of that.

I'll have more time with my space projects, he told himself. I don't have to play baseball. But he was just thinking up excuses, for he loved baseball more than anything.

Saturday afternoon, Larry Jones and Tommy Hart came to the house, dressed in brand-new baseball uniforms. They were carrying their spikes and gloves. Larry's was a catcher's mitt.

"Where were you yesterday afternoon?" Larry asked. He was almost as wide as he was tall. His hair was copper-colored, and he had freckles sprinkled around his nose.

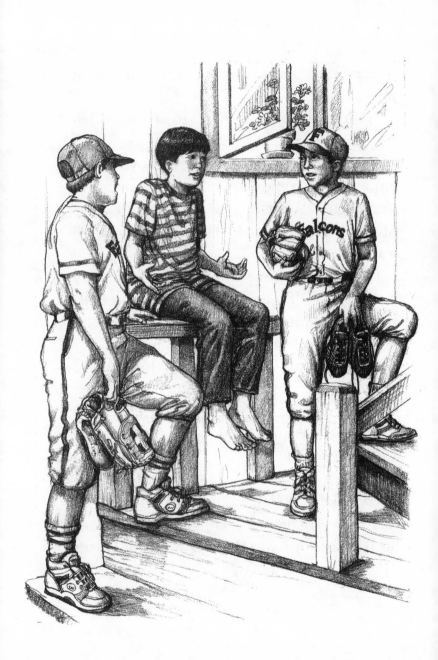

"Didn't you know Coach Bartlett was passing out the suits?"

"I got there too late," said Stan.

"You should've been there," said Tommy. "You would've gotten a suit." He was the team's pitcher, a tall, slender boy who could hit as well as he could throw.

"Was Gary there?" Stan asked quickly.

"Of course," replied Tommy. "You don't think he'd miss it, do you?"

"We're going down to the field, now," said Larry. "Jeb Newman is going to pick us up here."

"Here?" Stan frowned. "Why here?"

Larry shrugged his large shoulders. "Because we told him to. You're coming along, aren't you?"

"I don't have a suit," said Stan. "If Coach Bartlett had wanted to give me one, he would have brought it over by now — I guess."

"Our first league game is Monday," Tommy said. "Against the Jaguars."

Why are they telling me this? thought Stan. I don't want to hear it!

Just then Jeb Newman drove his car up to the curb. Beside him sat his brother Gary in baseball cap and uniform.

Larry and Tommy trotted to the car and got in.

"Aren't you coming?" Gary called.

Stan shook his head, turned, and went back into the house.

Outside, the car roared away from the curb.

··· 3

Three shelves lined one of the walls in Stan's room. His Dad had built them for him, and painted them blue. Half of the lowest shelf contained books. All kinds of books — adventure, science fiction, and sports.

The remainder of the shelf, and the other two, contained a variety of models. Airplanes, ships, submarines, rockets, and satellites. In one corner stood a table about four feet square. On it was a miniature space base similar to that of Cape Canaveral. Every piece had been put together and glued by Stan's own hands.

Right now Stan was assembling a space-station model. This he was going to suspend

609

by a string from the ceiling to give the illusion of a real space station in outer space.

"Stan!" It was Mom. "You have a friend here to see you!"

"Okay!" he answered. "Send him in!"

He couldn't leave his model now, not while he was holding two parts of it together, waiting for the glue to dry.

In a moment Tommy Hart came in. His face broadened in a smile as he looked at the many models that decorated the room.

"Boy!" he said. "Would I like something like this!"

Stan grinned with pride. "They were kits. Dad bought most of them for me. Others I got for doing odd jobs."

Tommy took a few moments gazing wonder-eyed at the models, then came and stood beside Stan. "We lost to the Jaguars Monday," he said unhappily. "Four to one."

"Who pitched?" asked Stan.

"I did. Did we look bad! Don missed two

at short, and Duffy misjudged a fly in center field with a man on."

He began telling about other incidents that resulted in their losing the game. Stan just listened. He wasn't interested in hearing a play-by-play description of the game, but he wouldn't tell Tommy that. He liked Tommy, and he wouldn't say anything to Tommy that might hurt him.

Mom's voice carried to him again from the kitchen. "Somebody else to see you, Stanley!"

By now the glue was dry. Stan left the partially completed space station on the bench and looked behind Tommy. The overweight catcher of the Falcons came strolling into the room, shouldering a baseball bat. Sporting a mischievous smile, he stopped in the middle of the room and stood admiring Stan's models.

"You going to be an astronaut?" he asked Stan.

"I'd like to," replied Stan.

"Me, too. But I don't think they'll make a space ship big enough to hold me," said Larry.

He walked up close to the table on which stood the space-base model.

"Gary Newman looked great on second," he said over his shoulder. "He didn't make an error and he hit the ball every time."

"Sure," said Tommy. "And always into somebody's hands."

"That's better than not hitting the ball at all," replied Larry. "I struck out once, and you did, too." He looked around at Stan. "Why didn't you come to the game, Stan?"

Stan colored. "Why should I? I didn't get a suit."

"You weren't there. You might have gotten one if you were there. You know what the guys are saying?"

"Larry," Tommy broke in. "Don't you think you're talking too much?"

Stan looked at Tommy and back at Larry.

"What are you guys trying to say?" he asked suspiciously.

Larry shrugged. "They're saying you didn't want to show up when the suits were given out because you were afraid you wouldn't get one!"

Stan swallowed. He got out of his chair quickly and faced Larry. "I wanted to go, but I couldn't get there! I was in a boat!"

"I know," said Larry in a softer voice. "We heard about it."

Stan frowned. So that was it. They had figured that would be the excuse I'd give for not being at the ball park.

His eyes narrowed. "You figured the same as they did, didn't you, Larry? You figured that I —"

"Oh, no, Stan! Not me! Honest!"

Larry's face reddened, and he backed away a little.

"Watch it, Larry!" yelled Tommy.

But it was too late. The top of Larry's bat

struck one of the rocket models standing on the top shelf. It fell to the floor and broke into a dozen pieces!

Stan stared at the pieces, then at Larry. Hurt choked him. Then anger rose so quickly in him he began shouting before he thought.

"You fat, clumsy ox! Look what you did! Why did you have to bring that lousy bat in here? Why —"

Larry stared at him, his face paling. Then he stooped and picked up the pieces of broken rocket model. His chubby hands were trembling.

"I'll pay for it," he murmured. "Tell me how much it was."

"I can't remember," snapped Stan.

Larry put the pieces on the bench beside the space-ship model Stan was working on, and walked to the door.

Suddenly he turned around. His face was beet red.

"I'm glad you're not on our team, Stan

Martin!" he cried angrily. "You know that? I'm real glad! You're just like your brother! Everybody knows he wasn't good either!"

The words fell on Stan like hailstones. He wanted to say something, but couldn't.

Larry left hastily, and Tommy, looking embarrassed, followed him out.

Hardly had they left when Phil came into the room. Surely he must have heard Larry's unkind and untrue remarks. But, if he had, he didn't show it.

"I have a couple of things here for you, little buddy," he said, a warm smile on his lips.

He handed Stan an envelope. Whatever the other thing was he held behind his back, out of Stan's sight.

Stan stared at the envelope. It was very strange. His name and address were made up of words cut out from a newspaper and pasted on the envelope!

He ripped open the end of it and pulled

out the letter. This, too, was written with words cut out from a newspaper. Stan read the letter and sucked in his breath.

DON'T QUIT! YOU HAVE ABILITY! STICK TO IT!

It wasn't signed.

··· 4

P hil!" Stan cried. "Read this! Who would send me a letter like this?"

Phil read the letter and whistled. "How do you like that?" he said. "Somebody's interested in you, little buddy, and wants to keep it a secret!"

"But why?"

Phil shrugged. "I don't know. Whoever it is must like you, that's for sure." He handed the letter back to Stan. "Well, that should be enough surprise for one day, but here's another."

He brought his other hand around from behind him, and gave Stan a gray box. Almost instantly Stan knew what was in it. He took it and opened it.

"My baseball suit!" he shouted.

He lifted the jersey out of the box, held it against himself for size, then looked at the number 10 sewn on the back.

"Saw Mr. Bartlett on the street," explained Phil. "He told me to give this to you, and for you to be at practice tonight at five."

After his excitement wore off a little, Stan telephoned Tommy Hart and told him the good news.

"See? Didn't I tell you?" cried Tommy. "Going to practice tonight?"

"I have a suit, haven't I?" replied Stan.

"I'll meet you in front of your house," said Tommy.

He was at Stan's house at a quarter of five. The two of them walked to the field, carrying their gloves and spikes. Stan felt as if he were dreaming. Was Coach Bartlett actually

choosing him over Gary Newman, or had the coach only picked him to warm the bench?

Some of the players were already at the field playing catch. However, there was one player in the infield working on grounders. It was Gary Newman. And hitting a ball to him was his brother Jeb.

"He really wants to make sure he plays, doesn't he?" said Tommy, a trace of disgust in his voice.

"He probably will, too," replied Stan. To himself he thought, *I wish somebody would work me out like that.*

Soon a car pulled up to the curb, stopped, and a tall, thin man wearing a T-shirt stepped out. From the trunk of the car he dragged out a huge, dirt-smudged bag and carried it toward the dugout. He spotted Stan and grinned.

"Hi, Stan! We missed you!"

Stan smiled bashfully.

Jeb quit hitting to Gary and retired to the

dugout to watch. Coach Bartlett put the boys through batting practice first, with Larry behind the plate and George Page throwing. Stan tried to avoid Larry as much as possible. When he batted he didn't speak, nor did Larry.

A left-hand hitter, Stan socked a couple of grounders, missed a pitch, and blasted a fly to right field.

After batting practice the coach asked Jeb to hit fly balls to the outfielders.

"Stan, alternate with Gary at second," he said.

It was as Stan had expected. Most of the other infielders had their positions pretty well cinched: Larry behind the plate; George Page at first; Jim Kendall at third; and Don Marion at short. They were a year or two older than Stan and Gary, more experienced and better ballplayers. It was at second base that the team was weakest.

Coach Bartlett knocked grounders to his

infielders till the sweat rolled down their faces and they showed signs of tiredness. Stan missed several. The coach would then hit him high bounders, with "handles" on them, which Stan gloved easily. But Gary had no trouble. He was fielding the grounders skillfully, and pegging them accurately to first.

"Okay, that's it," said the coach finally. "Bring it in."

Jeb helped the coach put the balls and equipment back into the big canvas bag. Stan, carrying a bat toward them, heard them talking, and hesitated a moment. Distinctly, he heard the coach say:

"He's going to be a real ballplayer. Watch him in two or three years."

"He loves it," said Jeb.

"Loves it? I've never seen a kid with so much interest and desire. Believe me, that kid's a natural!"

Stan knew they were talking about Gary.

Silently, he laid the bat down and walked away.

··· 5

The line-up for the Falcons in the game against the Steelers was as follows:

D. Marion	shortstop
J. Kendall	third base
F. Smith	left field
D. Powers	center field
G. Page	first base
G. Newman	second base
L. Jones	catcher
E. Lee	right field
T. Hart	pitcher

The Falcons, taking their first raps, got two runs in the first inning to start them off. The Steelers' pitcher, a small, broad-shouldered boy with hair that needed cutting, allowed a walk and two hits. One of them was a triple off the powerful bat of Bert "Duffy" Powers. Duffy, a tall, quiet boy with glasses, couldn't make it home, for George struck out and Gary popped to short.

The Steelers managed to put a man on first, but there he stayed. Tommy's straight ball was cutting the corners, and the umpire was calling them as he saw them.

Larry, leading off in the second inning, belted a long fly to center. The soaring meteor drew a quick response from the fans, but before the chubby catcher got halfway to first, the fielder caught the ball for the out.

Then Eddie Lee hit a zigzagging grounder to the pitcher. The pitcher fumbled it, and for a moment it looked as if Eddie might get on. But then the husky pitcher closed his hand on the ball, reared back, and heaved it to first. Eddie was out by half a step.

Tommy Hart waited for the one he

wanted. With a two-two count on him he belted a single between short and third.

Stan, sitting in the shade of the dugout, looked across at Mr. Bartlett standing in the third-base coaching box. Would the coach give Tommy the steal signal? Tommy was fast, but he was pitching and there were two outs. Stan waited anxiously to see what the coach would do.

The coach gave no signal, which meant for lead-off man Don Marion to hit away.

Don socked the second pitch high over second base. The shortstop and the second baseman both ran for it, but the Steelers' other outfielders yelled, "Barry! Barry!" The second baseman made the catch. Three outs.

Again the Steelers failed to score.

In the top of the third the Falcons put across three more runs, and in the fourth two more. It looked like a runaway for them.

Meanwhile, three grounders had zipped down to Gary at second, and he had fielded them all. Stan wondered if Coach Bartlett would put him in the game. He wouldn't mind playing now, especially since the Falcons were far in the lead.

In the bottom of the fourth inning his wish was granted. He replaced Gary at second. A high-bouncing grounder came to him, and for a moment a frightening sensation came over him. What if he muffed this one?

The next instant the ball struck the pocket of his glove. He yanked it out and snapped it to first.

"Out!" shouted the umpire.

The wave of fright left him. That, thought Stan, wasn't bad at all.

The next two men failed to reach first either.

With two outs in the fifth, Ronnie Woods, a left-hand hitter, pinch-hit for Frankie Smith. He looked awfully dangerous. But he missed two pitches, then popped to first to end the inning.

The Steelers went to the plate with determination. But Tommy, pitching one-hit ball so far, didn't let a man get to first.

Duffy led off in the sixth. Standing eagerly at the plate, waving his bat gently, he looked threatening. The first pitch came in and he swung.

Crack! It went sailing far out to left field! It cleared the fence by twenty feet!

But it was no homer. It was foul by ten feet.

"Straighten this one out, Duffy!" the boys on the bench yelled.

Blast! Another terrific poke out to left! But again it went foul.

Then Duffy let the third pitch go by.

"You're out!" cried the umpire.

Duffy whirled, stared at the man, then went sulking to the dugout.

"That blind bat," muttered Duffy. "It was way outside."

"George Page, then Stan Martin," said the scorekeeper. "Get on deck, Stan."

George walked to the plate, a bat on his

shoulder. Stan selected one from the dozen on the ground and swung it back and forth a few times. Then he knelt in the on-deck circle waiting for his turn. It came quickly. George popped the first pitch to third for the second out.

Stan stood nervously at the plate, batting left-handed.

"Wait for a good one!" he heard Coach Bartlett say.

The pitch came in chest-high. It was beautiful. It was the kind of pitch he liked. But he didn't swing.

"Strike one!"

Another pitch came in. Lower now, but not too low. He swung. *Crack!* A grounder down the first-base line. He started to run. The ball went foul halfway to first, and Stan went back to the plate.

"Ball!" An outside pitch.

"One and two!" said the umpire, announcing the count.

The next pitch came down the groove. Stan belted it. A line drive over the first baseman's head! Stan dropped the bat and raced to first.

He had done it. His first time at bat, and he had singled. He heard the praises from the fans, and he heard it from Coach Bartlett.

"Nice hit, Stanley, boy!"

What now? A steal? Would the coach have him try it with two outs?

The coach slipped his thumbs behind his belt. That didn't mean anything.

Larry took the first pitch. It was a ball.

The coach still had his thumbs behind his belt. Now he moved his hands along the belt to his hips. This meant something. The steal was on!

Stan waited till the pitcher climbed the mound, then took a safe lead off the bag. The pitcher lifted his arms, brought them down, looked over his shoulder at first, then threw home.

"Strike!" said the umpire.

Stan took off, his spikes pounding the ground, leaving puffs of dust behind him.

He slid into second. Dust clouded around him. The second baseman caught the peg from his catcher and slapped it on Stan. But Stan was already there.

Two outs, Stan on second, and the count on Larry was one ball, one strike. The stocky catcher dug in on the first pitch, and whacked it far out to deep center! He had hit one like this in the second inning.

The Steelers' center fielder turned around and bolted back. He was nearly against the center-field fence when he lifted his glove. The ball plopped into it and stuck there.

The fans groaned. This time Larry managed to get a little closer to first than he did before.

"Tough luck, Larry!" The boys on the bench echoed his feelings. "You'll get it over that fence yet!"

Stan had started running at the crack of the bat. Now, crossing home plate, he stopped a moment and smiled at the unlucky catcher.

"He played for you, Larry, or it would've been a hit," he said.

Larry paused, his eyes meeting Stan's for a moment while both of them thought back to that embarrassing incident in Stan's room when Larry, hurt from the shameful words Stan had called him, shouted an outburst back at Stan. Afterwards Stan had been sorry for what he'd said.

Suddenly a grin spread across Larry's sweating face.

"Thanks, Stan," he said.

And right away you could tell he had been sorry, too.

··· 6

The lead-off man for the Steelers walked, then raced to second base on a scratch hit to third. Jim Kendall charged the ball, but by the time he fielded it and snapped it to second, the runner was there.

"Let's get a double, Stan!" Don shouted from short.

A right-hander was batting. Although it was the bottom of the sixth inning and the Falcons were leading, 7 to 0, Stan felt nervous. A double play would mean two outs and only one more to get to complete the inning. Three more on top of that would complete the game.

But if he goofed on the play, the Steelers could start a rally. There were many games — even in the major leagues — when a losing team scored several runs in the closing innings of a game to win it.

Tommy got his signal from Larry and put his foot on the rubber. He took his stretch, checked the runners on first and second, then threw.

Crack! A sizzling grounder to short!

Stan ran to cover second. Don fielded the ball and snapped it to him. Nervously, Stan caught it. At the same time he feared the runner's bumping into him before he could throw the ball.

In one motion he turned his body to first and threw. Horror overwhelmed him as he saw his throw going too wide for George to catch. The ball just missed the runner, and went bouncing toward the fence.

There was his chance to pull off a good

play, and he had muffed it. Gary would have thrown it perfectly. *I bet right now he's laughing up his sleeve.*

Now it was one out and men on second and third.

Tommy worked hard on the batter. With two strikes and a ball on him, the hitter blasted a line drive to third. The ball traveled like a white bullet about seven feet off the ground. Jim lifted his hands. *Smack!* The ball struck his glove. But then it went through and fell to the ground!

The runner on third rushed back to tag up. Now, realizing that Jim had missed the hard-driven ball, he turned and streaked for home.

"Home, Jim! Home!" Don Marion shouted.

Jim picked up the ball and pegged it home. Larry, straddling the plate, caught the ball coming in like an arrow. He put it on the sliding runner, and the umpire jerked up his thumb.

"Out!"

Two outs, men on first and second. They hadn't tried to advance on the play.

The Steelers' next hitter waited out the pitches. Then, with a three-two count on him, he cut at a knee-high pitch. Whiff! Another strike-out for Tommy.

Coach Bartlett put in pinch-hitters in the top of the seventh, but nobody hit. The Steelers took their turn at bat for the last time in the game. Three men up, three men down. They lost, 7 to 0.

Stan didn't linger around to listen to the comments about the game. He saw Gary Newman's face and that was enough.

That evening Dottie, Stan's seventeen-year-old sister, got dressed to go out. It was a common routine, and Stan hardly thought about it.

When the front doorbell rang, Stan went to answer it. He found Jeb Newman standing there, and stared.

Jeb taking Dottie out? What was the matter with her head?

"Hi, Stan." Jeb greeted him with a smile. "Dottie, in?"

You know doggone well she's in, Stan thought. "Yes, she's in. Just a minute. Hey, Dottie!"

He hardly turned around, though, before she was there, smiling very politely and looking too pretty for a guy like Jeb Newman.

After they left, Stan closed the door disgustedly and turned on the television set in the living room. He watched the program with mild interest, for his mind was on the game he had played today.

Phil came home, wearing gray slacks and a fancy sport shirt.

He smiled at Stan. "Hi, little buddy. How'd you make out?"

"We won," Stan said. "Seven to nothing."

"Wow! Did you play?"

"A few innings."

"Any hits?"

"Singled." Stan paused. "I muffed on a double play."

Phil looked at him. His smile faded.

"Don Marion caught the ground ball and we got the man out at second. But I threw wild to first."

"They didn't get any runs, so what are you worried about?"

"They almost did, though, if Jim Kendall hadn't thrown a man out at home. He missed a line drive, but picked it up in time."

Phil pulled a hassock in front of Stan and sat on it. He placed his hands on Stan's knees and looked at his brother with a warm, kind light in his eyes.

"Little buddy," he said, "you're like me.

You get hurt easily, just the way I do. And neither one of us can help it. Tell me, how much do you like baseball?"

"I like it," Stan said. "I guess I like it better than football or basketball, even."

"It's a tough game," Phil said. "Sometimes you play your heart out, and you'll still fail. You'll sit back and wonder why you've failed. Why didn't you get that hit? Why didn't you catch that ball? Those things will run through your mind and sometimes you'll wish you had never started playing the game."

Stan stared at his brother. "Is that why you're not playing now, Phil?"

Phil shrugged, and avoiding Stan's eyes. "I did all right for a while. Then I missed a few grounders, and at the plate I'd either strike out or hit into somebody's hands. Couldn't do a thing right, so I was benched."

"Didn't they give you another chance?"

"Yes. But I was no longer a regular. I was

afraid that they were going to send me to a team in a lower league, and I didn't want that."

"So you didn't go back at all."

"That's right," said Phil.

"But it's different with you, Phil," said Stan. "You were playing professional."

"At one time I was your age and playing sand-lot ball too," replied Phil.

"But that letter I got," said Stan. "That letter printed from words cut out of a newspaper. It says I shouldn't quit. Who wouldn't want me to quit, Phil?"

Phil grinned and shook his head. "I don't know, little buddy," he said. "Obviously, somebody."

··· 7

Stan held the *Courier-Star* open to the sports pages, and was reading the Falcons' box score of the game with the Steelers.

	AB	H	RBI	R
Marion ss	2	1	0	2
eFinn	1	0	0	0
Kendall 3b	5	2	0	1
Smith lf	3	2	0	2
aWoods lf	1	0	0	0
Powers cf	3	2	4	1
Page lf	4	0	0	0
Newman 2b	3	2	0	1
bMartin 2b	1	1	0	0
Jones c	3	1	3	0
Lee rf	3	1	0	0

cCollins	1	0	0	0
Hart p	3	1	0	0
dR. Jones	1	0	0	0
Totals	34	13	7	7

a — Flied out for Smith in 5th; b — Singled for Newman in 6th; c — Struck out for Lee in 7th, d — Grounded out for Hart in 7th; e — Popped out for Marion in 7th.

Falcons . . .	203 200 0 —	7
Steelers . . .	000 000 0 —	0

Presently he sensed somebody watching him. He lowered the newspaper and saw Dottie standing behind him with her hands on her hips and a flattering smile on her lips.

"Bet I know what you're reading," she said.

He grinned, and looked back at the paper. "Maybe you do," he answered.

"Oh, don't be so rude," said Dottie. "You got a hit, and you guys won, didn't you? What more do you want?"

"Nothing," he said. He recalled that she had gone out with Jeb Newman the other night, and he went cold all over.

"Why did you go out with that Jeb Newman guy?" he said, talking through the paper. "What's the matter with Joe Warner? Or Tom Miller? You've been out with them before."

"There's nothing wrong with them," she said. "But Jeb's nice, too." She laughed. "You're just prejudiced."

He stared at her over the edge of the paper. "Preju-what?"

"Prejudiced. You don't like him because his brother Gary is working hard to be the regular second baseman on the team, and you want to play second base yourself."

He closed the paper hard, folded it, and tossed it on the coffee table.

"He tells you everything, doesn't he?" Stan said, and started to walk past his sister on his way out of the room.

644

She grabbed his arm. "Stan," she said, "don't be like that. Jeb is really a nice guy."

He looked up into her green eyes. There was a gentleness in them that brought a smile to his lips.

"Maybe you're right," he said. "Maybe I am preju — whatever that word is."

"Prejudiced." She laughed.

"Maybe I am prejudiced." He echoed her laughter, then turned, and walked out.

The Falcons practiced at five-thirty that afternoon. Jeb was hitting grounders to Gary when the rest of them arrived at the field. *Boy!* Stan thought. *Gary really wants to make sure he plays!*

Coach Bartlett had the boys bat around twice — hitting five and laying one down. Then he showed them how to bunt. Stan watched with strong interest. He had always thought that bunting was just for somebody who couldn't hit. But now he heard the coach explain how really important it was.

"A good bunt can advance a man from first to second," he said, "and put that man in a position to score. If a man is on third the batter can squeeze him in. A lot of games have been won with a run squeezed in, so don't take bunting lightly."

On Friday they played the Jaguars. Gary started at second. In the first two innings he handled three grounders without an error. The Jaguars played good defensive ball and began hitting Lefty Kellar hard. The score was tied in the fifth, 3-all. With one out and men on first and third, Coach Bartlett put Tommy Hart in to pitch.

A hit meant at least one run. An extra-base drive could mean two runs.

Tommy threw in some warm-up pitches, then waited for the hitter to enter the batting box. Tension mounted and the infielders began chattering in what sounded like a lot of jumbled words.

"Getimout, Tommy! Getimout!"

"Throweminthere, Tom! Strikeimout!"

Tommy stepped on the rubber, stretched, and delivered. *Crack!* The ball zipped across the infield close to second base. Gary ran hard, reached for the hop, caught it, and snapped the ball to shortstop Don Marion covering the bag. Don whipped the ball to first.

In time! A double play!

"Nice play, Gary," said the coach, as the second baseman came trotting in. "Fielded that ball like a major leaguer. Nice play, Don."

Then the Falcons broke the tie. With a man on first, Duffy Powers socked a double and George Page singled. The Falcons went ahead by two runs.

Stan replaced Gary at second. He snagged a pop fly, then bobbled a grounder. He picked up the ball quickly and, almost without looking, snapped the ball to first. The ball went wide, and the runner advanced to second.

However, the Jaguars didn't score. Neither did they push across any runs in the final inning, and the score ended with the Falcons coming out on top, 5 to 3.

On July 5, Stan played the first three innings and bobbled two grounders. One of them resulted in a run for the opponents, the Red Devils. But the Falcons managed to keep ahead from the first inning on and won again, 3 to 1.

We're lucky to win, thought Stan. *I'm playing as if I'm a real rookie!*

He was worried out there. He was thinking about how much better Gary Newman was than he. That was why he kept bobbling so many grounders.

Phil was right. You can love the game with all your heart. But your heart can get hurt awfully easy.

The same thing was happening to Stan that had happened to Phil.

··· 8

The hot July days skipped by quickly. Stan almost forgot about the mysterious letter he had received. He had thought that some member of his family had sent it — perhaps his Dad — but he wasn't· sure.

So far Phil hadn't seen the Falcons play. Stan didn't encourage him, either. Dad and Mom went as often as they could, and so did Dottie.

"I don't see what you're worried about," said Dad after the Falcons' game with the Clippers. "You got a hit and made two assists. Is that bad?"

It did not happen to be bad that time, but the Falcons had lost the game, 7 to 4. Then the Comets gave them a lacing, 6 to 2, a game in which Stan went without a hit. However, he didn't feel so bad. Some of the others went hitless, too, including Duffy Powers.

One warm afternoon, as they were riding in Phil's boat, Larry remarked to Stan and Tommy, "You know, there's one guy who surprises me on our ball team."

"Who?" said Stan.

They were discussing baseball, trying to figure out why the Falcons had lost their third game in a row yesterday. In that game they had gone two extra innings. Then a triple broke the tie, ending the game in the Red Devils' favor, 7 to 6.

"Gary Newman," said Larry. "That guy's really gone to town. Know what his batting average is?"

Stan turned away and looked at the waves swirling alongside the fast-moving boat. He knew, all right. And so did everybody else on the team.

"Three-seventy-two," said Tommy. "The highest on the team."

"And he hasn't missed many at second," went on Larry.

Maybe he didn't realize he was "rubbing it in" Stan. And maybe he did. It was a wonder Stan wasn't benched for good.

The boys had played catch on shore and had brought their gloves and a ball on board with them. Now Stan struck the dark, oily pocket of his fielder's glove hard with his right fist. Why did the guys keep bringing up Gary's name? He wished he had never heard of Gary Newman.

"Hey, you guys!" yelled Phil suddenly. "Look what's coming over that hill at our left!"

The three boys turned. A yell burst from all three. The northwestern sky was almost black. Mountainous clouds bore toward them, twisting in the sky before a strong wind.

A streak of lightning flashed and then thunder rumbled.

"We'd better head for shore right now!" Phil said, turning the wheel of the craft. "Put on your life jackets! We can't take any chances!"

The boys each turned to pick up a life jacket. As Stan reached for his, the boat turned and he lost his balance. Quickly, he caught himself, but his fielder's glove slipped from his hand and went over the edge.

"My glove!" he shouted. "Phil! My glove!"

Panic overtook him as he saw his almost-new glove riding the crest of a wave, then gradually sinking.

If he didn't do something right now, that glove would be gone forever!

Stan dived into the water and felt the pleasant shock of its warmth cover his body. He opened his eyes and looked around hastily. Then he rose, whipped the water from his head and leaped high to look for the glove. Again and again he leaped, searching the dark, greenish water.

Then he knew that the worst had happened. He'd never see that glove again.

... 9

You crazy fool!" yelled Phil as he slowed the boat alongside Stan so that Tommy and Larry could haul the boy in. "What're you trying to do? Drown?"

"I wanted to save my glove," Stan murmured hoarsely.

"Save your glove?" Larry echoed. "You make it sound as if it was human."

With his friends' help, Stan got into the boat and sat on the rear seat. Instantly, Phil increased the throttle, and the boat began speeding forward again.

"To blazes with the glove!" yelled Phil over his shoulder. "I'm trying to save us from being

655

hit by a storm and you want to save a glove! Try to top that, will you?"

Phil would say that, of course. Perhaps he had never felt the way Stan did about a glove. Perhaps that was why he didn't care about playing baseball any more.

"Here, put this on," said Tommy, and helped Stan with a life jacket.

Stan steadied himself against the bouncing of the boat. Already the waves were rolling high. Drops of water fell upon them. For a moment Stan wasn't sure whether they came from the water about them or the heavy clouds swirling overhead.

Again lightening pierced the sky for a moment and then abruptly vanished. Again thunder rumbled.

The boys hung on for dear life to the sides of the boat. Ahead of them the shoreline seemed to be rising and falling. Trees leaned under the power of the wind. Leaves broke loose from their branches, flew swiftly and crazily through the air. Birds swooped low and high, carried every which way by the wind. The drops fell thicker, and now Stan knew they were falling from those black clouds.

The boat lifted on the crest of a wave, then came down *smack!* The bow pierced the water, and gallons of the churning whiteness spilled into the boat, covering the boys' feet.

Phil hung desperately onto the wheel to keep the boat from getting out of his control. It was up to him now. It was a fight between him and the mad waters of the lake.

For a while the gap between the boat and the shore seemed to remain the same. Then slowly it closed, and Stan saw several men appear on the dock. They were waiting to help pull in the boat and secure it.

Finally the boat rocked close to the dock. The boys tossed out the rope. The men caught it, pulled the boat in against a pair of rubber tires, and secured it. The last *puff-puff* of the motor died away as Phil turned it off.

"Thanks, guys," he said gratefully. "We'd have a real damaged boat if it weren't for you."

"We were ready to call the Coast Guard," one of the men replied, grinning.

Hardly five minutes had passed when a car drove up, stopped with a sudden jerk, and three anxious-looking people jumped out.

"Stan! Phil! Are you all right?"

The boys grinned at Mom, Dad, and Dottie, who stared at them white-faced.

"All right?" echoed Phil innocently. "Why? Is something wrong?"

Dottie's green eyes flared. "Don't be smart, Philip Andrew Martin! We saw that storm coming, and we knew you were out on the lake. You and Stan — all of you! Of course, if we knew you were such a hot-shot pilot —"

"He is!" Stan cried out seriously. "He saved our lives!"

Dottie smiled. Her eyes softened.

"I'm not so sure about that," said Phil humbly.

"Well, I am!" said Stan.

"So are we," said Larry earnestly. "If it wasn't for Phil, we might have all drowned."

"Drowned? With your life jackets on?" Phil chuckled. Even with his face streaming wet from the rain, you could see it color a little. "Look, the four of us don't mind," he went on, pointing at himself and his three companions. "But don't you folks care about getting wet?"

"Yes, we do!" Dad yelled, and led the race to the car and its shelter from the storm.

··· *10*

On Thursday, July 21, Stan watched the start of the Clippers-Falcons game from the bench. Some of the boys sitting beside him, especially Larry's brother Ray, Ronnie Woods, and Mose Finn, chattered without letting up a minute. They seemed satisfied just wearing the Falcons' uniform. Fuzzy Collins was more quiet, like Stan.

"Come on, you guys," said Mose. "Where's that chatter?"

This nudged Stan and Fuzzy into some yelling, but not for long.

Stan didn't know about Fuzzy, nor did he

care very much. He had his own self to worry about.

He didn't like warming the bench three or four innings a game. Of course he knew all fifteen players couldn't play at the same time, although the better ones did play every inning.

"Got to keep in the better players so no team could shellac us," Coach Bennett once said.

Not playing regularly proved he wasn't one of the better ones. That was what griped him, and made him feel the way he did now. The season was almost half over, and he wasn't a bit better now than he had been at the beginning.

Phil was right. Don't get to love the game very much. You might get awfully discouraged.

I'm awfully discouraged now, thought Stan.

He watched the Clippers take their first

raps and go down under Left Kellar's fast-ball pitching. The Falcons came to bat. Frankie Smith smacked a solid single, but he didn't get past first.

The Clippers started off the second inning with a single, followed by a sacrifice bunt that put the man in scoring position. A double sent him around the bases. Another run scored before the Falcons could get the Clippers out.

That last hit was a hot grounder to Gary's left side. Gary almost had it. But the ball struck the tip of his glove and went bouncing to the outfield.

I could've caught that, Stan thought. *I would've kept that last run from scoring.*

It looked easy from the bench.

I have a hobby at home. My airplane and spaceship models. I can work on them. After a time I can forget baseball. A guy can forget it, can't he, if he's away from it for a while?

By the fifth inning the Clippers had a strong

hold of the game. They were leading, 4 to 0.

"Okay, Stan," said Coach Bartlett. "Get on second. Lots of hustle now."

Stan picked up the new glove Dad had bought him and raced out to his position at second. A moment later the Clippers' lead-off man beat out a dribbling grounder to third. The Falcons' infield moved in, expecting a bunt.

It was a bunt! The ball rolled toward first, just inside the foul line!

George Page charged in after it. Stan rushed to cover first. At the same time Lefty ran toward first, too.

"I'll cover, Lefty!" Stan yelled.

Lefty stopped. George fielded the ball, turned, and whipped it to first. The ball just missed the runner. Stan stretched, and caught the ball in time.

"Out!" cried the umpire.

Stan felt good as he hustled back into

position. The next hitter flied out and Lefty walked the third. Then a grounder was hit to short, and Don tossed the ball to Stan at second for the forced out.

He didn't get to bat this inning, but he would the next. The Clippers, hotter than fire, mowed down the Falcons one, two, three in the bottom of the sixth, then scored two more runs at their turn at bat.

With one out and a man on, Stan stepped to the plate. He took a called strike, then leaned into a shoulder-high pitch and swung with all his might.

"Strike two!" cried the umpire, as Stan's bat swished through the empty air.

He took a ball, and then another. Now the count was two and two.

Stan stepped out of the box and touched his sweating hands into the soft dirt. *I can't strike out*, he thought. *I just can't!*

He got back into the box, and the pitcher went into his stretch. The ball breezed in.

It looked a little inside, but it might cut the corner!

Stan swung.

Smack!

The sound was the ball hitting the pocket of the catcher's mitt.

"You're out!" yelled the umpire.

Stan went back to the dugout, sick at heart.

Fuzzy batted for Eddie Lee, and fanned, ending the ball game. The Clippers took it, 6 to 0.

Stan spent a lot of time the next day looking at the spaceship models in the Hobby Shop on Darby Street. He would earn money somehow — there were always people who wanted their lawns cut — and save it up to buy more models. He could spend hours and hours just assembling models. It wouldn't be long before he'd forget baseball altogether.

He didn't say much around the house, but

the way everybody looked at him they certainly must have suspected that he wasn't happy about something. Mom tried to pry the trouble out of him, but he told her that there was nothing wrong.

"I bet!" said Dottie, who was suspicious about anything.

The next day he got a letter. He stared at the address on the envelope. It was exactly like the one he had received before. The words were cut out of either a newspaper or a magazine.

He tore off the end of the envelope and took out the letter. This, too, was made up of cut-out words.

YOU ARE GIVING UP TOO EASILY. NO BOXER QUIT BECAUSE HE LOST A FIGHT. YOU LOVE BASEBALL. IT'S A GOOD GAME. STICK WITH IT.

The last three words were underlined twice in ink.

"Mom," he said, the letter trembling in

his hands, "who keeps sending me these letters?"

Mom shrugged her shoulders. "I don't know," she said. "But whoever it is must certainly know what's bothering you!"

··· *11*

Everybody in the family read the strange letter. If one of them had sent it, his — or her — face did not show it. Everyone acted just as surprised as Stan did, and looked at each other suspiciously, too.

Maybe it's somebody on the team, Stan thought. But who would care enough about him to send a letter like that?

Tommy Hart? Larry? Or could it be Coach Bartlett?

He did not mention the letters to any of his teammates. Maybe one of these days the person who had sent them would say something unintentionally that would give him away.

"Just the same, that letter makes good sense," Dad said. "Everybody should take its advice."

Phil's face colored a little, and he turned and walked away.

Beginning with the next practice, Stan played harder and harder. He tried to forget about himself and just do what he had to do, and do it the best he could.

He improved fast. Coach Bartlett noticed it.

"I've been noticing you, Stan," he said. "You've picked up a lot of spark lately. Just as if you've shaken off some kind of bugaboo. What's happened?"

Stan grinned shyly, and shrugged. "I don't know. Guess I'm just playing harder, that's all."

"Guess you are," said the coach. "Okay, get on second. Gary!" he shouted across the diamond. "Play short! I want to try something new!"

Gary looked puzzledly at him. "Short? But Coach, I've never played short."

"Don't say never," replied Coach Bartlett. "A good infielder plays any position in the infield. Your arm is strong. Get on short and don't argue."

Gary got on short, and Coach Bartlett began hitting grounders to him and Stan. They worked double plays. The coach showed Stan how to cover second and then throw to first when the ball was hit to short. Then he showed Gary how to work the play when the ball was hit to second.

"You're doing great," he commented after he had the boys sweating. "Something tells me you're going to turn into a great double-play combination."

Coach Bartlett said things like that. The kids liked him for it, even though what he said didn't always turn out to be true.

It was Wednesday, July 27, when the coach had Gary and Stan try out their new positions in a game. The new line-up was as follows:

J. Kendall	3b
S. Martin	2b
F. Smith	lf
D. Powers	cf
G. Page	1b
G. Newman	ss
L. Jones	c
E. Lee	rf
T. Hart	p

The Falcons had first raps against the Steelers. Jim walked, and Stan laid a beautiful bunt down the first-base line to put Jim in scoring position. Frankie socked two pitches back to the screen, then whiffed. Two outs.

Duffy Powers walked to the plate and smashed the first pitch to deep center for a triple. Jim scored, and then George beat out a dribbler to third, scoring Duffy.

Gary walked, and Stan was sure that the

Steelers' coach would put in a new pitcher. But he didn't, even when Larry singled and Eddie Lee singled right behind him. It was Tommy who ended the merry-go-round, hitting a ball to deep center which the center fielder caught almost without moving.

Score: 4 to 0.

The Steelers were helpless at the plate, but for the next several innings they held the Falcons to one hit. In the fifth the Falcons found their eye again, and blasted the ball for three runs. This time the Steelers' pitcher went to the showers.

At their turn at bat, the Steelers seemed to find their eye at last. The first two batters singled, and Tommy walked the third to load the bases.

Coach Bartlett waved the infielders in.

For the first time since the game had started, Stan felt scared. What should he do if the ball was hit to him? Throw home, or to second? He looked at Gary, and then at

Tommy. But Gary was leaning forward, his hands on his knees, chattering for all he was worth. He had lots of life, Gary did. Tommy was facing third, rubbing the ball, just taking his time. He didn't look worried at all.

The first pitch was a called strike. The second was in there, too. The batter swung. *Crack!* A hot grounder down to second, right at Stan!

He had to make his decision — right *now!* Home, or first?

He caught the hop, whipped it home. Out! Larry snapped the ball to third. Safe by half a step!

"Nice peg, Stan!" said Tommy, smiling.

One away. Still three on.

A high pop fly to third, going foul, with Mose Finn going under it. Mose had taken Jim's place. A warm relief came over Stan. *Mose will catch this ball and I won't have to worry about a double play,* he thought.

The ball came down, a small, white meteor. It struck Mose's glove, and bounced out!

"Get a basket!" somebody shouted from the stands.

"Butterfingers!" Stan muttered to himself.

The next pitch was a ground ball to short. Stan raced to cover second. Gary fielded the ball and snapped it hard to Stan.

The ball struck the thumb of Stan's glove and sailed past him!

He turned, ran after the ball, and picked it up. But it was too late. A runner had just crossed the plate.

"Come on, Stan!" shouted Gary, angrily. "Hold on to 'em!"

Stan blushed. Even though it was the Steelers' first run, Stan felt that it was his fault. Gary had thrown that ball a little too hard, but he still should have had it.

Tommy fanned the next man, and the boys hustled off the field.

"You threw that ball too hard, Gary," accused Coach Bartlett. "When you're that close to second, throw it easier. Watch it the next time."

Stan looked, baffled, at the coach, and then at Gary, who went silently to the dugout. So the coach had noticed. Suddenly, he felt a lot better.

The Falcons went on to win the game, 8 to 1.

··· 12

I need a vacation," said Phil just before August rolled around. "I haven't been away from home in a long time."

Dad smiled. "Where do you want to go?"

Phil shrugged. "South somewhere. Georgia. Florida. Just to see some country I haven't seen before."

Phil had no steady job. He had worked on construction for a while, on the new senior high school. Then he had had a job as a stock clerk in a computer factory. He seldom complained, but he hadn't acted satisfied with either job.

"Boy! Wish I could go with you," cried Stan.

"Maybe you can — sometime," Phil said, pinching Stan's nose. "But not this time."

"We'll miss you," Dottie said, her cheeks dimpling as she smiled. "But I think a two weeks' vacation will do you good."

Phil laughed. "Want to get rid of me?"

"Just for two weeks," replied his sister, and kissed him on the cheek.

Phil looked at Stan. "If you want any rides in the boat, little buddy, Dad will take you. Don't you ever take it out by yourself."

"Don't worry," said Stan. "Jeez, don't you think I know?"

Phil packed his suitcase, and Dad drove him to the bus station.

"Write," Dad said.

"I will," Phil promised.

Things did not go very well around second base during the practice sessions. Stan felt sure he knew what it was. Gary just didn't like the idea of Stan's taking over at second.

677

Was second base very different from shortstop? Stan didn't think so, yet it could be only for that reason that Gary acted that way.

Jeb was almost always at the practices, too, sitting in the dugout with his legs stretched out in front of him and his arms crossed over his chest. He had dated Dottie again and Stan didn't like that at all. There were so many real nice guys. Why did she have to go out with him?"

The funny part of it was, Stan really couldn't think of anything bad about Jeb. Maybe he just didn't *want* to like Jeb because he showed Gary pointers on the ball field. Phil never had done that with Stan.

In a way, when you thought about it, Phil was a strange sort of guy.

Gary played the entire game at short against the Red Devils. Once, a double-play ball, he threw the pill too hard to Stan just as he had done before, and Stan missed it.

The very next pitch was hit for a grounder and Stan didn't get his glove down low enough. The ball sizzled through his legs to the outfield and a run scored.

"The coach must be blind if he thinks you're an infielder," said Gary with a very angry look on his face.

A double drove in another run for the Red Devils. Stan was glad when Fuzzy Collins took his place in the fourth inning.

Two runs were all the Red Devils scored. The Falcons beat them, 5 to 2.

They trimmed the Comets, 11 to 1, and on August 4 they played the Steelers again. No team was worried about the Steelers. Whoever had named that team must have figured that they would be tough as nails. But the Steelers were in the cellar and by the looks of things would stay there.

The Falcons had a field day against them. Everybody batted around at least three times, and some four and five. Stan and Gary pulled off two sparkling double plays. Two other times Gary snapped the ball too wildly for Stan to catch. Gary said nothing at these times, as if he knew Stan couldn't possibly have caught those throws.

The Falcons had a lot of men left on. Otherwise the score would have been worse than 9 to 3.

Picture post cards came from Phil. They were stamped in Atlanta, Georgia; Memphis, Tennessee; and Nashville, Tennessee.

"Boy! He's really traveling!" murmured Stan excitedly.

Then, for a few days during the second week of Phil's vacation, there was no word from him.

"He's sent us a card almost every day," Mom said. "Guess he wants to rest a while."

But Mom looked worried. Of course there was no reason why she should be worried, but Mom was like that. Dad got a little disgusted with her.

"He's a man now, Jen. He can take care of himself. You have to get used to that fact."

"I know," Mom said quietly. "But it isn't easy."

And then, exactly on the day that was to end Phil's two weeks' vacation, Mom and Dad received a letter from him.

Hello, everybody! Sorry I haven't dropped you even a post card these last few days, but I've been very busy. Doing what? Well, listen! I have just signed with Harport! Yes, I'm back with them, and I'm happy! I'll have to come home for some of my things, and to tell my boss I'm quitting. Until then, be good and be cheerful!

Love,
Phil

··· 13

Phil flew home and Dad drove to the airport to meet him. Stan went along, too, excited as ever over the news about Phil's playing professional baseball again.

Phil had barely climbed down the steps from the plane when Stan rushed up to him and asked:

"How are you doing, Phil? Are you hitting that apple?"

Phil grinned, and pinched Stan's nose as he sometimes did. "Maybe not like Mantle, but I'm hitting. Let's wait till I get home and I'll tell you all about it. Right now I'm so hungry I could eat a bear!"

Mom and Dottie kissed Phil as if he had

been away a year. Then Mom cooked a quick meal and everybody sat around the table listening to Phil talk while he tried to eat.

"Oh, let the poor boy eat," said Mom.

But whenever Phil said anything, she was all ears too.

"So you took your vacation just for the purpose of trying out with Harport again," said Dad, grinning.

"That's right," answered Phil between bites, his glance swinging from one to the other. "I wanted to play baseball again. Matter of fact, nobody really knows how much I missed it and wanted to play."

His eyes rested on Stan for a moment, then turned away. I know, Stan thought. I know *exactly* how he felt.

Phil said he had to return to Harport day after tomorrow. They were playing a night game.

"Oh, boy!" said Stan, and looked up at Dad

with wide, eager eyes. "Can we go back with Phil, Dad? Can we see him play?"

"That's a good idea!" said Phil. Smiling, he tapped his left hip pocket where his wallet was. "I signed for a nice bonus. The trip will be on me. Better yet, how about Mom and Dottie going, too?"

"Nothing doing!" cried Mom. "No airplane trips for me! I'm keeping my feet on the ground!"

"Mom," said Dottie, "don't be so oldfashioned. We'll make the trip. Phil will buy us all round-trip tickets, and we'll go. Right, big brother?"

"Right!" said Phil.

Mom insisted she wasn't going by air, and that was that. She kept her word, too, at least until the next afternoon.

Once again Dad got disgusted with her.

"All right," he said. "If you're not going, neither am I."

"Oh, no," Mom said. "You're going. *I'm* staying home."

When the plane departed the next afternoon, Phil, Stan, Dottie, Dad *and* Mom were on it.

Stan laughed when the plane taxied down the long runway, and then took off. Mom had her eyes closed. It wasn't until the plane was quite high that she opened them again and dared a glance out of the window.

"Oh, my," she said.

She was quiet for a while, fascinated by the view passing slowly underneath them. The earth below stretched out like a giant patchwork quilt. Hills loomed in the distance. Rivers wound crookedly, finally emptying into small lakes that flashed the sunlight like tiny mirrors.

"This is beautiful," Mom finally said. "Really beautiful."

At her side, Dad grinned with satisfaction,

winked at Stan, and then leaned his head back to rest.

The game, played under lights, drew a large crowd. Stan and his family sat in reserved seats, directly behind the Harport dugout. Phil, dressed in his white uniform, winked at them as he walked past. Broad-shouldered and head held high, he looked even taller than he did in regular clothes.

The game got under way. Phil played short, and Stan watched him eagerly. It had been a long time since he had seen Phil play. Phil moved lightly on his feet, and he threw the ball like a bullet.

Each time a ball galloped down to short, Stan bit his lip. But Phil played the ball like the professional he was, catching the hop and whipping it to first for the put-out. Once he worked a double play without an assist. The ball was hit to his side of second base. Running hard, he nabbed the ball in his gloved hand, stepped on the bag, then pegged to first.

Then, in the fifth inning, he fumbled a hard-hit grounder. He finally picked up the ball and fired it to first, but the runner was already there.

"Oh-oh," muttered Dad.

Stan got nervous. How would Phil act now? Would that error bother him so that he might miss another? Or would he not play as well as he had been playing the earlier part of the game?

In the seventh inning a hard-driven ball headed between third and short. There were two outs, and a man was on third. Harport trailed by one run. This extra run would be an "insurance" run for the other team.

Phil's too far from it! thought Stan. He just can't possibly get that ball!

Then Phil stretched out his *bare right hand,* caught the ball, and pegged it to first!

The throw was long, swift, and accurate. It beat the runner by a step!

"Wow!" gasped Dad. "Did you see that?"

"Man, what a catch!" cried Stan.

The fans gave Phil a big hand.

So far, at the plate, Phil had grounded out and drawn a walk. Now, with a man on, he stepped into the batter's box again. He was a right-hand hitter. He stood tall and loose.

The pitches came in, and he looked them over carefully. At last he had a full count on him — three and two.

"This is the one that counts," whispered Stan excitedly.

The pitch came in, and Phil smacked it. It sailed far out to left, over the fielder's head! The ball struck the fence and bounced back. A run scored and Phil stopped on third base with a triple.

The next hitter scored Phil. Harport kept ahead the rest of the game and won it, 4 to 3.

The crowd cheered, and then began to drift out of the ball park.

Dad stood up, a pleased smile on his lips.

"Phil will stay with the game now," he said, almost to himself. "He's not afraid of losing any more. He's not afraid of making errors, or striking out. I wonder what made him change his mind?"

··· *14*

The family stayed at a motel that night. They saw Phil the next morning for a while, and both Dad and Stan praised him.

"Man, what a catch you made!" said Stan. "Didn't that ball sting?"

Phil grinned. "A little."

They spent a couple of hours with him, seeing some of the sights around the city. Then they had lunch with him. Later a taxi drove them to the airport, and they boarded their plane for home.

Stan watched clouds drift past the right wing of the big plane.

"I've been thinking about Phil, Dad," he said.

"You have?"

"Yes. I bet he's thought about those letters. Those mysterious letters I've been getting. What do you think, Dad?"

His father patted his knee and smiled. "I wouldn't be a bit surprised, son. Not surprised at all."

After the plane landed, Dad called a taxi to drive them home.

When Stan walked into his room, he found a package on his bed. It was box-shaped, and wrapped in red and white striped paper with a large bow. Stan looked for a tag but didn't find it.

"It *must* be mine," he said to himself, his heart tingling.

He took off the bow and the wrapping. The box clearly showed what the package contained. A *Voyager* model!

"Phil gave it to me!" he shouted.

Sure enough, there was a card inside the

box. *Hi, little buddy. I hope you like this. Phil.*

Stan carried it out to the living room, almost stumbling in his haste, and showed it to Mom, Dad, and Dottie. They acted surprised, but almost immediately he knew they were only pretending. They had known about the package all the time!

He spent the next morning putting the model together. In the afternoon he looked over the baseball schedule and discovered that the Falcons had a game with the Jaguars. They had split with the Jags before, so Stan wasn't worried.

Suddenly he remembered Gary whipping the ball to him so hard that he had to miss it. How could Coach Barrett expect to make a good combination around second base if Gary insisted on being bullheaded?

Mom, Dad, and Dottie came to the game and sat in the bleachers behind first base.

Stan wished they hadn't come. He and Gary were starting, and he knew that things weren't going to go just right between them.

Then he remembered the letters, and Phil. Phil had conquered the thing that had held him back from playing baseball. It must have been the letters — those strange, mysterious letters — that had changed Phil.

As long as I think about those letters I feel all right. It's as though they have some magic power.

The Jaguars were first up. A pop fly and two grounders to the infield took care of their first three men.

Jim Kendall, leading off for the Falcons, drew a walk, and Stan bunted him to second.

Frankie Smith, digging in hard, hit a dribbler down to second. He was thrown out, but Jim advanced to third. Then Duffy got up and lifted a high fly toward left field. It soared like a meteor. This ball was really going into orbit. Duffy tossed his bat aside and beat it for first.

But then the ball curved, and disappeared over the left-field fence!

"Foul ball!" boomed the umpire.

Duffy was nearly to second base. Shaking his head, he cut back across the diamond, picked up his bat, and tried it again. The Jaguars' pitcher slipped the next one by him. Then Duffy poled one to center field and the ball was caught.

Three away.

The Jaguars' clean-up man swung two bats from one shoulder to the other as he stood just outside the batter's box. Then he flipped one aside and stepped to the plate. He was a left-hand hitter and looked mighty dangerous.

The outfielders moved toward the right. Eddie Lee went back ten steps. In the field Stan and George Page backed to the edge of the grass.

Tommy got his signal, wound up, and delivered.

"Ball one!" shouted the umpire.

The next one was in there, and the batter swung. *Crack!* A high fly ball over second base!

Stan ran back for it, watching the ball constantly. Ahead of him he heard Eddie Lee coming toward him on a mad run, and a horrible fright went through him. He'd read about players colliding. Sometimes it resulted in a serious injury. That mustn't happen now! Not when he had a chance to nab that fly!

"Let me take it, Eddie!" he yelled desperately. "Let me take it!"

"Go ahead!" cried Eddie.

The ball came down swiftly over his left shoulder. Stan put out his glove. *Smack!* He had it!

"Nice catch, Stan!" said Eddie.

Cheers and loud applause greeted Stan as

he turned and pegged the ball in to Gary. A warm feeling overwhelmed him as he trotted back to his position. He noticed that Gary didn't say a word, but Stan didn't care now.

I'll play the best I can. I'll hustle after every ball. If I make an error I won't feel as if the world has dropped on my head. Even major leaguers miss them sometimes. I'll try not to worry, or get disgusted again. Those are the things I must remember. And if I must sit on the bench, so what? There's another day coming, and another game.

Tommy fanned the next batter, and the third batter popped out.

"Let's pick up some runs," urged Coach Bartlett as the Falcons came to bat.

But the innings slipped by, and they didn't get a man on base. That little right-hander on the mound for the Jaguars was pitching a great game. Frankie, Duffy, Stan, and a couple of others had gone down swinging at his fast ball.

"What's he got? Nothing!" grumbled Duffy. Yet the little pitcher had the Falcons eating out of his hand.

And then, in the fifth, with none on, the Jaguars' clean-up hitter broke the nothing-nothing tie. He poled one over the left-field fence for a home run.

··· 15

The long hit inspired the Jaguars. The next man singled. Then, even though Jim and George played in on the grass, a bunt got by Jim, and men were safe on first and second.

The Falcons' infield began to chatter seriously. Coach Bartlett had put substitutes in several positions, but still kept in Gary and Stan.

Then — a hard-hit ball down to short! Gary fielded it, pegged it to Stan!

A wild throw! It sailed past Stan, and the runners moved! Fuzzy Collins, now playing first, chased after the ball. The runners reached their bases and held up.

Bases loaded and no outs!

The infielders moved in. The Jaguars had one run, but a hit now could mean one or two more. Possibly three. It would be a shame to let the Jaguars plaster them with a shutout like that.

Tommy Hart worked hard on the batter and struck him out. Then a ground ball was hit to second, only a few feet from the bag. Stan raced for it and caught it in his gloved hand. He could touch the bag and throw to first. Or he could touch the runner coming from first and then throw it. But he might lose some precious time. He didn't dare risk it.

He tossed the ball easily and accurately to Gary. Gary stepped on the edge of the bag, then pegged the ball to first.

A double play!

Three outs, and the Falcons trotted in, glad that that hectic inning was over.

Coach Bartlett motioned to Gary. Stan,

sitting within earshot of them, heard the coach say:

"Gary, you had better change your attitude out there or I'll have to bench you the next game, our last of the season. I've warned you once before. I won't again. Knock that chip off your shoulder and play ball as you should. Don't think for one minute I haven't noticed how you've been acting toward Stan. I thought I was doing you a favor by putting you at short. Shortstop's about the toughest position on the diamond. You can field grounders well, and throw well. You could have thrown that ball to Stan for a double play easily, but you deliberately threw it hard and wild. You didn't make him look bad. You made yourself look bad."

Gary's face turned red, and he looked toward the end of the dugout. Jeb was sitting there, gazing out upon the field.

"Don't look at Jeb for sympathy," said the coach. "It's time you thought things out for yourself. Okay. That's all. But remember what I said. Get on deck. You're second batter."

Stan couldn't believe his ears. He realized he was staring and his mouth was open. He caught Larry looking at him, and blushed. Larry winked.

The Falcons failed to score at all, and the game went to the Jaguars, 1 to 0. It was still a shutout, but a very good game.

The Falcons closed the season on Friday against the Comets, who carried home the victory 8 to 2. Gary played. He and Stan worked a double play, and afterwards he flashed a grin to Stan to prove that the chip on his shoulder was gone forever.

The next day the *Courier-Star* printed the League standings.

Teams	Won	Lost	Games Behind
Jaguars	11	4	—
Clippers	10	5	1
Falcons	8	7	3

Comets	7	8	4
Red Devils	6	9	5
Steelers	3	12	8

"Well, we didn't do so bad. Did we, Dad?" said Stan.

Dad smiled. "Not at all. By the way, you received a letter in the mail."

He was holding it in his hand. Stan shivered as he saw the familiar printing on the envelope.

"Another one?" he cried.

He opened it with eager, trembling fingers. Then he pulled out the letter and read it.

CONGRATULATIONS! WE THINK YOU'VE LICKED IT. AND SO HAS PHIL. YOUR EVER-LOVING FANS, DOTTIE AND JEB.

Stan's eyes widened. "Dottie and Jeb?" he shouted.

Dad laughed. "That's right. They've been the writers of those mysterious letters."

Stan was flabbergasted. Then he chuckled. "Got any old newspapers, Dad?" he asked. "I'm going to answer that letter!"